Teachers Abroad Mysteries

#1 Revolution Revenge
#2 Oasis Assassin
#3 Turkish Delight Gone Sour
#4 Singapore Fling

Revolution Revenge

Phyllis Wachob

This novel is dedicated to all those who experienced the Revolution up close and personal.

Preface

Although some of the places and characters in this novel are real, for example, Tahrir Square, the Egyptian Museum, Hosni Mubarak, and Zahi Hawass, most are fictional. Those people and places of historical record are easily found in international media. However, there is no Hatshepsut's Mansions, Mr. David's Antiques or the American University of Egypt. In its essence, this is a work of fiction. Names, characters, places and incidents are either the product of the author's imagination or are used fictitiously, and any resemblance to actual persons, living or dead, businesses or establishments, events or locales is coincidental.

Cast of Characters

Barbie Falcon– English teacher at the American University of Egypt

Penelope Watson – English teacher at AUE and Barbie's roommate

Mohamed – *bowab* (doorman) of Hatshepsut's Mansions

Ahmed – Mohamed's cousin and assistant *bowab*

Mitch P – Assistant Professor of Arabic History at AUE

Rachel – Mitch's wife

Parker Hampton – Professor of Archeology at AUE and Head of the Department

Cornelius Smythe – Professor Emeritus of Archeology at AUE

Mary Bell – Professor Emerita of Political Science at AUE

Gamal McCall – Assistant Professor of Archeology at AUE

Tiffany – Gamal's girlfriend

W.B. Lee – Associate Professor of Archeology at AUE

Mercedes Radcliffe – W.B.'s wife

David – Antiquities dealer in the Khan el Khalili

Badboy – Barbie's cat

Chapter One: What Happened to the Internet?

"Where is he?" she mumbled to herself.

Barbie stood on the sidewalk just outside her apartment in Hatshepsut's Mansions on Al Sheikh Al Marsafi Street in Zamalek. The weak winter sunshine broke through the thick leaves of the tall trees that lined the street. Under their canopy, the air was still chilly and Barbie shivered as she pulled her light-weight jacket closer around her neck.

She fumbled in her oversized purse for her phone. I really need something so I won't keep losing my phone in this vast garbage dump, she thought. Finally, she clutched the small, dumb, but adequate for her needs, flip phone and opened the cover.

The screen was strangely configured. The time showed 9:34, the battery showed full bars, but the connectivity counter was blank. "Oh, come on!" she wailed loudly. "What now??" She closed her phone and opened it again. And again. There was no way she could make a call.

She stepped out into the street, hoping that the driver would come as she looked. She had negotiated with him the night before. Nine-fifteen exactly. She walked down the street to the corner where the street ended at the Cathedral, the 'Standing Rib Roast' of Zamalek. No one could tell Barbie when this building got its moniker, but it was obviously named this because of the modernist roof that consisted of soaring white beams that ran from the dome of the roof in an arched circle. All it lacked was white doily paper feet and it would have passed muster in any of the local French restaurants. Now, the yard was deserted.

She peeked down the street where the back entrance, the west gate of the Marriott Hotel, gave onto Zakareya Rizk Street. There were no private vehicles with idle drivers that could be her 'Mohamed the Driver' waiting at the corner. She glanced towards Twenty-Sixth of July Street, the main east-west street in Zamalek, and saw some foot traffic, all heading towards the bridge across the Nile River. More demonstrators heading to Tahrir, she noted to herself.

It had been an eventful few days, but so far nothing had impacted her life or those of the expats who lived near her. The Egyptians complaining again, they all thought. She personally thought the Egyptians had much to grumble about, but they complained and then shrugged. The recent events in Tunisia were a great impetus to Egyptians being more aggressive in complaining. However, Egyptians weren't as well organized, there were more of them and besides, so many seemed so comfortable in their complaints. Who didn't complain about Mubarak and his rich friends?

Barbie sighed and retraced her steps. She walked down to the corner coffee house which the expats who lived in Hatshepsut's Mansions favored. She looked at the round maidan still littered with yesterday's detritus and scanned the parked cars there. No one. Friday morning was the least busy time of the week and Barbie wasn't surprised at the quietness.

"Damn, damn, damn!" She checked her phone again. Still not working. Upstairs, she thought, I'll phone from upstairs.

She hurried up the ten wide white marble steps to the oversized front door and pulled on the long brass door handle. Slowly the door creaked open and Barbie scurried in through the opening. During the day, Mohamed the Bowab sat on an ancient wooden chair just inside the open door, inspecting all who dared to enter. He not only knew the tenants, but the tenants' friends and their friends' friends. Some of the tenants, like Professor Bell and Professor Smythe, had lived in their first floor apartments for many years. Others, such as Barbie and

Penelope, had only arrived last summer. By now, late January, Mohamed the Bowab knew every one of their friends as well. But Friday, until after the Prayer, was the one time of the week that no one expected Mohamed at his post.

Barbie looked at the lift. She could not get used to calling it an elevator, even though the other Americans called it that. Exposed on all sides, the inner workings were visible, as well as the passengers who rode in it. The lift and Barbie had issues. Although Barbie admired its ancient thick metal pulleys and antique pockmarked weight that rose and fell in counterpoint to the cage's rise and fall, she did not trust it. She had been caught more than once, five times to be exact. Not today. She ran up the remaining three flights to her apartment.

Finding her key was as problematic as finding her phone, but she hesitated to ring the bell. Even though Penelope was inside, she knew that she would not be awake and Barbie was not interested in rising the ire of her apartment mate. Not today. She had excluded Penelope from the outing because it was Penelope's birthday gift that she sought in the antique shop in the Khan el Khalili. She had arranged the trip early so that Penelope would not even want to go with her. To wake her up now would be defeating the purpose of sneaking out 'shortly after dawn' as her friend had called it.

Finally, she slipped the key in and gently turned the lock. She pushed the door open slowly, watching out for escaping animals. The black and white fur ball flew out the door from an unknown place near or more likely, behind the door. "Damn! Badboy, come here!!" she said lunging at the cat. Scooping him up from his usual 'hiding' place near the lift, she let herself into the apartment and closed the door with the minimum of fuss. She was still bewildered at her cat's strange desire to get out the door, but to go nowhere once he got out.

"Phone number, I need the guy's phone number. On Gertrude's email, I'm sure that's where it is," she whispered to herself.

Dumping her bag in a heap at the base of the office chair, she clicked the on button of her new computer. Wonderful musical tones rose and the screen flicked on to the screensaver.

It was a picture of Barbie and Penelope near a Sherpa's house in Nepal, their last vacation. Barbie jiggled her foot, urging the computer to warm up faster and give her the email page. Clicking the google page resulted in a small round circle that spun around and around and around. Barbie swerved the mouse to the small icon in the corner that showed the programs currently open. She looked at the five solid black bars that told her there was no connection.

No phone, no internet. "The government is scared, they have shut us down. They are so frightened of the students and the workers and the intelligentsia, that they have cut us off." Barbie didn't know she was speaking aloud until she heard Penelope behind her.

"What's happening? What are you talking about? I thought you were going out this morning?" Penelope peevishly murmured.

"It's started. The revolution has started. There's no phone service and no internet service. It's lucky we have water and electricity. We do have water, don't we? The government is scared and so they've shut off the means of communication. It's the way to stop the demonstrators."

"Yeah, you're right. If they can't text or call each other, then how will they know when to gather and where to go? Should stop all this!" Penelope looked at Barbie with a quizzical look.

"No one told Mubarak that there were demonstrations, riots, and revolutions before Facebook? Of course this isn't going to stop them! This is like throwing down the gauntlet. It's begun, the Egyptian Revolution has begun."

"Barbie, don't be melodramatic! Have you had breakfast? I'm starving. I'll cook eggs if you like." Penelope offered.

Barbie picked up her meowing cat and wandered into her bedroom. She was excited, and terrified. She had only once before been in the midst of civil unrest and that was for just a few minutes on a bus in India. This was the real thing. The shots that had been fired in the last few days were no longer just isolated policemen getting excited. This latest weapon against the people, cutting off communication, was the start of something much, much bigger. Would they be safe? Could they get out? Would they be forced out of here? What should they do? How could anyone tell them what they should be doing? Swirling questions made her dizzy.

She pulled open the tall French doors that led to a tiny balcony. Standing there, she crooked her head to get a view of a sliver of the Nile, just between the two large brick-colored new wings of the Marriott Hotel. Over the top of the palace, that was now the main dining and administrative part of the hotel, she could see the River Nile, the TV tower and the off-kilter floors of the Ramses Hilton Hotel. Just out of sight to the right was Tahrir Square. Liberation Square, the heart of modern Cairo, was now the center of the new liberation struggle of the long-suffering Egyptian people.

Chapter Two: Friday Noon at the Marriott

To be fair, Barbie thought, this was not the beginning of the Revolution; that started on Tuesday. They had all been warned to stay away from Tahrir, but that was easy. Although the American University of Egypt was only four short blocks away, it was still vacation and no one was interested in going into the office before they had to. Tuesday, January 25, was 'Police Day', a national holiday and the day chosen for demonstrations against the police. However, nothing that was planned impacted the expats, so they had all been blasé. Until today.

As Barbie happily ate the eggs that Penelope had made, the phone rang.

"I thought you said the phones were down?" Penelope shrieked.

"Well, the mobile network isn't working, but I guess revolutions are NOT coordinated by land lines," Barbie responded.

Penelope jumped up to answer it. "It's Rachel. UMM, ummmm, really! Hey Barbie, turn on the TV! No haven't heard from anyone. Barbie told me that the mobile network and internet are down. That's all. Wow, wow, WOW! Barbie," Penelope shouted. "Turn on the TV."

"Don't you remember," Barbie hissed. "The wind last week blew the dish down. We don't have a working TV. Ask Rache if you can watch hers."

"Yeah, I'll be down in a few minutes. WOW!" Penelope hung up. "It's all on CNN and BBC and Al Jazeera. Everybody has reporters there. And Mitch can translate the Arabic on the local stations. This is it, Barbie, this is the real thing. It is sooooo exciting."

Penelope and Barbie had been teachers together for years, but this was the first time they had ever shared an apartment. The contracts that they had signed to become English Instructors at AUE had stipulated one bedroom apartments, but the coordinator for housing had suggested this arrangement instead. They had a spacious apartment in one of the most sought after neighborhoods and most elegant apartment buildings in exchange for the two much smaller apartments. They each had a large bedroom, a bath, a large wardrobe and a small balcony off of each bedroom. They shared an enormous living room, dining room and small niche used as an office as well as the small kitchen. So far, the arrangement had worked well. Penelope had previously tolerated Badboy, but this time, being a live-in roomie, had even fallen for him a little, as all cat lovers did. She had even started to use his formal name, Zeus, when addressing him. She was a good cook, and Barbie let her do all the cooking she wanted, as Barbie was then left alone to clean up. They had taken frequent vacations together, so they knew that they could be tolerant of each other's schedules.

Barbie finished her eggs. "Well, I'm off to the Marriot. Professor Cornelius will be there, I'm sure. He'll be able to tell me something about it all. And you can get the skinny from Mitch. See you later."

Penelope agreed that it was a good plan and dashed off to her room to get ready to visit the downstairs neighbors. Another new set of AUE tenants, Mitchel and his wife Rachel, had moved in the same time as they. During orientation, the four had bonded and, as their apartments sat on top of each other, had taken to invading each other's space on a daily basis. Mitch, a professor of Arabic History, was the employee, and Rachel had tagged along. Mitch had a Polish father and was therefore stuck with an unpronounceable and unspellable name that began with 'P'. He was the only Mitch around, so no one confused him with anyone else. Mitch P it was. He was blond and blue-eyed, had unblemished skin, a square jaw, blessed with a set of shoulders that would be the envy of any football player, as well as lovely six-pack abs. Alas, Mitch was convinced he was not at all handsome, although his wife Rachel knew he was, and Barbie and Penelope knew he was, and quite a few of the guys at the local's teashop on Twenty-sixth of July knew he was. But Mitch was five foot five inches tall and was cursed with the notion that a short man could never be truly handsome. Rachel felt herself lucky to be his wife. And, Mitch was smart. He went through college and grad school on scholarships because he always got perfect scores on any exam he attempted, the highest grades in any class he took, and was always obsequious to the decision-makers. Mitch may not have known he was handsome, but he did know he was smart. And to the three 'girls', he was a godsend. He spoke Arabic. He spoke it very, very well, with a beautiful accent. He even spoke the local Egyptian Arabic well enough to pass for an Egyptian in places other than Egypt. He could sit on a bus or on a bench along the corniche and read a local newspaper, to the amazement of all who saw him. The females depended on him to speak for them, to translate TV, flyers, advertisements, whatever, and so, had been lazy about learning Arabic. He had only one cloud on his horizon; he was the only 'white boy' in an Arabic History Department.

While Penelope left amidst slamming doors, Barbie dawdled around her room, picking up clothes, storing shoes, giving Badboy a brushing. She repeatedly went out on the balcony to gaze out to see if the skyline had changed, or if there was noise, or if she could discern anything from looking across the Nile.

She went down the stairs and saw Mohamed returning to sit in his chair by the door. Mohamed was a giant of a man, standing well over six feet tall and sporting a huge belly that made his gallabeya billow in front. He wore a long pale cloth wrapped around his bald head which contrasted with his dark coffee colored skin. Because Mohamed had returned to his post, Barbie knew then that Friday prayers had finished and that Cornelius would undoubtedly be in his usual chair on the terrace.

The streets were busy. The foot traffic consisted mainly of men, as usual, but a significant number of women, especially younger women, mixed in. They were all headed towards the bridge. As she emerged into the street by the hotel, she glanced towards Twenty-Sixth of July Street. There, the crowds were thicker, so thick that they spilled into the street and the cars, that normally ruled the roadway, had slowed. As she watched, one small car simply disappeared into a scrum of bodies. One small boy dashed up and over the hood before the driver had a chance to react and honk his horn. Tentatively, Barbie walked to the corner and inched towards the front of the hotel which fronted the restaurant boats on the Nile. She shied away from the gangs of young men who shouted slogans, but they were in the minority. Frankly, it looked like a lot of people going to a festival or a really good shopping trip.

When she reached the front of the Marriott, she decided that she was better off inside with 'her own kind' instead of out on the streets. She walked across the marbled courtyard and approached the wide doors. Brass handles, too heavy for a normal person to use, were opened for her by a grandly dressed doorman. Immediately inside, a hideous, and flimsy, metal detector greeted her. Beside it was a moving rubber belt where Barbie flung her backpack. She smiled ever-so-sweetly to the burly attendant and waltzed through with a fling of her golden curls. Even though Barbie was on the other side of forty, she could still use the dumb blonde, flick the curls and flash the even white teeth to beguile mere earthlings like the attendants at a Cairene hotel.

Through the security maze, Barbie whizzed past the shops, bars and waiting areas on her way out to the terrace. When she had first seen the Marriott, on her third day in Cairo, Barbie had stood in awe of this part of the hotel. The Marriott has started life as a royal palace over a hundred years ago and many parts of the elaborate, lavish over-the-top decorations could still be seen. They had been smartened up, of course, but they were preserved to give 'guests' the impression that they were trespassing, eavesdropping or thrillingly included in a royal event. Flocked wallpaper, thick carpets, obsequious waiters, myriads of mirrors, grand staircases, elaborately painted ceilings, monstrous vases of fresh hothouse flowers, and an occasional sheik in flowing white robes with an entourage made the lobby a truly enchanting experience. Barbie loved it all, but had no time today to wallow in the decadence. She needed to get to the terrace.

Stepping down the wide staircase at the back of the lobby, she glanced to either side. The crowds had thinned considerably since last week. There was a flurry of excitement as a large tour group gathered to leave. Were they leaving early because of the 'troubles', or were they just leaving? The guests seemed a bit anxious, though, so it could be either. Or it could be that they felt lucky to get out today while the going was good? Would there be a mad rush to leave? She must find Cornelius Smythe and learn the true story.

The doors to the terrace opened slowly and she was greeted with the sight of the lush green gardens of the hotel. Formerly royal gardens, they had a formal layout, with copious bushes that flowered, lawns that somehow always seemed the same hue of green, and huge mature trees that rustled with a comforting sound. She stopped and looked left and right. He ought to be to the left, that was his usual place, but she saw no one down that way. A waiter approached and murmured something that perhaps was, "May I help you?"

"Is Professor Cornelius Smythe here, by any chance?" Barbie smiled brightly.

"Oh, my lovely girl," boomed from behind. "Have you come to help me while away the midday hours of Friday?"

"Certainly," Barbie turned her smile on Cornelius.

"I'm over here, my dear," Cornelius said and pointed towards a table that had a bottle of beer and a tall glass sitting on it. "What will you have, dear?"

"Tea," Barbie said over her shoulder to the waiter who had followed their progress.

"And another beer, you lovely boy," said the professor in an easy affectionate manner. "Ah, in the old days I had plenty of drinking companions, but 'Abdullah' Poole converted and no longer drinks. So, I am too often alone on my Friday."

Cornelius Smythe was the grand old man of the Archaeology Department at the American University of Egypt. He bragged openly about the days when he commanded legions of Egyptians excavating at 'his' digs in Cairo as well as Upper Egypt. Now, he played the elder statesman and pooh-poohed his continuing influence on Egyptology in Egypt. But everyone knew that was a lie. He had known everyone and still did. His fuzzy halo of snow white hair framed a pale face that often grew pink when he was out in the sun. He habitually wore a broad brimmed hat outside and he could be seen across the campus wearing the khaki hiking hat. His belly had become round with good living, and even though he was of less than average height, his booming voice and commanding presence made him seem bigger than he was. His costume today was a well-worn archeologist's shirt and shorts. His bony knees and white shins did not seem out of place in this outfit, although he was one of the very few men in Egypt to wear shorts.

As soon as she was seated, Barbie burst out with, "Professor Smythe, what is happening? The mobile phones are down, the Internet is cut off. What is going to happen to us?"

"The demonstrations you mean? Well, I suspect that they will come to nothing in the end. Might drive away the tourists, be inconvenient for us, but in the end, Egyptians do like their pharaohs. This is a culture that has great respect for the Big Man, they have never experienced anything else. They need the strong man to lead them, to direct them, to tell them what to think and do. They are simply not capable of democracy, no matter what they might think they want."

"But the young people, they have seen the world. They have Facebook, social media, they text each other incessantly. They are connected. Even Ahmed, the Boy Bowab, has a mobile phone."

"But it won't do him much good today, will it?"

"The government is scared. The government shut down the phones and the Internet, didn't it? Mubarak did that, didn't he? How can they do this?" Barbie wailed.

"Oh, you youngsters think life is bounded by the electronics of the world." Cornelius snorted in derision, "Real war, now that is entirely different. In real war, there is no electricity, no water, no food," he leaned forward, "and no cold beer!"

Barbie laughed as the waiter approached with her pot of hot water and a tea bag lying naked on a small plate. Barbie felt frustrated by not being able to immediately pop the tea bag into the water, already tepid she thought. At least she got proper milk and a bowl heaped with sugar cubes. She watched as all the various pieces were laid before her and the waiter stood and turned away. She put the tea bag into the water. "And the expats? What happens to expats during war?"

"During the war in '73, we were evacuated. It was the first time AUE was ever forced to evacuate the expats. What did we do? Just left, flew out, went home. Half came back the next fall, but many never came back. But it didn't matter, there are always more young adventurous people waiting in the wings and within a few years, we were back to strength."

"What will happen this time? Will we evacuate?"

"Frankly my dear, I certainly hope not. I want to be here. I want to experience this. It's different this time." Cornelius cooed softly as he saw the waiter approach with a fresh bottle of cold beer.

"Will you go to Tahrir?"

"Oh, heaven's no. But I will be sure to send my boy out and he'll come back and tell me all." Cornelius referred to his live-in house boy, hardly a boy at 35, who was immensely useful as a source of what was happening on the street. More than once Cornelius had referred to this 'source' of news in juxtaposition to what Mitch reported he had read in the papers.

"What does he say about what's happening now?"

"He hasn't been out yet, not to Tahrir. But this afternoon I expect I'll hear all about what is truly going on."

"So, if I really need to know, I need to come to you?"

"My dear," he patted Barbie's knee gently. "You are always welcome. My liquor cabinet is well-stocked and fresh tea always available."

"Are we safe?" Barbie crinkled her forehead. "I mean, being evacuated or not being evacuated does not really depend on whether we are truly safe or not, does it?"

Cornelius paused and drank deeply of his tall beer glass. "From whom?"

Barbie, too, hesitated. She had never given this idea any thought. "Rioters, the government?"

Cornelius chuckled. "My dear, in this part of the world, no one knows who is friend or foe. Today a friend, tonight, we never know. There are men who inhabit the shadows. The time to settle scores is nebulous, unknown. There are enemies who have been forced to compromise, and now they need to show their stripes, declare who is the enemy and who is their patron. It can be exhilarating. 'Workers of the world unite!' But the reality is: who pays the salaries, who controls the utilities, who makes the country run?"

Barbie had no way to respond to this rambling speech, so she sipped her tea: expensive, cold, cheap, and stale. Why was she always lulled into ordering it here? It was as if she expected, or hoped, that she could get a decent cup of British tea at this so obviously British or European palace. "Will Mubarak quit?"

"Unlikely. This rabble is just that, rabble. No organization, no agenda. Facebook? Pah!?" Cornelius's Boston Brahmin accent became thicker as he said this, his roots as an upper-class elite showing through.

"In this garden, I always feel so far from Egypt. It seems strange to come here and talk about Egypt. I feel like I'm in some country house garden in England or France or somewhere terribly civilized."

Cornelius answered her. "Yes, it has always been that way. That's why I like it. One day a week, at least, I am home."

"That's silly Cornelius. You've lived in Egypt for almost 50 years. How could this not be your home?"

They sat in companionable silence for a few minutes.

"I asked you if Mubarak would quit and you said he wouldn't, but is it possible that he will be forced to go?" Barbie ventured.

"Well of course he will someday. El Din in Tunisia was forced out, never thought he would end that way. And of course there is a kind of precedence for being 'forced' out. So, maybe Mubarak will go. Ask Gertrude, why don't you? Professor Bell, that is."

"Her name is Mary, isn't it?"

"Yes, but if anyone knows the politics, our very own 'Gertrude Bell' does."

Chapter Three: Evening of Chaos

Barbie entered the apartment with her hair dripping. Penelope looked up from her place on the couch where she sat with Badboy curled against her leg and a book in her lap. "You've been to the club? Swimming? On a day like today, the Gezira Club is open?"

"Why not?" Barbie retorted. "So what are you doing that is different?"

Penelope grinned and patted the cat. Penelope was a placid person. She could get excited when provoked, but her outlook on life was one of serenity and quiet joy. She loved animals and was always trying to adopt Zamalek's stray dogs. Barbie objected, as did Mohamed the Bowab, so Penelope cajoled others into taking them. She had grown up in southern California with dogs and thought that everyone should own one or two and that they were not only Man's Best Friend, but Penelope's as well. She sported short, curly brown hair, large glasses that she needed to see, but was always misplacing, a round pale face sprinkled with freckles and a large bosom that strained to be contained. Craving excitement and adventure, she had chosen to become an English teacher abroad to escape the boredom of an LA lifestyle. She had worked with Barbie at a few other schools and they had leapt together at the chance to come to Cairo, their most exotic posting so far. Penelope Watson had loved the life of an expat teacher but for one thing.

Her prince in shining armor, her soulmate, the love of her life, eluded coming to meet her. At 39, though she hated to admit it, she had almost given up. A small well of hope and yearning still bubbled within her secret thoughts and occasionally came to the fore. Barbie knew it was there and was quick to tease Penelope if she was found with a romantic novel, made a comment on the handsomeness or suitability of a man her age, or in any way lowered her guard. Today, she had thought Barbie was busy and had pulled out a sinfully delicious romantic novel, which she now stuffed under the pillows. A swift distasteful glance from Barbie let Penelope know that it had been noted, but that Barbie was in no mood to comment at the moment.

"There is a revolution going on outside and you go to the most exclusive sports club in Cairo and go swimming. The end of the world as we know it and you do laps!" Penelope jumped in before Barbie could make a comment.

Barbie shrugged, "It was open, everything seemed normal. By the way, have you seen Ahmed? Do you know if he is coming for his lesson or not?"

"Actually, I saw him earlier. He seemed excited and was very much on edge. He was running an errand for someone, I believe, so he didn't stop to chat," Penelope answered. "By the way, how is he doing with his English?"

"Great, just a super student. He gets it that you have to work at it from all angles, that language is not just the alphabet and the texts, but it is also listening and trying to speak and trying all the time to increase vocabulary and grammar. He is constantly coming to me with new words to find out their meaning. Unfortunately, many of them are of the 'four-letter' variety and I try to discourage him. But he knows that there are 'men' words and 'lady' words and he says he'll go ask someone else. Actually, often it is Gamal that he turns to these days. Oh well, better a man discuss slang words for a woman's private parts or curse words than me."

Ahmed was a relative of Mohamed the Bowab. No one was ever sure what exactly the relationship was, but it was unnecessary in Egypt. Cousin was a single word in English, but it covered multiple relationships in Arabic. Ahmed, who like all Egyptians, had no last name or family name, only a string of father's, grandfather's and great-grandfather's names appended to his own, was happy to be called simply Ahmed. He came from the same small village in Upper Egypt as Mohamed and was sent to 'learn a trade', that is, to be a bowab, or door keeper. The job was part security guard, part butler, part gofer, and in an apartment building as large and important as this, someone to 'be' there to turn away the riff-raff and note the comings and goings of people. Ahmed was short for his age of twelve, thin, often unwashed (although improving since taking English lessons) with soft brown eyes that saw everything, everywhere. His ability to function in English would help tremendously in getting a good job later on. He had been to the village school for five years, but in the last few years had begun to be exasperated with the boring teachers, the restrictions of the school, and the feeling that he had learned as much as he was going to from the poorly run village establishment. The suggestion that a job in Cairo might be more suitable filled him with immense excitement. He had arrived the day after Barbie and Penelope in late August and had instantly won the hearts of all who met him. He had figured out that the few polite phrases he knew were much appreciated by the foreigners and that they won him treats of food and then errands. While he ran errands, he learned the neighborhood and got tips from the foreigners. There were lots of big tips for a twelve-year-old from Upper Egypt. Mohamed kept control of these tips and showed him how to use them to buy the jeans he craved, the baseball cap, and the tee-shirt with the logo of the Ahly football team. But he also showed him how to save the majority of the ten and twenty pound notes and to divide them between sending home to his mother and saving for the future. Ahmed was overwhelmed with his good luck at coming here. When he discovered that the blonde lady who was so nice to him was an English teacher, he shyly approached her and offered to pay for lessons. Barbie had laughed in his face, but immediately said yes, waived the fee and began daily (or almost daily) lessons with homework. The homework was fun and consisted of writing down words from signs in the neighborhood, words that he had overheard, and phrases that puzzled him. He thought this very useful. Grammar was easy as he was not overwhelmed with it, only being corrected when he became unintelligible. In the last two weeks before the winter break, Barbie had come up with some colorful story books that she encouraged Ahmed to read on his own. They went over them together when Ahmed became frustrated by not understanding the words. He discovered that he had a dictionary on his second-hand phone and was learning to use it. He and Barbie met for about forty-five minutes or an hour, usually in the late afternoon. The last class had not ended with a plan for the next one. "I don't know if he'll want to study English today or not," Barbie sighed.

Penelope sat up, and pushed the cat off of her. "What is happening outside?"

"Not much. There was a lot of foot traffic towards Tahrir earlier, but near the club, the cars just circled as usual. Friday, even this one, seems to be a bit quiet. I'll tell you later what the great Professor Cornelius Smythe said. Basically, he thinks it will all blow over. I'm going to take a nap." Turning to the cat, she said, "Wanna come and sleep with me, you wanton animal?"

The room was dark when Barbie woke. She turned to her bedside clock. After six, and she had completely missed her chance with a lesson with Ahmed. It wasn't the first time and in fact, he would undoubtedly appear tomorrow and want a 'double lesson' because he had missed today. Barbie thought that maybe it wasn't too late, given the bizarre nature of the day, so she got up, put on a thick sweater and went downstairs to look for Ahmed.

Mohamed was sitting on the hard wooden chair in the lobby by the front door.

"Masaa' il kheer," Barbie greeted him with her best imitation of 'Good evening' in Cairene Arabic.

"Masaa' il nuur," came the response.

"Ahmed???" Barbie used body language to look around and shrug her shoulders.

"I dunno," Mohamed responded. "Walid come, walid go, walid no say where."

Barbie smiled at Mohamed's use of the word 'walid' (boy) in Arabic. It was a multifunctional word for any boy, your own son, an unknown child, or in this case, the wayward cousin.

"Miss," Mohamed furrowed his forehead as he addressed her. "Miss no go. No go out. Danger. Men no good."

Barbie answered, "Yes, big problem today. Tahrir big problem. No phone, no computer. Big problem. Better stay house."

"Better stay house," Mohamed repeated.

"Don't worry, Mohamed, I will stay here." At that Barbie opened the big glass doors and slithered out to the front steps. She sat on the steps and took in the atmosphere.

It was eerily quiet here. The calm before the storm? There were no cars on the streets where there usually were many. The foot traffic had lessened as well. Hatshepsut's Mansions sat in a strategic location in Zamalek. On a quiet back alley, it faced only another block of flats and a small coffee shop on the corner. But a few steps to the right was the Cathedral and just around the corner, the back entrance to the Marriott Hotel. There was no direct egress to Twenty-sixth of July Street, but a three minute stroll brought the walker to this main thoroughfare of Zamalek. Directly across the narrow busy street was Thomas' Pizza and next door to that, Drinkies, the purveyor of liquor in this part of the city. The supermarkets were further away, but food was available for the hungry expat. Both establishments delivered. It was an ideal place to live as an expat. Taxis always cruised Twenty-sixth of July Street and for a price, were willing to take a person anywhere.

As nothing seemed to be happening and Barbie felt the chill, she decided to go in. The lobby of the 'Mansions,' as the inhabitants called it, was a spacious hall. In the center towards the back was the infamous lift, on either side were doors to the large downstairs apartments. To the right was Professor Cornelius Smythe. No one was able to tell Barbie how long he had lived there, and even he was mysteriously vague on the date he moved in. To the left was Professor Mary Bell, the one

Cornelius referred to as 'Gertrude', although, of course, that was NOT her name. Also, in the back near the lift was a door that went downstairs. Barbie knew that this is where Mohamed and Ahmed lived. She had never seen it, and really didn't want to, leaving the boys some privacy. There were windows around to the sides and back of the building, and obviously there were wires for electricity, gas pipes and other equipment that Mohamed controlled.

In an attempt to keep in shape, Barbie walked up the stairs. The downstairs apartments were high-ceilinged, and the first flight of stairs was longer than the others. The apartments from the second floor on up were lower. The second floor had four apartments and so were smaller than the ones on the gracious ground floor. As she passed them she thought about who was back from winter vacation and who was still gone. The second floor only had two inhabited apartments, two being reserved for short term visiting professors or other VIP visitors. The front right apartment was occupied by Professor Parker Hampton, the Head of the Archeology Department at AUE. As most of the archeologists in the department were Egyptologists, as was Professor Hampton, he had an extremely high profile both within and without Egypt. His majestic profile was often seen on book covers, National Geographic TV programs and as advertisements for the department. Barbie thought he was terribly stuck up, but he was a lofty Professor, Head of the Department, and Barbie was an Instructor.

The apartment at the other end of the hall was occupied by 'W.B' Lee and his wife Mercedes Radcliffe. She always introduced herself using her own last name, as if she was a bit ashamed to be married to the rough and ready W.B. Barbie didn't like either of them, but she knew they were in residence as she had seen them the day before. The next floor also had four apartments, again only two of them had current occupants. To the right rear was Mitch and Rachel's apartment. The one in the front was a big question mark. The woman who had lived there had been, so the rumor went, denied tenure and she had simply left without finishing out her contract. Barbie was glad that, so far, the Instructors were not included in the evil system of personal vendettas and blackballing colleagues they didn't like, or those who may threaten them for fame and advancement.

At the other end of the hall was Gamal McCall's apartment. He too had returned from the mid-winter break, and Barbie knew why. As a new Assistant Professor, he, like Mitch, had to put in 50-60 hour work weeks year-round in order to attain the coveted tenure. Failure to do so meant leaving. Gamal was in the new 'class' of AUE hires, so Barbie and Penelope had gotten to know him well. Half Egyptian (the Gamal part) and half American (McCall), he was young, loved to party and was a fun addition to the Drinkies and Thomas' group. He was also an Egyptologist and therefore one of the core money makers at AUE. Across the hallway from him was another not yet returned couple. And when she reached the top floor, hers, she sighed with annoyance. Her fellow teacher Llian was not back yet, and the Presidential interns that lived directly across from Barbie were also not back. At least there was still the really young couple to the left, they were here. Barbie hadn't seen them in a few days, so maybe they had taken the opportunity to do some traveling before school started in eight days.

Barbie entered the apartment and smelled garlic, onions and sizzling fat. "Spaghetti ready in a few seconds. Have a good rest? Did you meet Ahmed?" Penelope called from the kitchen.

"No Ahmed, good nap, why don't we have a TV? I really need to know what's happening."

"Downstairs, they won't mind. Especially if I bring them some of the homemade bread."

Within twenty minutes, the two were on Mitch and Rachel's doorstep with the aromatic homemade sweet bread. For the next hour, the four sat and watched CNN, BBC, Al Jazeera and a station from Iran. The estimates of the crowds varied enormously depending on who reported the numbers. What was not different was the growing crowds in Tahrir. No traffic was allowed and the round center island was full of people who were stationary, but around the main island was a sea of circling bodies. It was impossible to imagine what was really happening.

"Will our classes start in a few days?" Penelope asked.

Mitch furrowed his brow and looked at the crowds on the screen. "If Mubarak doesn't go now, and this continues, then no. We will NOT have classes next week."

Barbie chimed in, "Cornelius thinks he won't go."

The TV announcers showed the signs carried by the crowd. "Irhal." (Leave.) "We won't go until he goes."

"Well," Mitch declared. "There is your answer. He either goes in guns blazing and massacres the lot, and he stays, but everyone will hate him and he needs to be in fear of his life. Or he resigns and goes into exile. It wouldn't be the first time in Egypt."

"Has he said anything yet?" Penelope asked.

"No. We need to wait. Egyptians are good at waiting you know."

Barbie heaved herself up from the couch and announced her departure. "Need to feed the cat."

Upstairs she busied herself with food and water, calling Badboy as she did so. As it was unlike him not to come immediately, Barbie went looking for him. After five minutes looking in the obvious spots, she then looked in the not so obvious ones. She went out onto her balcony and called loudly. She listened for his strong meow and thought she heard something, faint though it was. "You got out again, you Badboy. I'll find you."

She rushed down the stairs, calling the cat, "Here, Kitty, Kitty, Kitty." At each floor, she paused to listen for an answer. No sound came from the central stairwell or the lobby. No one was in the lobby, which seemed strange to Barbie as Mohamed usually kept guard. His wooden chair sat by the front door but was conspicuously empty.

Mindful of his earlier warning, Barbie cautiously pulled the front door open. "Here Kitty!" she called and listened. Again, the faint answer that she had heard upstairs came to her. "I'm coming Kitty. Where are you?"

At the street level, Barbie stopped and called again. To her left she heard the faint meows. Cautiously she walked to the edge of the building. "Kitty?"

This time the response was clear and Barbie was sure the voice belonged to Badboy. The side of the building held a space that contained a large garbage bin and enough room to also hold larger throwaways. Now the space was entirely in the dark. Shadows from the streetlamps meant that Barbie could see nothing in the space, although she heard Badboy's meow. "Come out of there, you silly thing!"

Badboy meowed again, twice, louder, but did not move out of the darkness. Barbie squatted down, stuck out her hand and wiggled it. "Come on kitty, sweet kitty." The response was a loud meow, but still no movement. "Are you caught in something? Why don't you come out?"

Remembering the small light on her key ring, for power outages while trying to fit the key into the lock, Barbie pulled the key from her pocket. She flipped on the switch and shone the feeble light into the depths of the bin area. Two green globes gleamed in the reflection. "Meow!!"

"Come here!!!" Barbie used the flashlight to negotiate the rough ground, strewn with garbage and slick with putrid refuse. Slowly, she crept forward, keeping the cat's eyes in her beam. She saw a dirty rag, a rough brown bit of clothing like a gallabeya, and then a pair of running shoes. The shoes were attached to a pair of feet ,as the bottoms showed themselves towards Barbie.

Mesmerized, Barbie crept forward and flashed her light at the pile of clothes and the shoes. Badboy sat practically on top of the mound and meowed again as Barbie's brain took in the dark liquid and the handle of the knife. A bit of a sleeve covered the face and Barbie watched in fascination as her arm reached out and gently pulled the cloth back, revealing the familiar face of Ahmed.

Someone started screaming then. Loud, piercing screams that were accompanied by gulps of air and newer, louder screams. Barbie stood up and still the screams filled the air. It

wasn't until she had attracted a small crowd that she realized
that it was she who screamed.

Chapter Four: The Friday Night of Anger

Barbie sat on her bed, the dim light of a bedside lamp the only illumination. Hunched up, her arms around her legs, tears streaked down her cheeks. She had been dragged away by her friends, as Mohamed the Bowab 'took care of' the dead body of his cousin. Now, she sniffled and murmured again and again, "Why little Ahmed? Who could do that to a child? Why would anyone do that? Is this part of the whole thing? The uprising, the violence, the chaos out there? What could he have to do with it? So where did he die? How did he get here? Or did someone kill him here? Why? Why did this happen?"

Penelope, from her mattress on the floor, tried to soothe her friend, when in reality, she felt like crying and letting go too. Why did Barbie get to do it and not her? She remembered that it was Barbie, in all her innocence looking for her cat, who had found his body. "Barbie, I really don't know those answers. And I don't know if we'll ever know. I feel so sad…"

Mohamed had come running at Barbie's screams and immediately had taken charge. He had called loudly and other bowabs arrived within a minute. Badboy was unusually compliant as he was gathered up and returned to his home on the fourth floor. In Barbie's arms, he quivered, but behaved. It was probably for the best, as Barbie's distress was broadcast to the neighborhood, and the sooner she left, with her loud screams and panicky wails, the better. The situation was best left to the bowab and his cronies.

"Don't worry about all of this. Concentrate on us, on how we are trying to stay safe. As long as we are inside, nothing can happen to us." Penelope used her best 'soothing voice', the one she used for students who had failed an important exam.

Barbie sniffled and was about to reply about the uselessness of Penelope's platitudes when they heard an ominous rumble from outside, like a storm or a garbage truck coming by. It did not stop, as thunder or trucks did, but continued as a distant roar. "Up to the roof, we have to try to see what we can." Barbie pulled back the covers, wiped her face with a clean tissue and stuffed her feet into slippers.

They both quickly managed to get out the door, without letting the cat out. He had recovered from his earlier despair and was ready to join the adventure. As they mounted the dimly lit staircase, they heard commotion from the floor below. Penelope looked over the railings to see Mitch and Rachel making their way up to the roof as well.

The air was cold, but the night reflected the mild coolness of a January in Cairo. The four immediately went to the back side of the building, the side with the view of the Nile. The river was obstructed somewhat by the twin towers of the Marriott, but they could still see the inky blackness of the Nile and the sparkling waves where the water picked up the lights. Cairo, a city of upwards of 20 million, stayed lit all night, as most cities do in the twenty-first century, obscuring the stars completely and only letting the moon glow faintly. Now the sky showed a faint pinkish-orange glow and it came from across the Nile, slightly upriver from where they stood watching.

"Is Tahrir on fire?" Rachel asked. If the emotions of anger, frustration, and fear mixed with hope could light a fire, then Tahrir was on fire. But no one believed in spontaneous combustion. "I'm cold, I'm going in, catch you guys later."

"Mitch," Barbie asked. "What will happen to Ahmed? What are the funeral customs here? Will they call the police? Sorry, that was a stupid question. At a time like this, he is lucky to be noticed. But what will happen?"

Mitch was a thoughtful man, not given to outbursts or quick answers. He shrugged and muttered under his breath.

"Okay, okay. I know that Egypt operates in the past century or centuries, especially in places like Upper Egypt, but surely, even a small boy is worth something to his mother?"

Mitch faced Barbie. "Maybe. Remember, they sent him here to get rid of him to a certain extent. For him, it was a splendid opportunity, but I really think that they didn't care much about him. That's what I've gathered from Mohamed. His death is a tragedy, but as you said, it is a tragedy that belongs to a previous century. Too many boys like Ahmed. There are millions of them in Egypt: uneducated, no skills, no money, nowhere to go. They gather at the gates of the football clubs, waiting for something to happen. They have no occupations, no jobs, no money to get married, no hope, no future. They are the ones who are out at Tahrir now. Nothing else to do.

"Sorry, you asked about funeral arrangements. If he lives in Upper Egypt, he has a family plot and should be buried there. They will try to get his body home as soon as they can, tomorrow morning if possible. With all of this, who knows if he will make it in time? He needs to be buried before the next sunset."

"Could we help with money or something?" Barbie asked. "It's the least we can do."

"I'm sure it will be appreciated. We can ask Mohamed. I'll do that if you'd like."

"And we can ask the others if they want to help," Penelope answered.

"But what about the fact that he was obviously murdered? There was a knife sticking out of his chest, I saw it! If this was at home, or if he wasn't a small boy from the back of beyond, something would be done," Barbie said indignantly.

"Mohamed said there would be no police. I think he is afraid. There is looting and arson. Didn't you see the TV pictures with the burning cars and all that chaos? Who cares about one more 'throwaway kid'?"

The door to the rooftop burst open and Rachel stumbled out, now dressed more warmly. "The orange glow, the thing that's burning, is the NDP building. That's the headquarters of Mubarak's party. They lit it on fire. Can you imagine?"

"That's right next door to the Egyptian Museum!" Mitch added. "My God, what must be happening there? Some people in this building might be awfully worried if they start burning the museum as well."

"What reason would someone have for torching the museum? Surely they have guards or something? And besides, that contains National Treasures, the nation's patrimony!" Penelope was indignant.

"A nation's patrimony! Don't you think those young men with no future would like to get ahold of some of that patrimony? Sell that gold. Maybe even burn it? Besides," Mitch added, "there are a number of radical Islamic scholars who think that Egypt should get rid of all those statues and paintings. Depictions of the human body, you know, and many of them naked! Let's just hope the museum is safe."

"Who is around now that could do something? Cornelius Smythe is here. He would be very unsettled, I'm sure, if someone disturbed the treasures. Could he do anything though?" Barbie said.

As one, they had all decided to abandon the rooftop and slowly began to make their way down the stairs. "Oh my god," Barbie stopped. "Cornelius' apartment is just above the place where I found the… I found Ahmed. Did anyone see Professor Smythe? Do you think he is safe?"

"Don't worry, I saw him through the doorway." Rachel volunteered. "His man came to the door to see what it was all about, and I saw him in the hallway. He was not really dressed to come out, but he got the message. He seemed a bit shocked, but maybe it was that time of night and he'd had all he could take for the day. I think it would take a bit to shock him. But what about Parker Hampton, his apartment is directly above Professor Smythe's? Did anyone see him?"

"I don't know if he is back from vacation or not. Not that I have much to do with him, being head of the Archaeology

Department is about as far away from us lowly English teachers as you can get," Penelope answered. "I frankly don't keep track of my neighbors very well."

"W.B. and Mercedes are back from the holiday break, I saw them today," Mitch added. "And I think I heard them talking with Gamal, but I'm not sure. I was leaving and I heard noises in the hallway and definitely heard W.B. You do know how loud and penetrating his voice is! And then there was a woman's voice. I assumed it was Mercedes, seeing as how she lives with him. Then I heard another man's voice and just assumed it was Gamal. I didn't wait for him to come up to our floor, or maybe he was going out ahead of me. They can be very chummy, those three!"

"So everyone else hasn't come back from vacation yet?" Barbie asked.

"Let's see," said Rachel in her 'organize now' voice. "Professors Bell and Smythe on the first floor. Accounted for. Professor Hampton and Professor Lee and wife Mercedes on the second floor. There are two empty apartments there, so all accounted for on the second floor. Then the third floor. We are here, Gamal, or rather Professor McCall, is here."

"We think," interrupted Penelope. "I haven't seen him, but Mitch heard him, so count him as here."

"Okay, then we have the couple, Gene is his name, and I'm not really sure what her name is. She is elusive to say the least. They are in the apartment catty-corner from us. But I'm sure they're not back yet. I remember her bragging about staying with family until the very last minute. And then, the poisoned woman, poor thing."

"Poisoned?" Penelope shrieked. "She's NOT??!!"

"Of course she's not dead, she's just been denied tenure. Same thing! And that's why I say 'poor thing', because she'll be lucky to get anything after this. She may not even come back. I saw her as she was leaving and she seemed to be taking a lot with her for a short holiday. I wouldn't blame her, just cut and run, leave it all here, let someone else deal with it. So, she's not here. So that's the third floor. And you two on the fourth."

Barbie broke in, "And that's all. Llian hasn't come back, and the couple that lives in the corner apartment, Jack and Markie, haven't been seen and the apartment across from us has no one for the moment."

"Pretty thin ranks, then, isn't it?" Rachel noted. "I mean, if I weren't already here, I might think of not coming now, delay a bit. You know what I mean? Avoid the problems. But I think that we need to know who is here and who isn't. Who we need to watch for, check on, you know. Like a civil disaster. Watch out for your neighbors!"

"Hey, isn't the university supposed to be doing that for us? Aren't they responsible?" Penelope countered.

Mitch chuckled. "No, they're not 'responsible'. It's every man for himself. Check your contract."

"I'm off to bed. I don't know if I can sleep, but I need to at least try." Barbie stopped at their door and opened it, careful to not let the cat out. Penelope joined her and Mitch and Rachel continued on down to the next floor.

Barbie went to bed while Penelope fussed in the kitchen. Soon they were both in Barbie's room with Penelope on the floor. Badboy was so happy to have a choice of sleeping companion that he failed to settle down and made a loop from bed to bed as both tried to find elusive sleep.

Finally, Penelope sat up and pushed the cat away. "How can I sleep?" she asked.

Barbie sat up as well. Just then, they heard a commotion in the stairwell. It came through as a faint noise, but they could tell that it wasn't as faint as it appeared in the room. They both got up and pulled on more clothes.

Barbie got to the door first, but was suddenly afraid to open it. Finally, she pulled it open and stuck her head out. Penelope was immediately behind her. There was a clang, followed by a bang far down the stairwell. Then footsteps sounded on the floor.

"Mitch," hissed Barbie. "Is that you?"

The footsteps hesitated momentarily, then resumed. The front door opened and closed with a loud clang deep below them.

No further noise came, so the two teachers pulled back inside the apartment. For the first time, Barbie noticed that there was only the one lock on the door. There was no chain, no dead bolt lock, nothing as a secondary defense against intruders. It had never occurred to her to need anything else – until now. After shutting and locking the door, she placed a chair against the door, propping it under the doorknob.

"Fat lot of good that will do us if the hordes come looking for us!" Penelope complained.

As they entered the bedroom, Barbie noticed an 'off' odor. Not the odor of cat, unwashed dishes, dirty clothes or other normal odors of a lived-in house. This was chemical, acrid, sharp, and hard to pin down. She sat in the bed, covers pulled up around her. Tears forced themselves out of her tired eyes.

"This has been a horrible day. Why Ahmed? Who did this? Why? When did this happen? Where? Why Ahmed?" Barbie mumbled between sniffles and tears of fear, exhaustion and grief.

"Where? What do you mean by 'where'? You mean you think that whoever did this didn't do it here, alongside the house? Where you found him? That maybe someone murdered him elsewhere and dumped him here?"

"Penelope, what are you talking about?" Barbie wiped her face and looked towards her friend in the dark.

"Well, you asked where he was killed. And indicated that it might not have been here. I mean, what did the body look like? Did it look like he had been killed right there in the space next to the garbage?"

"Well, no, it didn't look like that at all. I was too shocked and there was blood and stuff. But now that I think of it, he was lying on his back, all 'laid out,' I suppose. He looked like a dead person in a coffin. With a knife in his chest. It didn't look like it was random, or 'just happened' or an opportunistic attack. It looked like he had been stuck with a knife, died and then was laid out like that, in a dark place, where he might not be found until morning."

"Barbie, are you saying that this didn't have anything to do with this uprising, this revolution thing at all? Do you think it could be personal? Do you think that someone found him somewhere else and brought him here? There was nothing going on around here; no shots, no people threatening anyone, nothing that was revolutionary at all. Just us, just going about our business. I mean, the club was open, the Marriott was open, it all seemed so normal. So why here? Why Ahmed? Is that what you're saying?"

"I think I'm tired and confused. I don't know what to think about any of this. Why is there such chaos here? Why are we caught in it? Penelope, should we leave? Should we just get out now? Are we safe? Is it really dangerous out there and we don't see it? I mean, this is a foreign country. We can't always understand and know what's happening. We don't know the culture, the signs, hell, we don't even know the language. We just walk around pretending we are safe and that our friends, the Egyptians, will take care of us."

Penelope laughed bleakly. "We live in Zamalek. It's the safest place in Egypt right now. You know, the Americans live just two streets over. Nothing is going to happen to us. And besides, we can't do anything tonight. Wait until morning, then we can think some more about it. We need to sleep. Here, take your cat, he is always good for making you warm and sleepy."

"He's a bit dirty; maybe I should give him a bath. Or maybe not. At least wash some of this evil smelling garbage off of him." Barbie got up and took the cat to the bathroom.

Penelope drifted off to sleep as the sound of the water sloshing over Badboy's dirty feet and Barbie's murmurings to him became soft and rhythmic.

Soon they all slept. In the distance, the uprising continued, sending distant sounds through the windows.

Barbie woke with a start. She stared at the clock on her bedside table. There was a 3 and a 2 and a 1, but she couldn't focus on the numbers to tell her what time it was. She heard the noise again from outside. This wasn't from the distance, but here, in the neighborhood, near the building.

She jumped up and raced to the balcony, flinging open the French windows. The smell was still there. Tear gas? Fireworks? Gun smells? The sound came again, a person running, footfalls hitting the ground in a rhythm. He or she stopped, turned, ran the other way, finally fading in the distance. Another thump sounded nearby, a garbage can was knocked over? Something cracked on the ground followed by more thumps. Barbie strained her eyes, but could see nothing. The noise was near, but hidden from view. It could be nothing more than a feral dog being chased, someone or something raiding the garbage. Someone running, someone who shouldn't be there? But who and where? Finally silence reigned and Barbie pulled her cat back inside, latched the door and went back to bed.

Cairo did not sleep peacefully that night.

Chapter Five: Irhal (Leave)

The morning was quiet. Barbie and Penelope normally woke to the noise of traffic, schoolkids, and people starting their days. But the noise level on this Saturday morning, January 29, was far less than usual, and both had been sleep deprived the night before, so slept on. Even the cat took the opportunity to sleep in.

Over breakfast, they steadfastly kept away from conversation about the events of the previous night, and concentrated on food, the current state of their larder and who would set about rectifying the shortcomings. They ate the last of their by now stale bread and counted less than a breakfast's worth of eggs in the fridge. Coffee was in good supply, thanks to Barbie's recent trip to the Yemeni Coffee Company on Bustan Street across from the Bab el Luk Market. She had bought two kilos worth to avoid a repeat trip soon, which meant they had plenty.

"We really need to stock up on things: bread, eggs, maybe UHT milk, cans of things. And batteries, candles…" Penelope enumerated.

"You mean hoarding? That's not fair, or very humane. Think about the poor who can't afford high prices for things, "Barbie countered.

The phone rang. Penelope picked it up, but no one was on the line. She put it down and scowled. Her mobile phone rang and she raced to her bedroom to answer.

"Rachel, thank God, the phones are working again. Uh, okay, you were just calling to check if the phone was working. Well, I guess it is! What's up? What's the news? Oh my God, the headquarters burned down? Really, to the ground? Oh, didn't know that. The Egyptian museum looted? Ooooo, as feared, worse that we feared. No police? Nowhere? All gone? What will happen? Oh, the army is in charge? Well, no one liked the police anyway. They were useless. And the enemies of the demonstrators. So, who's in Tahrir? Full? You're kidding. I must see this. Is it on TV? All stations, yeah, got it. And they've been there all night? Wow, full, all night? Tents? Awnings? Cars and jeeps on fire? Wow, things are moving along. We will definitely come and watch later, okay? Thanks for all the updates. We really need to go shopping. Food, that's right. Oh, great, come with us? When? Okay, noon, an hour from now. Thanks for the info!"

"I can't believe this is happening. Here in Cairo, just across the Nile. We are caught in history!" Barbie marveled.

"I'd rather have food than history. So, the phones are working, maybe the internet? I'll give it a try."

Penelope disappeared into her bedroom where she had set up her laptop. "Nooooo," she wailed a few minutes later.

Within an hour, Barbie and Penelope had appeared at Rachel and Mitch's door, asking to be allowed to watch the TV. Barbie commented on the stories she had heard from her mother about sidling up to neighbors' houses, hoping to be invited in to watch the first TV on the block. "I feel like this is the 50s and you guys have a TV and we don't, so we have to beg to watch."

Rachel gave Barbie an arched look and said nothing. The four watched the news blips from a number of channels and got only the barest of information from any. The pictures from the square were horrifying in the change that had taken place in the last few days. From a series of traffic circles to an occupying army, albeit one that bore no arms, the major open space had been utterly transformed.

"Well, let us brave the streets and shopping of Zamalek." Penelope jumped up and grabbed her shopping bags.

Mitch opted to stay and monitor the news, while the females braved the shopping. They had heard nothing about hoarding or the availability of food, but they feared the worst.

They walked out the main door, not stopping to talk with Mohamed, who was in earnest conversation with another bowab. Barbie felt bad about not being able to say anything this morning, but she also understood that their doorman was a very busy man, especially today. They turned to the right at the bottom of the stairs and walked the few yards to the corner. The main feeling was one of quietness.

They glanced across the street at the Church yard, often full on a Saturday with Sudanese refugees and their children. None were there. Turning right again, they walked the short distance to the next corner, which was directly across from the northernmost back entrance to the Marriott. There were a few taxi drivers hanging around outside, as usual, but fewer than normal. No cars moved on this street. They turned left, walked past the back of the church and came to Twenty-sixth of July Street, the major thoroughfare in Zamalek. Marveling at the absence of traffic, they crossed the street, stopping directly in front of Thomas's Pizza. It was a staple of expats in Zamalek, even in Cairo, but they were surprised to see the place open and serving customers. The small liquor store next door, Drinkie's, remained shut, however.

In silence they walked down the dirty sidewalk, always being careful to watch their feet to avoid trash, uneven pavement and the merchandise sellers that frequently crowded the cement. They listened to the murmured conversations, the small nuances of feeling that came to them from the few pedestrians. Saturday morning was usually a very busy day in Zamalek. Schools were generally in session for half a day and so schoolchildren spilled onto the sidewalks at noon, flush with an afternoon off to shop, eat forbidden foods or just exercise their freedom. Today was still the school holiday, but few children were seen. Shops were shut that usually would be open, with metal doors pulled down and locked with heavy metal hoops embedded in the cement at the doorway. No vendors lined the streets. The lone newspaper man stood beside his forlorn collection of papers, now days old as no new ones had been flown in from London, Paris, Rome or Berlin. The local papers appeared to contain only the barest of news and were not selling well.

"Look," pointed out Rachel, indicating the small grocery store across the street that everyone called the 'Palestinian Market,' as the owner was one of the many displaced Palestinians in Cairo. The door was open and patrons stood outside, facing the crowded entrance. An angry woman burst through the tight mob and expressed great satisfaction at her exit, bags of groceries in hand. She called over her shoulder at someone and the patrons on either side of her mumbled their dissatisfaction at her rudeness. An upper-class woman, doing her own shopping in Zamalek, perhaps she felt justified in her outburst of annoyance.

"Metro, on to Metro," Barbie mumbled as she turned her back on the scene across the street.

Even the air felt thick with rumbles of dissatisfaction. The young felt dissatisfied with their lives and yearned for change, violent if necessary; the upper-classes felt angry and cheated of their smooth lives of servants, servile shopkeepers and ease of movement. Today, no one was satisfied with what they had. Waiting, they were all waiting. The disenfranchised waited for change, the formerly satisfied waited for things to return to the way they were.

As the three shoppers neared the corner where Metro Supermarket had claimed the basement space, they saw a scrum of cars, shoppers laden with bags, and angry would-be customers who wanted nothing more than to get into the store and purchase their goods and join the finished shoppers on the sidewalk. Gingerly, the three entered and grabbed a cart. Rachel pushed, while Barbie and Penelope tried to grab things off the shelves and sort them into two piles.

The shoppers in Metro were determined. They dragged the few children in firm tow and yelled at husbands and wives to get various items. Carts traveled at a high speed, as if wheeling around the store faster would accomplish the task better and quicker. Some who had not managed to snag a cart clung to one or two bulging baskets, from which items continuously escaped, bouncing off the carts they encountered and creating piles of damaged goods on the floor. Within a minute of arriving at the store, the three expats felt besieged by the crowds, the situation and their own desperation to not be left without provisions for the coming storm.

"Let's get bread," Penelope yelled. "We need some fresh bread."

Rachel obligingly wheeled the cart with a wonky front wheel, down the aisle of bread. "Oh no," she wailed, stopping directly in front of a completely empty series of shelves that normally held loaves and loaves of bread. There was no white bread, brown bread, local bread, fancy bakery bread, loaves that had already been toasted: nothing lay on the shelves. A few packages of crackers, the local equivalent of digestive-type biscuits, lay on the bottom shelf, one package torn and the contents spilling onto the floor. "There is no bread."

"No, here's a loaf," Rachel called as she hauled a plastic wrapped wad of sliced bread out from a lower shelf.

"Euww, it's been opened and look, someone has taken a few slices." Barbie grimaced at the destruction.

"Put it back, put it back," Rachel said, pushing the cart to the end of the aisle. "I guess we really do have enough. I could make my own, I guess.

"Eggs, we need eggs," Penelope said.

But no full cartons remained on the shelf, only opened ones with cracked, leaking eggs were left. The girls trawled the aisles, trying to find food to stock up on. Canned meat was available, although none really wanted to buy the cans decorated with pictures of placid cows, tuna swimming the seas or bright looking chickens. Fake pictures of fake food. The aisle that held canned vegetables was well-stocked and the three shoppers tried to find a few cans 'just in case' no fresh vegetables were available. They saw locals loading up on canned beans and Barbie grabbed a few as well. At a sidelong look from Penelope, Barbie defended herself. "Good source of protein. We might need it. Also can be eaten cold!"

"I'd rather have nothing than that!" Penelope declared.

"You may get nothing. Careful what you wish for," Rachel interjected. She, too, reluctantly added some cans of beans and vegetables to the cart.

The pathetic pile of fresh goods had been carefully picked over. "Carrots, potatoes, cabbage, all good to stock up on!" Barbie declared as she carefully went through the bins, squeezing and gazing at each vegetable that went into the cart.

"Cat food?" Penelope asked.

"Ah, the thoughtful one stocked up last week and had them deliver at least a month's worth. Badboy can always eat what we do, and if he doesn't like it, he can go on a diet." Barbie added.

"So are we ready to face the scrum?" Rachel asked, looking askance at the crowd that passed for a checkout line.

One store employee unsuccessfully asked patrons to go into one line or the other, trying to sort them out by the total load of the cart, whether they were able to carry their purchases themselves or demanded delivery, which was promised, but not in the next few hours, or by some other designation Barbie couldn't fathom. Old customers, new customers, rich or poor??

Once outside, they heaved a sigh of relief. Even though they might not like all the food they purchased, they reasoned that it would get them through the next few days at least. Even demonstrators had to eat, so food was a basic commodity and likely to be allowed to be delivered.

Not far from the Metro doorway, a young man leaned over a sign on the street. He used a magic marker to write his message. He traced over the letters carefully in another color, all the better to see his words. Noticing the audience, he stood up, "Irhal," he read. "It means 'go away'". He mimicked kicking a football. "Mubarak, go away!"

An older Egyptian man, wearing a threadbare, outmoded brown suit stopped and faced the girls. "Actually, a better translation is 'leave'. These young hooligans think they can topple a government with their signs and their marches. Humph."

The young man's hair was pasted into a fashionable wave on the top of his head. He wore a bright T-shirt advertising his football affiliation and the ubiquitous blue jeans, torn at the knee. It was unclear whether they were torn because he had worn them so much, or whether he had bought them in this condition. He launched into a passionate soliloquy in Arabic, obviously aimed at the old man and other passers-by who could understand. The expats stood fascinated as this confrontation took place. When he had had his say, he turned to the English speakers and said, "This old man, he is wrong. He is old man, he never know freedom and democracy, he don't know how to say. We are new Egyptian, we have different way. We want democracy, we want freedom. We say, 'Mubarak, Irhal.' We don't want you. We want freedom, we want democracy."

The old man backed away, distancing himself from the young man on the sidewalk who had now gathered a larger crowd. "Nothing but football hooligans. They have nothing better to do than hang around the football stadiums, wasting their time, living off the earnings of their hard-working parents. What a disgrace for Egypt." He muttered these last remarks to the three expats and they smiled back at him, in a vain attempt to placate him and show some semblance of solidarity. They understood quite well that their jobs at the university put them on par with the upper-classes of Egypt, even though they themselves might not be classified in the same social class back home where they came from. Their Egyptian colleagues belonged to this class, and their students did as well.

Barbie pulled on the arms of the other two. "I think what we have witnessed is a classic neo-colonial racist encounter between old Egyptian, upper-class money and lower-class outcast youth. Let's just keep moving along."

Rachel agreed. "Wow, I bet Mitch could turn this encounter into a full one-hour lecture on the changing dynamics on social class and allegiance in the Middle East. That was classic, that was. Young man pitting himself against the old man, who represents money, power, cultural capital. And the young man, with that hair style, that t-shirt and his broken English, standing up to that. He surely had courage. The world is changing, our little world right here, changing before our eyes."

Barbie looked back at the scene of the commotion. Now, smaller groups had gathered and there was a stand-off of sorts. Soon, it faded away and within a block, nothing could be seen of what had happened. However, just ahead of them they saw a group of young people gathering and marching down the street together. This time there were a lot of females in the group, some with and some without headscarves. As they passed, they heard over and over, "Tahrir".

They looked at one another, frightened this time. "Allah, what is happening here?" wailed Penelope.

Chapter Six: What Happened at the Egyptian Museum

Before Barbie and Penelope could put away their groceries, Rachel appeared at the door. "C'mon, you have got to see this stuff. Come and watch TV. Mitch has gone out, don't know where. But you have to come, you will NOT believe it."

Rachel had come to Egypt as a newly-married faculty wife. She was hopelessly in love with the brilliant, but at times moody, Mitch. Her curly brown hair had become an unmanageable frizzy cloud because of the harsh water in Cairo. She tried a string of products in an attempt to tame her tresses and the girls had laughed over the failed results of each one. When recounting these stories, her eyes sparkled with mischievous delight and red spots of color sprouted on her cheeks. Her ample figure had attracted much attention from the legions of young men of Cairo and she had taken to spending her days inside cooking and watching TV, until her husband and friends returned from their jobs. Cornelius Smythe had wickedly suggested that the cooking of food and eating of bonbons in front of the TV had only added curves and thus added to her attractions in the eyes of Egyptian men.

As the expats watched TV, history unfolded before them. It was surreal.

"Here we are," Barbie said. "We are watching BBC with their cameras and newscasters at a place less than a mile from here, letting them tell us all about what is happening. How can they really know?"

"Well, they are also talking to the government and looking at other places in Egypt and we aren't. We're just sitting here in Zamalek."

"Look, it's Alexandria. Dead, people are dead. They are shooting people there! And the numbers from Cairo. God, maybe we should be scared."

"They are not attacking us. But wait, look at that."

The three created a running commentary as they watched the pictures from the screen. When one channel started a repeat of an earlier video or commentary, they changed to another channel, handing off the remote to whoever insisted on manipulating it.

They watched in fascination as channel after channel reported the break-in at the Egyptian Museum. The Czar of Antiquities was reported to have said that only minor damage was done and nothing of importance was missing. A photo of Zahi Hawass with his characteristic leather hat was flashed onto the screen. Shouts of incredulity greeted this apparition. "How could this happen? How could they allow this to happen? Guards? Someone must care!"

The scene on the TV cut to Tahrir Square which was filling rapidly with people. Spots on the screen showed places where a car or vehicle was burning, sending gray clouds of smoke into the air. A close up showed one stuck into a subway entrance effectively blocking the ingress and egress, not that anyone was using the Cairo Metro system to commute to Tahrir these days.

The front door to the apartment opened and Mitch fell in.

"Hi, Mitch," Barbie greeted the occupant of the apartment. "As you can see, we are here again to watch TV. Hope that's okay with you?" She smiled a fake 'happy' smile, willing Mitch to forgive the intrusion for yet another day.

"Yeah. Hi girls. What are the talking heads telling us now?" Mitch took off his jacket and sat in front of the TV himself.

"Tahrir, the Museum, burning cars, more people killed, deaths in Alexandria, demonstrations…."

"Where've you been?" asked Rachel.

"Trying to find Gamal to see if he knew anything more about the museum. I knocked at his door, but no answer, so I figured he was out. But then I ran into Parker Hampton who was just leaving and asked him. I'd rather have asked Gamal, but I guess I can get the information wherever I can. But he was spooked today. He said he was on his way to the museum or to the antiquities department here in Zamalek to check on things. He kept checking his phone and I had the feeling that he wasn't the only one who was upset."

"We heard the Antiquities Czar's statement on the TV," put in Penelope.

"I guess that might make all the Egyptologists shudder. I had the impression that Parker was VERY upset about the break-in, and the 'looting' as he called it. I guess there was more damage than Hawass let on. Anyway, Professor Hampton shoved me out of his way and dashed downstairs to take this phone call, all before I had a chance to ask him if he'd seen Gamal."

"Are we worried about Gamal?" Barbie asked. "Do you think he can't take care of himself? I mean, we all know his Arabic is not so good, but he can pass can't he, at least on looks, for an Egyptian? And well, he might be at the Great Czar's side, helping count the missing pieces, don't you think? But maybe you are right, we need to keep track of people, just because we have no one else. The American Embassy said they'd make sure we have transportation if we want to leave, but the word 'evacuation' was not on their lips."

"Well, Gamal is not here now and we don't know if he was here last night. Maybe he spent the night in Tahrir? When do you busybodies want to start worrying? What's to eat?" Mitch headed for the kitchen.

"Did you find Mohamed? Is there anything we can do about Ahmed?" Barbie called, following him into the kitchen.

"No Mohamed either. I looked in all the normal places and called his name. The bowab across the street, the one they called Mohamed Mohamed, who fills in for our Mohamed, showed his face and shook his head at me. I didn't want to ask, figuring it was something to do with our little Ahmed and that this could keep until later. I took a turn around the neighborhood, checking out the American's enclave, and found some plain clothes marines standing around with bulky jackets. Very, very casual. And the Coffee Bean coffee shop, just opposite, doing a great business. Expat haven."

Barbie and Mitch cut cheese, found some crackers, a few still edible apples, a box of chocolate chip cookies and made tea. Mitch looked askance at the recent acquisitions and sighed.

"C'mon, Mitch, did you expect this to be a 'gourmet' revolution? You are being fed, count your blessings," Barbie called over her shoulder as she carried lunch on a tray into the living room where Penelope and Rachel sat glued to the TV screen.

"More information about the Museum. Apparently the army said they were protecting the building, but the rooftop was breached. Can you believe that?" Rachel reported.

Mitch answered, "No, I can't. How can you get to the rooftop without passing the army? It's a stand-alone building. They'd have to use a helicopter to get there, or pass through Army lines. Guess which they did?"

"Be quiet Mitch, and listen. And they said that a few of the artifacts were found in the garden this morning. Probably dropped by the culprits. And that they know who did it," Rachel continued.

"Wow, round up the usual suspects. Look, if they got in one time, they can do it again. It's like getting the wolves to guard the hen house. The army, seriously?"

"That's what they said on TV," Rachel defended her news.

"How much of that can we believe?" put in Barbie. "How much do they really know, those reporters? And how much of what they are being fed is the truth in any case? They are out there talking to people in the square, but who are they? Are they 'leaders'? Are there any leaders? Mitch, can we believe that the Museum is safe now?"

"I don't think we can take anything at face value. Not now. I mean, Parker was off trying to get information, maybe offering to help protect things. Maybe the university has a place that is more secure, or they can store the really valuable things in the Embassy. I'm not sure the US is seen in the best light right now, but it may be the best thing for the antiquities," Mitch said.

"How important is the university's department in helping to protect the museum? I know that the whole Archeology Department is deeply involved in the museum work. The whole department has permits for digs, lots of them, and they work in the efforts to stop looting tombs and the antiquities trade in general. This break-in would devastate them all wouldn't it?" Barbie asked.

Penelope gasped. "But I thought they all hated each other!"

"Well, that wouldn't stop them from being very unhappy about this. Even though they hate each other, what university department doesn't, that doesn't mean that some of them might be glad that thieves broke in and stole or destroyed artifacts. Especially ones in the museum! They might, just might, be united on one thing," Mitch added.

"Maybe that's where Gamal is, for once cooperating with his Head of Department." Rachel said. "I remember when he first got here, Gamal was excited to work with him. But a week later, he was grousing. I guess all Assistant Professors have to bow down to the almighty HOD."

Mitch chuckled briefly. "Almighty Head of Department, you're right. But at least Gamal could go to Cornelius and complain. I mean, Professor Emeritus Smythe holds no official power, but he can give poor Gamal an ear and maybe some advice about navigating the treacherous waters of the American University in Egypt's Archaeology Department. He still has a finger in the pie, sitting on committees and things."

Rachel added, "Maybe Parker Hampton is jealous of Gamal? I mean Gamal is half-Egyptian, even if he can't speak much Arabic. It must rankle a bit that he is so good-looking and so wonderfully friendly to everyone, so congenial and so collegial. No one dislikes Gamal, so maybe there is a reason to be jealous. And his doctoral work, wasn't it something similar to Parker's? Maybe Parker feels threatened by someone up and coming?"

"Don't forget, Gamal is junior faculty. He is absolutely, absolutely no threat to Professor Parker Hampton."

"But I thought he had connections. You know, Egyptian connections, through his mother's family. I heard him once talking about going to see digs done by his uncles and cousins. I think that maybe it was because there were ties, influences. That because he knows people, he has more clout than Parker the Pr… Sorry, I won't say that," Rachel said.

"Wow," Penelope said. "I didn't know you knew him that well! Tell us more."

"We had a few chats during that first week and I thought he felt as much of an outsider as I did. Of course that's not true, he just had a way of being so friendly. So I heard the whole story. Egyptian mother studying in the US, falls for the handsome young professor at the university. Her family not particularly happy, but a strong-willed woman and a young man very much in love. And that although he is McCall, his mother insisted on an Egyptian name, Gamal. He thought it was neat and he had supportive friends who let him know that you could be a Gamal and still be an all-American boy who played baseball. He didn't think he was going to be an archaeologist like others in his family, but just after he graduated, with a degree in psychology, he came to Egypt for a short season to help his uncle on a dig and got hooked. He went to graduate school and did some work at other places that have really strong Egyptology departments in England and Europe, so he is really and truly extremely well educated in his field. Not that Parker has a real reason to dislike him, or really fear him, but Gamal has connections. I mean deep connections. He knows everybody in the business, all the professionals, the archeologists, the dealers, even the Czar is an acquaintance."

"Uncle Zahi, huh?" Mitch asked.

"Rachel, Mitch, stop, listen to this." Barbie had drifted back to the TV and now called their attention to the latest news.

The announcer had the Egyptian Museum to his back and in that earnestness of on-the-scene reporters now declared that the Army had taken over the security at the Museum, which housed 'National Treasures' such at the golden mask from King Tut's tomb. The break-in had been minor, only a few cabinets were broken into and a few items taken, mostly from the minor finds in King Tut's tomb. "Antiquities Czar Hawass has expressed his dismay at this tragic break-in, but believes that the army will be able to protect these unique treasures. We have been told that when demonstrators found out that someone had breached security, they united with the army, locking arms in an attempt to build a security wall around the world famous site. The Army is now firmly in command of Tahrir Square, where the Museum sits on the northwest corner. Meanwhile, in Port Said, reports are coming in of dead and wounded from Friday night's clashes…"

"Better in the hands of the army than some of the demonstrators, and of course, whoever broke in. This is terrible," declared Penelope.

"The NDP headquarters that were burnt last night are directly adjacent, don't you know? If demonstrators can get into the headquarters and burn it, then the Museum next door would be easy. Especially if you are talking about bribing the guards. Then it would be easy to just show your money and your Egyptian bona fides and you are in." Mitch said.

A knock on the door startled all of them. Mitch went to answer, being mindful of his three 'ladies' and the danger that might lurk outside the apartment door. When he opened it, the ladies were startled to see Mohamed. His chin looked even more unshaven than usual and his turban lay askew. He spoke to Mitch in rapid-fire Arabic, which Mitch tried desperately to slow down. Mohamed slipped something out of his pocket and showed to Mitch, who took it and looked incredulously. More earnest speech passed between the two. In the end, Mitch agreed, "Tayyib."

As soon as Mitch closed the door, the three jumped on him, "What, what?"

In answer he took the small card passed to him by Mohamed. "They found this."

It was an ID card from AUE, a card they were all familiar with. The square picture in the center of the card was of a smiling, young Arab-looking man, one they knew well. "Gamal McCall," whispered Rachel.

"Where did they find it?" Penelope's voice cracked.

"You know they are taking all the dead bodies to the mosques. It is just a precaution, and someone wants to count them and if no one knows who the person is, they need to identify the body. They found this card on a body. They identified it as Gamal."

"But where did they find him? Where did they find the body?" Rachel said, anguish squeezing from her voice.

"They said they found it at the Egyptian Museum, outside in the grounds. He was found dead sometime early today, but no one could identify him until just recently, when they searched his pockets."

"No, it can't be another one; that is two in two days. This can't be happening." Barbie fought back tears, trying to control her wavering throat.

"Sorry, I have to go." Mitch took back the card from Rachel's hand.

Chapter Seven: Bring My Brother Home

Mitch disappeared into the bedroom and the three heard drawers opening and closing, and then the closet door banged open. Not having anything more to say, they waited for Mitch, the TV blaring behind them.

Mitch reappeared dressed in a gallabeya and was wrapping a small towel around his head. "Damn," he said, throwing the towel to the floor. "Mohamed will have to give me one. He looked at his feet, now clad in cheap shower slippers. "Too clean, all of it. My feet are too clean, my slippers are too clean, my gallabeya has no spots on it. At least it fits, thanks to that shopping trip to Tunisia."

"We laughed at you, we thought you'd never wear it. But why are you wearing it now?" Rachel asked the obvious question.

"I'm going with Mohamed to get Gamal's body from the mosque. We need to get it out before the authorities figure out he died and try to make political hay out of it." Mitch answered enigmatically. "What am I going to wear on my head?"

"You have the keffiyah that you bought. You did buy it, didn't you? I'm sure you bought the whole outfit. It should be in the same drawer as your other hats." Rachel suggested.

Mitch reappeared with the pale blue keffiyah dragging on the floor behind him. "I'll get Mohamed to tie it for me. It wouldn't do trying to pass as an Arab with a drooping keffiyah."

"Pass as an Arab?" Rachel gasped.

"Eyes, Mitch, eyes. You can cover up your blond hair, you can pass off the pale skin, but what will you do with your eyes?" Penelope immediately threw herself into the game.

"What's wrong?"

"They are blue, not dark blue, or semi-blue, but as blue as the Polish skies in summer!" Penelope pointed out.

"Sunglasses, that will do it. And besides, I'm not passing as Egyptian, but maybe Tunisian or Lebanese. I could never get the accent perfect enough, someone would out me. But a foreigner, I can do. I'll be Gamal's Lebanese cousin, come to identify him and collect his remains." Mitch emptied his pockets. "And no ID. Too risky. Mohamed can use his ID if we need any."

Mitch was interrupted by the TV announcer's declaration of a curfew. "Although yesterday's curfew of 6 pm was widely ignored, army officials have once again declared a curfew for Cairo, Alexandria and Suez starting at 4 pm today."

Mitch looked at his watch, "Just after three now. Gotta go." He took the watch off his wrist and deftly slipped it into his pocket through the hole in the side of the gallabeya, as if he had been wearing this costume for years.

A knock on the door alerted them to the waiting Mohamed. Rachel handed Mitch a pair of aviator sunglasses, which he scowled at, but put on his face. Mohamed greeted him at the door, and a tiny smile lurked momentarily at Mitch's appearance, despite the tragedies of the last few days.

"When are you coming back?" called Rachel as the door closed on the two.

A noncommittal 'humph' was heard just as the door slammed shut.

"What will he do? 'Collect the body', what does that mean?" Penelope asked.

Rachel shook her head. "I don't know what he means. But if he died last night or early this morning, they will try to bury him soon. I guess what he means to do is snatch the body now so the government doesn't find out. By 'political hay', I guess he means that they could use this occasion to say that foreigners are butting their noses into the business of Egypt. I mean, where does the US stand in all of this? At the moment, all the US Embassy is saying is that citizens can get out. But the US isn't taking sides on this. And no one wants to get Gamal mixed up in this. You heard him, 'They said he died at the museum last night.' Someone could think he was part of the gang breaking in."

"Never, he would never do anything like that," Penelope put in.

"We know that, but the government? Maybe they wouldn't see it the same way."

Barbie hadn't taken part in this discussion until now. "And what about the demonstrators, the anti-Mubarak people? What might they feel about Gamal, or any American getting mixed up in this? I mean, I know where I stand in all of this, but I am sure there are Americans who firmly believe that Mubarak is the good guy and the demonstrators are the bad guys. And if they see Gamal as 'joining the anti-government forces', they might say that he was being 'anti-US?' That is a load of 'bleep', but someone might just use that against the university, against us, his colleagues. I see the point of getting his body out of there and somewhere safer, so no one can use him for political purposes. What I am having trouble with is really believing Gamal is dead. What happened?"

Rachel's phone rang and she ran to get it. "Oh hi, Mitch. Yes, yes of course. We won't say anything to anyone. You're right, can't trust anyone. Bye."

Rachel looked at her two companions. "You heard."

"Yeah," they said in unison.

"He was on the Lion Bridge, on foot. Lots of people. He's thinking that the crowd will just swallow him up." Rachel reported on Mitch's conversation.

"Ahmed, now Gamal. This is real."

"The army authorities are warning residents of Cairo, Alexandria and Suez that a curfew has been declared from 4 pm. The army has warned all residents to stay inside. In the meantime, Tahrir Square has begun to fill to overflowing, all streets and bridges that approach the Square are choked with pedestrians streaming towards the center of this…" Rachel reached over and turned off the TV.

"Yeah, that's another thing Mitch said. He said, 'Don't go out.' We need bread, let's go."

The three grabbed their purses and shopping bags. Barbie thought that if she was to be caught in a revolution, it was best to be in the company of others who also felt the same way she did. If the 'authorities' said to do, or especially not to do something, the best course of action was to immediately do the opposite. She had operated on this principle her whole life and had never regretted it, with the sole exception of the man she had married.

"Do you think we should take our ID?" Penelope asked

"Definitely not, except maybe our AUE ID. That's better than a passport in Egypt any day. Maybe put the big money in money belts?" Rachel answered.

"No big money. If we need big money, we are in real trouble. Just enough for the bread and little else. Our head scarves, just in case. And a warmish jacket. What if we get caught out there?" Barbie commented.

Within minutes, they were on their way down the stairs. "It feels funny, sneaking around without Mohamed not being here. He always asks where we are going. At first, I thought it was cute. Then it got to be really intrusive, so I started lying to him, or saying, 'Shopping' all the time. Now I wish he were here, and that we could tell him where we are going. Someone needs to know where we are, don't they? We don't want to end up like Gamal," Penelope said in a small voice.

"Or Ahmed," added Barbie.

Outside, the weak January sunshine filtered through the large trees on the street where Hatshepsut's Mansions stood. The three shivered at the cold, the thought of the cold, and the tension that hovered everywhere. Penelope lifted her nose in the air and sniffed. "Burning things," she declared. Rachel turned and looked all around. The sidewalk was almost empty. Even the neighborhood's feral dogs had taken shelter. This time, they took the other way out to Twenty-sixth of July Street, going left at the corner by the cathedral and then taking a right at the next corner. On the broad Twenty-sixth of July Street, they saw more pedestrians and a few cars, and they could hear from the elevated street above them, that no cars were moving towards the opposite side, towards Tahrir.

Penelope spotted them first, among the other pedestrians along the street, a small group of other AUE teachers on the north side. They motioned for the three to come over. Glad to have someone else to talk with, the three dashed across the street, dodging the traffic as usual. They formed a huddle on the street in front of the now closed exchange shop that sported an enormous dollar bill in the window.

"What's the news?" Rachel asked with innocence, well aware that the three probably possessed more real news than the others, but unwilling to disclose the fact.

The group discussed the curfew, telephone connections, calls home, whether they would leave or not, the food situation, and especially the lack of bread and wine. "Essentials in my book," said one with more than a touch of insouciance, as befitting an absent-minded Professor of Philosophy. A few raised eyebrows met this remark, but the talk then fell to the best place to get bread.

"You know there is NONE in the stores, but there is a government bakery around the corner on Brazil Street. It's got just a tiny hole in the wall to the outside, and there are long lines, but I've heard they are still baking," said one.

"The chaff-filled stuff with bits of hair and burned things on it is not my idea of bread, but if that is all there is, bring it on. I can eat it," said Barbie with a distasteful twist to her lips.

"Do you guys have enough water? Metro is still delivering and I have filled up all my empty bottles," said another.

Penelope looked alarmed, "Yeah, I guess we should fill up, I think I just threw out a few empties last week."

"I rescued them, don't worry," Barbie reassured Penelope. "I come from earthquake country, remember. We always have water around. I don't let empty bottles go lightly." She turned to others in the group. "Is everyone at your place accounted for?"

"Don't know. How can we connect with people? Our internet is still out, I'm assuming yours is too. It's such a confusing time of the year. Half the profs are still on vacation, the others are due to return any day, in fact, one was due today and called from the airport. He was stuck there, no transportation. We kind of urged him to stay put and catch the next flight out. I mean, I didn't sign up for this and I know that he didn't."

"Did he go?" Barbie asked.

"Last we heard he was still waiting, camping out at the airport. We saw a brief news report. I guess getting to and from the airport is as bad as anything. They've cancelled flights in. Everyone still at home is not about to fly into chaos, and so fewer planes were coming in. And every tourist in Egypt, and this is the high season you realize, wants out NOW. So the airport looks like a cross between a refugee camp and a storm shelter."

"But some embassies are evacuating their people," another one chimed in.

"But not the Americans. Only 'non-essential' Embassy staff and families. Even if you want to go, you have to pay. Not a freebie that comes with the passport," a tall, thin man added.

"But I heard the British University and German University are sending their foreign teachers home, evacuating."

"I'll believe it when I see it. I just worry about what is going to happen to us? To Egypt? What's next?"

Before anyone could answer, a young man carrying a broom handle approached them. "It's not safe. Go home."

"What, what do you mean?" Penelope looked around and suddenly realized that the group consisted of six females and one male, a vulnerable grouping in Egypt.

"Go to your house, and stay away from the streets. It is dangerous now." The man moved off, walking purposefully down the street.

"Does anyone know what that was about?" Rachel asked.

They all shrugged and looked puzzled. A glance at the street revealed fewer than normal pedestrians and even fewer cars. No one looked menacing or out of place. What did the man know that they didn't?

"They are just Zamalekites, just 'us'," said one looking at the people.

The young man in the group looked at the three Hatshepsut's Mansions girls. "So, what is happening in your neck of the woods?"

Rachel looked startled and mumbled, "Nothing much."

"A few of the teachers aren't here right now. Llian, you remember her? She's still away and due back today or tomorrow. So, we're not sure she can get from the airport home or not. But the two old ones, you know the Professors Emeriti, they are okay. Mostly staying inside, kind of quiet like." Barbie brightly informed whoever would listen.

"Did you hear about the Egyptian Museum? Wow, wasn't that something! And the Antiquities guru on TV, 'All is safe.' Doesn't the head of the Archeology Department live in your building?" the man asked.

Rachel's eyes grew wide as the questions got closer and closer to the secret they were told to keep. "Yes, Professor Parker Hampton lives in our building. We've seen him, he's safe. I don't think he is involved in the museum thing at all. My husband saw him today, in fact. I think he said he was on his way to see what could be done, or something like that. All taken care of. No worries."

"Anyone been to Tahrir yet?" the man persisted.

"No, we haven't been, have you?" Barbie said.

"No, not yet. I'm thinking of tomorrow. They say they are calling on all Egyptians to turn out, protest the take-over by the army and push Mubarak to leave. I'm thinking of my own sign and what I'll say on it."

"No fear on your part, I see," said Penelope brightly.

"If the Egyptians aren't afraid, I'm not either. Well, see you guys around. Call if you need some courage, or food or water!" He waved as the group left, walking towards the bridge over the Nile that separated them from the tumultuous activities in Tahrir and environs.

"I'm calling Mitch. This is all getting really, really weird." Rachel got her phone out and called Mitch. She tried once and let it ring until it got the 'leave a message' part and she hung up. She called again. The two watched her intently as she waited on the noisy sidewalk.

Finally, Mitch answered, but only with an Arabic 'Alo.' Rachel spoke in a low voice. "Speak in German if you can't speak English. But is everything okay?"

This was met with another grunt as Barbie and Penelope leaned in to hear answers. "Have you got there yet? Have you found him?"

"Yah, gut," came the answer.

"We didn't stay in. We went out and now it is getting really weird out here. We're heading home now. But we still don't have any bread." Rachel said into the phone.

This was met with silence, or perhaps Mitch was not in a position to say anything. "Well, bye, see you later." Rachel waited a bit and then Mitch uttered another noncommittal grunt. She closed the call.

Evening had begun to close around them as they stood on the street. From out of a dark alleyway across the street, they saw a large man wearing a gallabeya walk menacingly onto the sidewalk on the main street. He carried a large two by four, muddy and ragged at one end, looking like it had been stolen from a building site. His large eyes under deep brows stared at them. Barbie wanted to, but dared not, stare back at this Neanderthal as he purposefully walked down the middle of the sidewalk, swinging his crude weapon in time with his long steps.

"Do you think it's too late to go get bread?" Penelope asked.

"Yes," came the simultaneous answer.

"We need to get home," Barbie declared. She shuddered in the cool wisp of air that suddenly appeared from out of an alleyway behind them. She noticed that there were no more foreigners on the streets and the women, too, had all gone in.

Now, only youth ruled the streets of Zamalek. "The back way. Now."

They scurried across the street to the sounds of stores being closed. Metal door covers came down with a rattling river sound and ended with a sharp metal 'clunk' as the door hit the ground. The owners quickly locked the doors with large padlocks that attached to sunken metal eyes in the ground and then walked away. Presumably they also had cash in their pockets and wanted nothing to do with the unknown elements in the streets at the moment.

As they wound their way through the back alleys, Barbie peered into the deepening gloom towards the street corners where she knew the embassies always had police posted. They were generally young recruits from the provinces, armed with impossibly old and, Barbie hoped, unloaded weapons. Today, the young man at the corner who always greeted her cheerfully was absent and no one had taken his place. She looked down another street and saw no young policeman in his too-large uniform sitting, standing or sleeping in the tiny covered box in front of the Dutch Embassy. "No police," she said quietly. "We were told they had been 'called back', but I really didn't believe it. No one is there, no one."

"What does that mean?" Penelope asked.

"I'm not sure," Barbie answered, "but nothing good. We might laugh at them, poke fun of their guns and uniforms, but I always felt they were on my side. I always thought as I walked down the street late at night that if some man jumped me, they would be there to protect me or at least shout out. And there are so many of them here in Zamalek, that I always felt comfortable. A cop on every corner. But if they're gone, what does that mean for us?"

Quietly the girls walked through the narrow alleyways, coming across another small group of men 'armed' with sticks. One even held a short piece of plumbing pipe.

They arrived at the large stairway of Hatshepsut's Mansions from the south because of their roundabout return, only to see a large taxi arrive at the same time. Mitch jumped out of the front seat, followed by the much larger Mohamed. The driver got out and nervously opened the back door.

Standing a little away from the vehicle, the three watched in fascination as Mohamed whistled to summon the neighboring bowab, who instantly crept from the shadows of his building. The three men, with the help of the driver, extracted a large, heavy package from the back seat. Mohamed held the center as Mitch and the neighbor bowab clutched the two ends. The taxi driver did not wait for money or chat, but as soon as the package had been unloaded, re-entered the car, started it and pulled away with a screech.

Mitch noticed the three in the shadows and hissed like an Egyptian at Rachel. "Key, get Gamal's house key."

The three men struggled with the long paper-wrapped package up the steps and into the lobby. Barbie rushed forward to call the ancient lift, as Mohamed left momentarily to step lightly into the bowels of the building. A too-wide and too-short piece of plywood accompanied Mohamed as he reappeared before the lift arrived.

In the meantime, Rachel ran up the stairs and Barbie could hear a door opening and closing above. Barbie pulled the door of the tiny lift open as soon as it arrived and closed it behind the three men and the package. Penelope followed Rachel on foot up the stairs. Barbie now ran to get the door when it stopped, as she realized that the lift was full and the package was wedged in a way that would make it almost impossible for any of the occupants of the lift to open the door. The tiny cage looked vulnerable and far too open for this nefarious endeavor. As the ancient machine rose with the usual rattles and creaks, Barbie talked to herself, "Oh, please, don't let anyone else see this. Let this be quiet, for once!"

At the third floor, the three women met the lift and Barbie opened the door. The lift, as usual, had not stopped even with the floor and Barbie warned the men to be careful at they carried their burden, now made more stable with the plywood, out of the lift. They could not see their feet, and the weight as well as the shape of the awkward burden made the journey perilous. Rachel met them at the door of the apartment just down the hallway from hers. She entered first and flipped the light switch. Nothing happened. She tried a lamp, with the same results.

The men carried their burden in the door, using the feeble light from the hallway. Barbie tried the kitchen light, which blinked on, throwing a rectangle of feeble yellow light into the main room. The package was first set on the floor, but Mitch insisted that it be lifted onto the couch, as if someone had come in and laid down for a nap.

The two Egyptians departed quickly. Barbie saw a look of despair on Mohamed's face as he quickly shut the door behind him. Using the feeble light from the kitchen, Mitch cut the string that bound the paper-wrapped bundle. Pulling back layers of paper, a white shroud came into view.

Gingerly, Mitch pulled the fabric back until he had uncovered two eyes, staring straight ahead.

Chapter Eight: Curfew

"On the balcony! You want to put him on the balcony?" Barbie almost screamed at this unbelievable request.

"It's cooler out there. And, do you guys have any ice? Any that you have, and see if you can find any at Llian's house, or anywhere else you can. Go, quietly." Mitch had ditched the gallabeya and keffiyah. Now he demanded their help in transferring Gamal's corpse to the shady part of the balcony on the east side of the house. A large tree gave shade for most of the day, and the afternoon sun never made it to that spot. It was always cool there and the coolness of the night would help preserve the body.

As soon as they had helped Mitch move Gamal from the couch, they raced to get ice. Penelope was the first to return with a bucket, garnered from Llian's freezer compartment. She said she felt distinctly queasy contemplating the corpse, but she murmured to herself, "If they can stand it, so can I. If they can stand it, so can I."

Mitch arranged the ice cubes in plastic bags, tucking them into the paper wrappings and the shroud. He covered Gamal's face and put some ice there as well. As the early evening darkness deepened, they left the body in peace and retreated inside. Mitch found the fuse box and fixed the blown fuse and the lights in the living room came on. None wanted to sit down, or stay long, but before they left, Mitch wanted to get their stories straight.

"No one must know he's here, although it will be obvious shortly that he is 'missing'. I don't know who else may have keys to this apartment, but we need to try and keep everyone out of here. As far as I know, we are the only ones who know he is here. Mohamed might talk, he may be forced to. The other bowab can play dumb really well. Saidis are good at that. You know what they say about people from Upper Egypt? That they are stupid, slow, make good servants because they keep their business to themselves. Well, Mohamed is no dummy, but he can act like one when he needs to. So until we, or I, can figure this out, we need to be really quiet about this."

Mitch carefully locked the door and pocketed the key. Knowing that other keys were out there did not make any of them happy. They had each been issued five keys when they moved in. They learned quickly to let a neighbor have a key in case they locked themselves out, and they were certain that Mohamed had a key. They were also in no doubt that the University housing department had a way to access their apartments as well. No one wanted to ask if Gamal's own key had been found in his possession.

"I think we could use some food, at least some tea," Rachel said as they followed her to her apartment. Mitch came in and sat in the comfortable arm chair placed in front of the TV, which he switched on with the remote. The droning of the announcers sounded on every channel, recalling the conversations with reporters in the square, those seen in glorious shots standing high above the fray in Tahrir, and reporters from other cities in Egypt. Their world was full of the momentous events.

"Isn't there anything else on TV?" Penelope whined.

Mitch swiftly surfed through a number of their favorite channels until he came to a rerun of 'Friends'. Phoebe made yet another lame joke and offered to sing a song. Penelope piped up. "This isn't funny. It is not entertaining, it is not real life and how can we sit here and watch this muck, when life is out there!"

"I think what she means Mitch, is that she wants to go back to the Uprising." Barbie said as she brought some food from the kitchen into the living room. "Sorry for once more intruding, but the TV… Besides, I don't think I could stand to be alone at this point."

They ate in silence for a while. Then Penelope sat up and said, "Damn, I meant to call my parents. Have you guys called home? Do they even know what's happening here?"

"I usually use Skype and so that's out at the moment," replied Rachel. "But I guess we could use our phones to call. It might take minutes though, a lot of them."

"What about the land lines, can't we do that?" Barbie asked. It was obvious now that they had completely forgotten about their families and whether they might be worried or not. "Oh, I forgot, they only work in Egypt, unless you book an international call. So, mobile phones are it."

"I don't have many minutes left. I really want to keep them for an emergency," added Rachel. She looked at Penelope.

"Hey, don't look at me. I don't have any more than you guys do. I forgot about going to the store and getting more minutes. But isn't there a way to call the phone company and add minutes? Like link it to your bank account?"

"Yeah," Mitch conceded, "but I don't think the banks are open at all. All that I saw today were closed and the lines at the ATMs were long."

"Well, I've got money, but we have to connect with the phone company. Mitch, do you know how to do that?" Barbie asked.

"I can try." Mitch pulled out his phone and proceeded to run through menus and punch in numbers. At one point, he seemed to have figured out which number to call, but there was no answer. A busy signal sang on and on.

"Has anyone gotten a phone call from home on our landlines? I mean, they know our numbers, don't they?" Rachel looked puzzled. "Do they think that everything is just normal here? Aren't they watching TV or reading the papers? Where are their heads?"

"Don't blame them. Most of our families just have no clue where we are, what we're doing or even if this thing is real or not." Barbie looked depressed. "I wonder if they know how serious it is. Maybe they are just waiting for us to call them, but they don't know what the situation is. Have they ever had their internet turned off, or their phones go dead because the government did it to them? Maybe they just don't know. Actually, my parents might think it's quite an adventure. Old hippies, you know."

"Well, I think mine would be horrified if they knew how dangerous all this is. I'll think about using some minutes to call. Wrong time now, though. Saturday morning, too early." Penelope turned towards the TV that Mitch had switched back to the happenings in Cairo.

The news of the curfew, that was being widely flouted, was being broadcast on all channels. Mitch turned to an Arabic station and reported that the newscasters were unrelenting in their urgings for the populace to stay inside and obey the wishes of their leaders. "This must be a government station," Mitch said. "Wait, now they are explaining why. The police have all gone home, now the army is in charge."

"So, what difference does that make?" Penelope asked. "I mean, police, army, they are all controlled by the government, aren't they?"

"I think there is a general perception that the army is more professional, that they are well-trained and that their major job is to protect the populace, not harass them. The police are definitely the bad guys in this scenario. They are the ones who killed the businessman in Alexandria that started all this. And they are the ones who have been shooting people, not the army. The army can possibly gain the people's trust. Wow, look now! Look, tanks in Tahrir, the Army being welcomed! Wow, look at that!"

As if on cue, the cameras panned across the square as Army tanks rolled in among the people. They had to slow down as the crowds surrounded them and shouted. The announcer was excited by this as well, the words tumbling out of his mouth as he reported the first time that the Tahrir Square demonstrators welcomed anything smacking of authority. Far away shots showed the immense crowds that swelled the square, despite (or perhaps because of) the curfew. Not just men, but women and children thronged the open space. On the previously green lawn spaces, tents had sprouted and now covered the spaces with wisps of nylon. Banners and placards everywhere showed support for the demonstrators and against President Mubarak.

As they watched, a photo of Mohammed el Baradei, the Western-respected former UN inspector, was shown. An announcer said that el Baradei had showed up in Tahrir and made a statement. "The people have broken the barrier of fear. There is no going back." The announcer also remarked that the presence of this figure in the square seemed a bit unusual, as he was reported to be under arrest. "But as you can see, he is here, with us, in Tahrir Square."

A knock on the door startled them all. Mitch rose to answer it as the three women crowded behind him. Mohamed the bowab conferred with Mitch in rapid-fire Arabic. Barbie noticed that Parker Hampton and W.B. Lee hovered in the dim light of the lobby behind Mohamed. Their faces were serious, verging on frightened.

Mitch closed the door, grabbed his jacket and a flashlight and looked at the three women. "The men are being requested to meet." He opened the door and went out quickly, shutting it firmly behind him.

"This is not good," Rachel said. "They need the men, but not us. Does this have to do with fighting? Why can't we go?"

"You want to go too? Out there? Into the night?" Penelope asked.

"Reports of fatalities are coming in, from many places in the country. It was reported that over 100 people have died since the beginning of the protests on January 25. Most of these are reported to have been killed by authorities, but evidence is lacking as to the exact number and names. Chaos in some neighborhoods has prevented authorities from accurately counting those who have died. Bodies have been taken to mosques, families notified and bodies removed for burial without proper notification. Hundreds of injuries have been treated by local doctors or at home, and again, no accurate count of these is available."

"Well, we know of one, at least," said Barbie, sudden tears springing to her eyes. "Poor Ahmed, what did he do to deserve that? It just seems impossible that he could get messed up with something like that kind of violence. How did it possibly happen? And then, Gamal. That is even worse. We don't know anything about that. When or how. Presumably shot by police. This is way too much for me to handle."

"And the communication. I think that is the worst. We don't know anything except what they tell us on the TV and what we hear from the other expats." Penelope added.

"And what kind of reliability do you think both of those sources have?" added Rachel.

"What I can't stand, or understand, is why there have been two from this building? What are the odds? I mean, it's not like we are the instigators of the plot or anything. Why us, and why a little kid who isn't old enough to understand? And Gamal. What kind of business did he get involved in that put him in so much danger?" Barbie stood and reached for another tissue.

"What makes you think they are so separate? Maybe the two deaths are related?" Penelope said. "I mean, Ahmed was found here on Friday night and Gamal this morning at the Museum, but they were often together you know. Maybe they were somehow or other involved in something else together. That would explain two deaths in one house, especially when they knew each other. Maybe the police targeted one, or both of them. We don't really know where they were yesterday, during all the commotion in the square. They could have been anywhere."

"Penelope Watson, you have a very good mind. I think frankly you are right, I think there is a connection. Ahmed and Gamal often went places together. You know that Gamal's Arabic wasn't all that good and he used Ahmed to translate for him. If Gamal was going to the square and maybe to the Museum, maybe he asked Ahmed to come with him?"

"But, Ahmed was killed here." Rachel pointed out, "That's a long way from the Museum. And if they are connected, why were the two bodies found so far from each other?"

"Stop, stop, this is really creeping me out. Next you'll be saying that Gamal killed Ahmed, or the other way around, or that… Just stop, the whole thing is terrible. Maybe I should go home." Barbie sniffled and burst into tears again.

"Hey," Penelope said, reaching over to hug Barbie. "You found the dead body of a friend. That is heavy shit for anyone. And I don't think that one death has anything to do with the other. This revolution has got all of us in a tizzy. Poor Ahmed could have been killed by a number of people. Even though we think Zamalek is safe, it's not always safe for a small boy who likes to spy on people, run errands for people who buy drugs or alcohol in back alleys or any one of a number of things that I am sure Ahmed did. Please don't forget who he was. He was smart and funny and would do just about anything for a pound. He defied authority whenever and wherever he could. He was a naughty boy."

"But he wasn't bad!" Barbie defended the dead.

"I never said he was, just loved the game." Penelope pointed out.

"Could it have been by mistake? Maybe the killer was looking for someone else and mistook Ahmed for that person in the dark? Maybe they killed Ahmed thinking he was involved in something he wasn't. Or maybe as a warning to someone else not to mess with them? There are so many other possibilities that we haven't thought of yet. But please, don't say that Gamal was mixed up in it. I hope not; I pray not."

"How did he die?" Penelope asked quietly.

Barbie looked at Penelope, her friend, who had dared to ask the awful question. She knew the answer to it, but had tried to block it for the past day. She had tried to put it to the back of her mind and not think about it. She had tried to pretend to be Scarlet O'Hara who put things off until tomorrow or sometime in the future. She had not wanted to face the fact of his death and the manner of it. But she knew. She had seen, had even touched the cheap knife. It was available in all the souvenir stores, not expensive or hard to find. And she had seen it, sticking out at an angle just to the left of the sternum. It had been thrust into his heart just underneath the ribcage. She shivered at the thought.

Mitch burst into the room. Rachel and Penelope jumped up at his entrance and asked what was happening.

He threw himself into the easy chair and shook his head in amazement. "It's like a home security thing. You know the police have gone; they've been gone since last night. There hasn't been any one protecting or watching us for more than a day. We have been on our own, so to speak. The army have moved in, but they sit on their tanks and 'protect' buildings, for heaven's sake. What about purse snatchings, petty theft and break-ins? Anyway, there has been a movement, kind of a grassroots thing, all over Cairo. We are dividing the neighborhoods up into sectors and we will station men out and about all night. Kind of a neighborhood watch or homeland security sort of thing. It sounds really crazy, but because there is no police protection, we need to do something. Anyway, I went to a meeting with the 'guys' and we agreed on strategy. I'll take my turn sometime early in the morning."

"That's insane," said Rachel. "Just the men, the 'girls' don't get to defend ourselves?"

"Sometimes Rachel, you are too much of a feminist! This isn't a country that honors that AT ALL. The thugs out there would just as soon rape you as anything. There are rumors that the government has deliberately opened the prisons and let the bad guys out. You know how Mubarak has said that without him there would be chaos, that we need him to keep the peace and if he left, the country would disintegrate? Well, they say that he did this, let out the prisoners and told the police to go home, just to prove his point. Can you imagine? If that's true, then we do need to defend ourselves."

"This is incredible. This is just totally unbelievable." Penelope said. "This whole thing keeps getting weirder and weirder and worse and worse."

"Well, I'm going to bed to see if I can get some sleep before I brave the cold and ennui of taking my turn at guard duty. Good night all." Mitch stood and headed for the bedroom.

Barbie jumped up and stopped him, saying to him in a low voice. "I was just thinking about Ahmed, about what happened to him. Do you think it could have been the thugs last night?"

"Yes, I do, definitely. Now we know a bit more, it appears more and more that way. Sorry."

"But how did Gamal die? I know this may sound strange, but there have been two from this apartment building. It just seems so unpredictable, so coincidental. I mean, were they related at all? We know they knew each other, maybe…" Barbie whispered so that the others couldn't hear.

Mitch looked at her with hooded eyes, with a look that cast warnings at her. "Why do you ask?"

"Because of Ahmed, because of the way he was killed. He wasn't shot by the police. It was more intimate than that, wasn't it? To be stabbed like that, it had to be more personal." Barbie thought that Mitch was delaying, did not want to tell her the details, and so spare her the awfulness of the two deaths.

"Do not say anything to anyone. Do not spread any rumors. Not a word to anyone, you understand?"

Barbie nodded cautiously.

"He was stabbed in the chest, here." Mitch pointed to a point, low on his chest. He clenched his fist around a make-believe knife and thrust it upward. "Just like Ahmed."

Chapter Nine: Homeland Security

The three 'girls' were eating again a half hour later when Mitch emerged from the bedroom. He mumbled, "Couldn't sleep."

"Oh, I'm sorry honey, was the TV keeping you awake?" Rachel jumped up to soothe him.

"Naw, just jumpy, nervous, like everyone else. What's the latest on the news?" Mitch asked as he flopped into a chair. Barbie thought he looked spooked and shaken. They all felt it, but she knew that he bore the brunt of the secretiveness, the deaths and the uncertainty of the demonstrations.

"Well, tell us more about this meeting. Who was there? Where was it? Who called it? Everything, no secrecy because it was only men," Penelope demanded.

Mitch ate stale potato chips as he recounted the details of the meeting. "Actually, it was rather large, but just people from these few buildings on the street. It was held in the lobby downstairs, but we moved out into the street later to get the feel of what we were to check and how to do it. I think the idea was to figure out how to defend the street if a crowd of undesirables came along. We talked about roadblocks and how to set them up. Did you know that there was a retired army general living next door? I mean, I think I've seen him around, but I had no idea that he was such an important person. He was the one who came up with the roadblock idea."

"Were there Egyptians and expats?" asked Barbie. She knew that the neighborhood contained both, but the picture of this motley crew of residents was vague and fuzzy.

"Yeah, it was a collection of just about all the 'men' in the neighborhood. That includes all social classes. The bowabs were there and some of the small shop owners wanted to stay in their shops to protect them, so they were all counted as temporary residents. So, yes, all kinds, all shades, all classes of people. We were told to arm ourselves. Of course the general has actual guns, but he only hinted at that. And I for one, do not want to encounter my neighbor with a gun, for fear of their stupidity. So I think we are going for the broomstick variety."

"That's what we saw this afternoon! The guys with broomsticks and one with a pipe, they were part of this. And that's why they were being so insistent that we 'go home'." Barbie said.

"Well, part of the problem is knowing who is a Zamalekite and who isn't. So they suggested ideas about how to distinguish 'us' from 'them'. It was almost ridiculous, but they do have a point. We might have to wear armbands or something."

"Does this sound sort of familiar? Something like yellow armbands with the Star of David on them?" Barbie jumped up, genuinely horrified at the thought.

"No, no, not like that. But if strangers do come in, at least we will know they don't belong here, because they won't be wearing the armbands. That's the reasoning. But hey, I'm just reporting here. Don't shoot me, just because I'm the messenger." Mitch flinched at Barbie's words.

"Well, are these to be black armbands for mourning or white ones, or red ones steeped in blood?" Barbie carried on.

Mitch lowered his head. "I think they were talking about blue ones."

"Blue, now what color of blue? True blue or pale blue. And who will supply these armbands? Do we get them for free or do we have to pay for them?"

"Barbie, listen to me. This was a suggestion. And I think it best that you not wear one."

"Then I can be a citizen of Cairo, a citizen of the world, and not be 'identified' as one kind of person or another. What about the people who live in Maadi, what color will they be?"

"I don't know. But it was a suggestion."

"And what other suggestions did they have?" Rachel asked, trying to deflect the conversation.

"Well, the home guards idea was to get people to defend the island. I think the general and others were afraid of people coming across the bridge from Agouza. You know that Zamalek is basically a high-class suburb, and perhaps there are a lot of people here who support Mubarak, or who are more on the side of peaceful change, or at least not in favor of demonstrations…"

"Like the general?"

"Like the General. Wow Barbie, your parents and school did a real number on you, didn't they?" Mitch cocked his head at her.

"Oh, no, more like my contrary nature. So, go on."

"They are still trying to figure out this thing about sending the police home and opening the prisons. It appears that the police stations all over Cairo are empty. So that means that there are guns out there, taken home by the police, or looted from the police stations by the prisoners as they left. But this we know: there are more weapons on the streets now, and they are not necessarily in the hands of people that are friendly with the population. So that is a very good reason to have these guards everywhere. We don't know who has weapons, of what kinds, and what they might do to someone. Actually, the police are laying very, very low. Some of those criminals that escaped are supposedly 'looking for' the cops that put them away. It is a time for revenge."

"You mean the revolution could be an excuse to exact revenge? Under the guise of 'protecting nascent democracy', criminals, and others, could use this for personal gain? Hmmm. Actually, a very clever idea. But what have we done?" Barbie looked at Mitch for answers.

"We don't know. There are just lots and lots of rumors."

"So, do you think revenge was what got Ahmed?" Barbie asked in a small voice.

"I don't know Barbie. It could have been. His life was not an open book to anyone. He was secretive. He was also bold. He could have crossed the wrong person. And we must remember this. It is not our business. Given this whole chaotic situation, we may never know." Mitch looked at Barbie again, daring her to deny his words.

Barbie stared back and nodded her head, assenting to his assessment. "So what else did you learn in this meeting?"

"It was pretty classist, if you ask me. We don't talk too much about social class in America, but this meeting brought home to me where we stand in Egypt. We are upper-class. We, by virtue of our nationality and working for the AUE, are classified that way. I certainly wouldn't call myself upper-class," he chuckled and shook his head. "But we are. And those people who have no money, no education, no cultural capital, they are not. And the unspoken message I got today was that we need to defend ourselves against those lower-class persons who might try to cross the bridge and murder us in our sleep. It was a weird combination of football hooligans, unemployed, those not from here, that is, Upper Egypt, the poor…"

"The huddled masses yearning to breathe free."

"Only in America do we want those, Barbie. No, as I said, this was not the Egyptians of Zamalek's finest hour. And no one wants a repeat of last night. The burning of the NDP headquarters, the prison breakouts, the break-in at the Museum, the gunshots heard all over Maadi. They are hoping that these home guards can contain or deflect that behavior. And I, for one, am against violence and chaos. So, I will go and do my duty. Oh my gosh," Mitch looked at his watch. "I completely forgot. There's a meeting of AUE staff tonight."

"When were you going to tell us that? You were off to bed not too long ago." Rachel looked at her husband angrily.

"You haven't missed it, it's in 20 minutes. At Professor Smythe's apartment."

Just then, the TV announcer came into focus and the running commentary on the bottom of the screen caused all of them to turn. Rachel turned the TV up.

"Unconfirmed reports are coming in that plain clothes gunmen are shooting demonstrators. The demonstrators have told reporters that undercover police have been told to shoot at certain persons, targeting ringleaders and others who have been identified from the social media sites. When confronted, these citizens have fled with their weapons. Our cameras have been unable to capture any of the reported gunmen, nor have any of them stayed around to volunteer any information about who is paying them or what they are doing with the high-end weapons they are carrying. One demonstrator said, 'You know they are special forces; you just need to look at them. They are well-dressed, they are well-fed, and they move with confidence. They are not members of the Ultras.' Our reporters are attempting to verify these reports and interview the gunmen if possible. Please stay tuned for more reports."

"Ultras?" asked Penelope.

"Football fans. The Zamalek fan club calls themselves the Ultras White Knights. It's a cross between a gang and a football fan club. The members are very intense and some of this violence seemed to be between the football fans and the police. It is a long standing feud."

"Wow, I've got to look in on the cat before that meeting. I don't want him to have any reason to get out again." Barbie left and ran up the stairs.

Meowing hungrily as Barbie sneaked in the door, Badboy rubbed her ankles and purred as she attempted to get to the kitchen to get his food. Barbie watched as he gulped down half of his food and then as he looked for his litter box.

"Oh, I forgot little one. I put it out on the balcony while Miss Penelope is sleeping in my room." Barbie went with the cat to the balcony.

Badboy stepped out and looked around. As he scratched in his box, Barbie looked out on the scene. It was much the same as last night. There was menace in the air, and a strange smell rose from below to envelope her. Uncollected garbage, tear gas, fear? Barbie ruminated.

She looked down and to her left and then she realized that she had a good view of Gamal's balcony. She had never given it a thought before now, but she could see the dim outlines of two chairs with a large package spread between them. As she watched, a dim light spilled out of the window and a form appeared. She caught her breath until she was sure it was Mitch. The cat meowed.

Mitch looked up. "Barbie, is that you?" he asked.

"I hope so," she hissed. "What are you doing?"

"Do you have any more ice?"

"Not really. I know that we filled the trays up, but with our old fridge, I'm not sure they have frozen again. What's the matter?"

"Well, it's just that this is a dead body and we really need to keep it cold. We can't put it in a fridge because it's too big. The only thing we can do is try to keep it as cool as possible. The night air helps, but we need more ice."

"I'll check," she said, turning to go into the apartment.

She realized what the smell had been on the balcony. It was the smell of death.

Chapter Ten: A Gathering of Expats

The four knocked on the door to Professor Cornelius Smythe's apartment, which was opened by his live-in houseboy. Barbie thought his name was Mohammed, or one of the many variations, but was unsure, so just greeted him warmly in English. "Good evening."

She got a slight smile and a bow, but no verbal greeting in return. He offered to take their coats and helped them to hang them up on a large coat rack in the wide entryway. A huge shoebox occupied one corner and a full-length mirror hung beside the coat rack. The entryway was a room unto itself, decorated in what Barbie recognized as AUE issued furniture and some lovingly restored antiques. A few photos adorned the remaining wall space, showing Cornelius in his younger years, with a full head of light-brown hair, standing at the edge of a pit, gallabeya-clad workers gathered in the background.

The main room was already half-full, and more chairs were delivered from the dining room as they approached. The comfy seats were taken; the couch had three seated, plus one perched on either end. Cornelius held court in the large armchair that faced the large-screen TV that perched where the old-fashioned fireplace used to be. Barbie noted that the damn thing had been turned off for a few minutes for the meeting.

"Hello, hello," greeted Mercedes, wife of W.B. "Now that you English teachers are here, you can help us with the latest word game. What do you call a group of expats? A congress of expats? A herd of expats?"

"How about 'a blunder of expats'?" someone called out.

"A deportation of expats?' giggled another.

"Or a manifest of expats, as in a list of people on the flight."

"An intoxication of expatriates, or an ostentation of…"

"An oblivion of expats, as in no one really knows what is happening."

"An expaggle of expats."

"Really you know, the proper word for it is 'absquatulation', sort of a combination of abscond and squat. Isn't that what we do, leave our own countries, running away from something or someone and then squat in another place. I'm sure that is what the proper term is," Cornelius declared in a commanding voice from his chair.

"I'd check the internet on that, but we haven't any at the moment," tossed out another expat.

As the group helped themselves to drink and food, Barbie looked around the apartment as she wandered into the kitchen to get a glass of water. It was a typical Egyptian apartment of the age. The fireplace might once have been a good idea, but the air pollution was now so bad in Cairo that Barbie couldn't imagine what the populace would do with added smoke from fires to keep warm in the mild winters. She had been assured that winters in the past had been much colder than at present. The living room was spacious, about twenty by twenty feet, and held the usual assortment of comfortable, but casual overstuffed furniture. By contrast, the dining room next to it, was more old-fashioned. A huge oval table, able to seat at least twelve, held center place in the room that had in the past been designated as the 'ladies' room' and even now could be cut off from the main reception room by a curtain. It was as large as the living room and also contained a matching buffet and cabinet for dishes. All were elaborately carved and painted a muted brown and gold. Barbie had seen bilious green, baby blue, puke-yellow and brown and just plain dirty brown inlaid and carved furniture. It must have appealed to Egyptians in the past, as much of the furniture was still for sale, and that made in the older parts of Cairo was of a faux French of the nineteenth century. Threadbare carpets of an ancient age lay on the floor. She knew that Cornelius had been in Egypt in time to see the last flood and she wondered if he had owned these carpets since then. There was a further room off the dining room that held a smaller collection of chairs, a desk and a computer. Cornelius Smythe might have had eight decades behind him, but he was not behind the modern times. A wide hallway penetrated further into the apartment. She wandered further, looking into rooms, and readying her excuse if any should challenge her, of seeking the facilities. One bedroom held a double bed, a huge wardrobe and matching vanity and a chest of drawers. As it was dark, Barbie was unable to ascertain the color that it was supposed to have been, perhaps a soothing pink/red combination. Again, this bedroom was more spacious than hers. Further along the corridor, she pushed open another door to yet another large bedroom, obviously unoccupied and reserved for guests. At last she came to the bathroom, entered and locked the door. This room was twice the size of her own apartment's bathroom, but the space was needed as there was a washing machine, a large gas-powered hot water heater, a huge bathtub, a bidet as well as a toilet, spacious sink and a large closet for linens. Barbie used the facilities and gently dried her hands on the clean, fluffy towel.

As she exited, she wandered back to the kitchen looking for a drink of water. She stood and gazed around the large kitchen, unusual in an apartment in Cairo. Just then, a door opened from the end of the kitchen, and Cornelius' man came in. Barbie could just make out a small room behind. She realized that this was a servant's room. The extra space here and on the other side, in Professors Mary Bell's apartment, was what took up so much of the building's first floor. There were windows that overlooked the front of the building, facing on Al-Sheikh Al Masrafy, as well as windows in the rear.

"Madam, may I help?" he asked, shutting the door behind him very firmly.

"Water, I wanted a glass of water."

"It is on the table in the dining room."

"Yes, oh yes, thank you."

Barbie smiled but stood her ground as he left the room with a pointed backward glance at his closed door.

She realized that Cornelius' apartment must be at least 75% bigger than the smaller two-bedroom apartments upstairs. She had never been in this part of the flat and she now swung around, trying to orient herself in this space. She turned and faced the living room, now becoming noisier as more guests arrived. In her mind, she plotted the front of the building, the back of the building, and the front door that led to the center of the building. She looked at the closed door and realized that this small room, if it had a window, overlooked the side of the building where the large garbage bin stood, beside which she had found the body of Ahmed. Noise out there could have been heard in this small room. And if there was a door that went out from this room to the garbage area, a servants' door, then it might have been possible that…

"Barbie," hissed Penelope. "We're about to start this meeting." Penelope stood at the door to the kitchen, the manservant hovering behind her.

"Oh, sorry, I was just coming." She hurried to the living room and realized that any hope of a seat had been missed because of her wanderings. She counted the people, starting with those from this building. Professor Bell was here, as well as Mercedes and W.B. Of course, she thought, Gamal was here, in the building, just lying upstairs in no condition to join them. As she peeked around, she saw Professor Hampton slip into the shadows of the doorway to the entry hall. She looked for Llian, not really expecting to find her, but hoping perhaps that she had returned from vacation. Also, the couple from across the way was not yet back. There were others from the neighboring buildings. Standing behind the couch were two more English teachers and two Egyptian faculty members, one of them accompanied by his wife. A biology professor, a handsome Frenchman, sat opposite her. There were also three people she had never met before, and two more that she recognized as AUE faculty, but whose names she did not know.

Cornelius was holding court; there was no other way to describe the pomposity of his orders to the new comers to help themselves to food and drink. His own glass sat in the table beside him, jealously guarded by his clenched fist around it. Barbie recognized the clear amber liquid as his favorite whiskey.

"Hmm, ladies and gentlemen, let us begin. As the senior person in this neighborhood from the university, I've been asked to fill you in on what the administration is doing. First of all, there are no evacuation orders. We are not the US embassy, we are a private institution, and you are all here in a private capacity. Even though we are the 'American' university, we are made up of many nationalities. Therefore, you need to look to your own national embassy for instructions for evacuation or not. The second thing I need to say is that you may leave if you feel as though it is best. Many with children have left or are planning to leave, so that is up to you, but you need to do what you feel best. Our classes were not scheduled to start for another week, and the administration is hoping that all of this will die down before then. But, if it hasn't, further decisions need to be made. Although the university is not far from the action in Tahrir, it is far enough away so that we should be able to get to our offices and classrooms as long as there is no open warfare. We all realize that the last few days have been filled with chaos, so of course we won't go to our offices."

"But what about the curfew?" someone called out.

"The curfew is a problem, I know. Although the university must honor the curfew, as private citizens it is up to you. I would take care."

"Can we get back to the evacuation? I heard on the TV that the airport is chaos. All the tourists are crowding onto the planes and that even getting to the airport is a nightmare."

"Yes, let me read what the university has said." Cornelius pulled out a crumpled paper from his pants pocket and fumbled for his glasses. Over his shoulder, his manservant handed them to him, as if this request was a frequent one. "Shukran," Cornelius whispered.

"If any faculty or staff wish to leave, they must make sure that their head of department or supervisor is advised of the fact that they will no longer be in the country. You must let the university know where you are and how they can reach you. Phone numbers and so forth. No one here has internet access, do they? Anyway, if you wish to take advantage of the US evacuation efforts, you must make your way to the airport. The US government has promised that anyone who wishes to leave will be accommodated with transportation out of the country. However, the destinations are limited. Athens is one, Cyprus is another. There has been some talk of Rome or Istanbul as well. In any case, you have NO way of knowing in advance where you will go, or even when you will go. They suggest that you bring as little luggage as possible, but you must carry to the airport three days' worth of food and drinking water, as the supplies at the airport are extremely limited. Also, you must pay full economy fare for this service, but you don't need to pay in advance. You may sign a promissory note that you will repay this amount in the future. When you get to your destination, wherever it is, you are on your own at that point."

"I don't believe this!" the wife of one of the faculty members, that Barbie had never met, yelled. "They can't do this to us. They are responsible for us. The university needs to help us, not just tell us, 'Go to the airport'. This is outrageous. They are just like vampires, throwing us to the wolves."

Penelope leaned over to whisper to Rachel, "A bit of mixed metaphors there."

"They need to evacuate us! Now! I didn't sign up for this! This is not what I was promised!" The wife burst into tears and her husband reluctantly put his arm around her to comfort her. Barbie could only imagine how and why this couple made the decision to come to Egypt. It wasn't always so easy on the spouse who did not have the contract to leave everything and come to an unknown country and culture. Many a shaky marriage did not last through a foreign posting, she thought. She pushed away thoughts about the longevity of this marriage, or this posting.

Mitch spoke up now, trying to get more information, but also trying to avoid the topic as he glanced at Rachel. "What did the university administrators, specifically the president, say about going to the Square?"

"Ah, a good question, my boy! They remind us that we are strangers in this country, citizens of other countries with different laws and customs, so we must be careful of obeying the laws of this country. The president was particularly wary of the curfew. He said that we must pay attention to it and that violation of the curfew is against the law."

"But everyone is out in the street and the square, even though there is a curfew. Do they know it exists?" asked someone from the rear.

"Of course, Egyptians do what they need to do," continued Cornelius. "But as Americans, this is what the university administration advises us. BUT, we are here in the capacity of private citizens, and the president acknowledges that we can act as we see fit, the university has no hold on us; they cannot tell us what we must do."

"Well, I want to be evacuated immediately!" the hysterical wife continued.

"My dear good lady. I suggest you wait until morning. The dawn brings new light and you may find that things look brighter, or at least you will be able to get a taxi then. Mind the three days of food and water requirement."

"I want to go home now. How am I supposed to do that, there is a curfew!" she retorted.

"You only live a block away, maybe Cornelius can walk you," added a snarky voice from the shadows. Barbie suspected it came from Parker Hampton, but couldn't be sure.

"My dear lady, if you are unable to make it, we can ask Mohamed, our bowab, to accompany you, or if you are frightened of him, he can be frightening I know, there are empty apartments where you may rest your delightful self for the night."

The wife was guided slowly by her husband off to the kitchen. Whispered words of comfort could be heard as they exited the room.

"What about money?" the French biology professor asked. "I have almost no Egyptian pounds left and the ATMs are empty, or refusing to dispense large amounts. Twenty pounds is not a great fortune."

"Oh yes," Cornelius continued. "There is also information about that. How did the administration know that so many of us would be caught off guard, with little or no money in our pockets? In any case, if you feel as though you are unable to attend to your needs, the university has established a loan for you, until the banks reopen."

"How much can we get, I'm thinking of a couple of thousand pounds. I have dry cleaning to pick up and my cupboards are empty. What am I supposed to eat?" complained a voice from the rear.

"I am afraid that the dry cleaning may have to wait. The university is willing to lend you 250 pounds." Cornelius smiled broadly.

Hoots of laughter greeted this announcement. "Two hundred and fifty pounds, that's not enough to buy dinner out. How am I supposed to live on 250 pounds, until when?" Mercedes asked angrily.

Barbie snorted at this admission of extravagance of payment for dinner. She whispered to Penelope at her side, "Where does she eat all the time? The Ramses Hilton, the Four Seasons? Fifty bucks for dinner?"

"I think the ATMs at the Marriott are still working. Have you tried the two at the southern entrance? They are kind of stuck away and at least one of them gives dollars. I think that may be a better currency than Egyptian pounds," offered one of the Egyptians.

"Oh, I have Euros," said the Frenchman. "That should work." Murmurs of thinking out loud greeted this as the expats thought of alternatives to Egyptian pounds in their hands.

A loud knocking at the door interrupted the excited murmurs of the absquatulation of expats. Cornelius raised his head and someone near the door opened it. The crowd tried to peer out into the lobby, trying to see who had missed this valuable meeting.

                    Phyllis Wachob

It was the towering Mohamed, the bowab. He wore a puzzled face at finding so many of his irregular soldiers at the same place. "It is time!" he announced in clear English.

"Guard duty," said the Frenchman. "I am on first watch. Who goes with me?" He entered the vestibule and rummaged through the coats and bags piled there. "Ah, my weapon," he announced as he held up a long round wooden stick about a yard long and an inch thick.

"Nice stick, very beautiful in fact,' remarked one of the Egyptians. "But what is this, this white powder on it?"

"Oh, it must be flour. This is a special weapon, lent to me by my wonderful wife. She would not let me go unarmed, so she found the best for me. It is her special rolling pin, for making the French pastries."

Chapter Eleven: What to Do About Our Brother

As Barbie brushed her teeth, she was glad it was not an activity that demanded a lot of concentration, as her head was twirling with thoughts on the revolution, the deaths, and whether they should evacuate or not. She couldn't imagine trying to sleep. Penelope was asleep in Barbie's bedroom, on a mattress on the floor, but still Barbie knew she would toss and turn if she went to bed. Barbie understood Penelope's reasons for invading Barbie's privacy, and she didn't really blame her. She might have moved into Penelope's room, if her friend had not taken the initiative. The cat lay curled up next to Penelope, hopefully bringing some warmth and kindness.

Penelope had had a crying fit before she went to sleep, asking the hard questions that neither could answer about what was going to happen, what they should do and where all this was heading for themselves and the university. They talked about the future of their jobs, whether they would still have them when 'it was all over.' They wondered if they would get paid or not, how they might look for other jobs with no internet and no sign of it. It seemed foolish to simply leave and try to find jobs elsewhere as it was the middle of the school year. But they both knew places where jobs were to be had at any time of the year.

Barbie rinsed her mouth and prepared for bed. She looked in on Penelope, now softly snoring. The cat looked up at her and Barbie called softly to him. He got up and followed her to the living room. Barbie sat on the couch, pulled up an afghan and Badboy found a warm spot near her hip. She reviewed the conversation she had had with Penelope when they returned from Professor Smythe's apartment. Barbie had tried to make things look rosy, although she didn't feel it, and didn't think they were especially promising. Penelope had said it, "Ahmed is dead, Gamal is dead. This is more than just a 'civil disturbance.'" Although Barbie had tried to put a positive spin on it, she now admitted that Penelope was right. This was deadly serious.

They had rehashed between them information that they had gleaned from Mitch, the newscasts and what they knew or suspected. Barbie had maintained that it was a revolution, like the American Revolution. Gunshots were fired on both sides, people had died. But Penelope had pointed out that in the case of America and England, that the oppressors and the oppressed were separated by an entire ocean and that was in the days when internet did not bring the world together instantly. It was foolish to think that what they experienced was in any way comparable to the American Revolution. Besides, the American colonists had never said they wanted the removal of King George, just that they didn't want him as their king. But this was a large group of people who wanted to get rid of their elected leader. It was Mitch who pointed out all the ways in which Mubarak had cheated and stolen the elections, especially the last one. Therefore, they could quite legitimately say that Mubarak was not their chosen leader. Mitch had said it so eloquently. "The Egyptian people had been ruled by foreigners for 2000 years. Is was only in 1952 that they had their own leader. But since then, the 'pharaohs' have been dictators, stealing money from the treasury to wage hopeless wars, enrich their families and friends and consolidate their power. They trampled the rights of the citizens, and they neglected to make sure that the fellaheen (peasants) benefited from the riches of Egypt."

Barbie thought of her students, many of them upper class, but many from that rising middle class that led the demonstrators in the Square. She thought of the household maids, the doormen, the janitors at the club and at the campus, and the 'tea boys' who raced through the streets with tiny cups of tea for whoever had called and ordered it from the teashops. She thought of the women who sat on street corners selling vegetables, the young men who worked in the shops in Zamalek with so little to show for it at the end of the day. They were ordered around by their bosses, but were never able to save enough to become a 'boss' themselves. She thought of all of these people, always so kind to her, polite, smiling and proud to be Egyptian. They deserved better than they were getting. These thoughts led to Ahmed, and she tried to hold back her tears, once again. This was a revolution for him, for Ahmed to experience democracy, freedom of speech, a better education than what was offered in his small town, a chance to broaden his horizon and a chance at life. But he would never see it. He had become a casualty of this fight between the dictator and the stifled voices of the people.

"You will not go unnoticed. You will not have died in vain! I swear it, my little friend Ahmed. I will not rest until I can find out what happened. And if I can, I will avenge your senseless death!" Barbie swore to herself. She let the tears roll down her face as Badboy moved closer, in a cat attempt at comfort.

Suddenly, Penelope was in the doorway. "I'm scared."

Barbie, in her usual role of 'comforting older sister,' wiped the tears from her eyes and patted the couch. "Have a seat. I think we are all scared. I don't know how you can sleep at all."

"Not much. I worry about everything. I go to sleep, but my brain won't rest; it just starts in twirling and whirling, thinking about everything. I worry about us. What we will do if this gets worse? What will happen to Egypt? What about poor little Ahmed? What happened to him? How can they go on killing little boys? And I worry about the young foolish men out in the square. You heard what el Baradei said, 'The people have lost their fear.' Fear is what keeps us safe. Running away when the big bad wolf comes is a very good idea! But they aren't running; they are defying the wolf."

"They do it because they want a better life. They want some self-determination. I can understand that. I'm an American, and I know that my life is infinitely better off because I was born in that country. I have a voice in what happens to me. I can vote, I can complain without fear of being put in jail and tortured, I can choose where to go and what to do. I'm not tied down by tradition, poor education, or prejudice. They are our brothers, they are humans, people of this world. I need to care about them as if they are family." Barbie's voice rose as she spoke, until she almost shouted.

"Barbie, calm down. No need to get hysterical. But I am seriously considering leaving. I don't know how my family feels, but I know they must be worried, just a little at least. Which reminds me, I can call now. They'll be awake. How much would it cost, do you think?" Penelope looked for her phone and her address book with phone numbers.

"The phone call or the flight? And don't forget the hotels, meals, etc. That may be more than the flight. Where would you go? Where would you stay? At least here you have free housing." Barbie reminded her.

"And no bread."

"I do not believe for one second that we will suffer from lack of food. In months maybe, but not in a week or so. It is just a civil disturbance. It has taken the form of a revolution, but it is really limited. Just think of it as making history. We are in the midst of history in the making. In years to come, we can tell people, 'I was there. I was in Cairo during the revolution.'"

"I need to call my family. I'm not so sure I want to be in a revolution." Penelope opened her address book, looking for the phone number of her parents.

"Well, I want to be here; I want this to be MY time, my opportunity to be in the middle of things." Barbie countered.

"What about Ahmed? You could end up like him, dead in a back alley!"

"Don't be so melodramatic. I know there is some danger out there, but not for us. And look at it this way. We are citizens of the world. We owe it to the Egyptian people, our brothers, to stand with them in their fight against tyranny!" Barbie stood.

"Are we all expected to sing the 'Marseillaise' together now?" Penelope asked, one hand on her phone, one hand keeping the place in her small book.

"What are you talking about?" Barbie asked. A heartbeat later, she smiled. "Very funny, we are NOT in Casablanca now. But you may be partially right. Oh, make your phone call." Barbie got up, gathered her quilt around her and let Penelope have some privacy.

Even though she was in another room, she listened to Penelope's part of the phone call as she very quickly gave a run down on the events.

"No, no, no. I am NOT in danger. But we don't know what will happen. That is the worst thing. Yeah, yeah, yeah, I've got money if I need to get out. As long as my credit card still works. I have to go. If you need to contact me, you can try this mobile number, although I don't know if it will work. This phone call is very expensive and we all need to save our telephone minutes for emergencies. We are not sure we'll be able to buy more. Bye, wish us all luck!" Penelope closed her phone and came into the bedroom. "Well, that is done. They were remarkably unconcerned. They just thought it was a little riot or something. They had no idea. Well, if I'm going to stay, then it is better that they don't know anything."

They both went to bed then. Barbie refused to look at the time, but she lay awake for hours thinking through the events of the last twenty-four hours again and again. There was nothing to get up for tomorrow so she could sleep when the Sandman came. Today had been busy enough so that she should have felt sleepy. Badboy jumped down and scratched at the French window. She let him out onto the balcony to use his litter box, which she had transferred out there. He casually strolled over to it and raked at the sandy litter. Barbie followed him out and stood there, hugging her arms and trying to take in the night sky. The glow that she had seen the night before was gone, but she knew that less than a mile away, thousands were spending yet another night in Tahrir Square, camping out and holding the front lines. As Badboy finished and slipped back into the bedroom, Barbie looked down to the body on the balcony below. She wondered if it had begun to deteriorate further.

"Ssss, Barbie, is that you?" Mitch's voice floated up to her.

"Yeah, where did you come from? I didn't see you."

"We need some help. The time has come. Get dressed and come down and help." Mitch said very quietly.

Barbie quietly dressed, as Badboy stood by and watched. She left her nightgown on, but put pants on underneath, and a jacket over it all. There was a tail from her nightgown hanging out the back of her jacket, but she didn't notice it. When she moved to the door, Badboy started to follow. "No way, Buddy. You can stay here!" She held him back with her foot as she gently closed the door.

The lobby appeared even darker than before as if the lights had been changed for ones of a lower wattage. Maybe there was a brown out. Quietly she descended and when she got to Gamal's, she put her ear to the door and listened. She turned the doorknob quietly and let herself inside. Slowly and silently, she went through the apartment, now with only a few lights on, and went to the bedroom. On the balcony, she saw a number of dark figures. She recognized Mitch's short stocky form and Mohamed's tall, broad figure. Mohamed wore his usual gallabeya, which gave him away, somewhat. One other figure, wearing dark clothes, seemed to be in charge.

"Who's this?" said the unknown man.

"A friend, she knows," Mitch said succinctly.

"I guess we need her. Is she strong enough?" Unknown asked again.

Barbie looked hard at the man. The features were dark like an Egyptian, but the voice was tinged with a southern American accent. She recognized the haircut and how he held his body. She knew he was military. "I am strong enough," Barbie answered. "And I can speak."

The four maneuvered the dead body into the apartment and to the door. Mitch was instructed to make sure the coast was clear. Barbie was instructed to call the lift and help with the buttons. As before, she ran down the stairs to reach the bottom to open the door for the three men carrying the heavy bundle. As she opened the door, she realized that a car waited outside, at the foot of the grand entrance stairway. Normally Mohamed kept this area cleared for loading. Now, they were loading.

It was an SUV, of some indeterminate dark color, with a section in the back that could take lots of equipment or suitcases or in this case, a body. The driver, another man dressed in black, jumped out and opened the rear for them. Barbie tried to peek inside, but realized the windows were all darkened. The interior was also dark, and as the streetlights, too, were at their dimmest, Barbie could see little. As the body was gently shoved into the back, Mitch reached into an inside jacket pocket and brought out a small booklet. Barbie could just see the embossed gold lettering on the front, with the eagle clutching his arrows. A US passport. A sliver of a white card, a business card, Barbie thought, stuck out of it like a bookmark. Quickly, Mitch slipped the small booklet into the shroud and folded it over.

"Good to go," Mitch whispered.

"All the documents there?" asked the man in black.

Mitch nodded. The driver and the man in black swiftly got into the car and it smoothly, but hastily, drove away.

Barbie and Mitch stood watching the car leave and Barbie whispered. "All the documents? I saw his passport."

"AUE ID card. You said yourself that it was better than a passport. I hope they let him go home peacefully, and quietly."

"So, he is going home?" Barbie asked.

"Inshallah, God willing."

They walked to the top of the staircase and watched the night. There was a light in the sky that Barbie realized was a dawn light. They sat on the top step to rest a minute. Mitch pulled out a cigarette and lit it.

"No, Mitch, you don't smoke!" Barbie protested. She moved away from the offending stick.

"I gave it up, but now, I think I need it again." Mitch drew hungrily on the cigarette, filling his lungs with tar and nicotine.

Barbie, sensing a presence behind them, looked around to find Mohamed standing in the shadows of the front door. His face was blank, with the inscrutable look that good servants cultivate. When he saw Barbie watching him, he withdrew deeper into the shadows.

Chapter Twelve: The Calm before the Storm

Mitch finished his cigarette and pulled out the pack in his pocket and looked at it. He put it back. Barbie wanted to question Mitch about a lot of things, but decided now was not the time.

They heard a noise from the street so stood and craned their necks to see what it was. A group of expats, including one from last evening's meeting, came striding down the street.

"A night of triumph over fear and terror!" shouted one, as he passed the two on the steps. The men brandished their weapons, including a cast iron frying pan.

"Catch anyone?" Mitch called to them. They laughed and then two peeled off to go to their homes, leaving a few to carry on.

"Damn, I think I missed my turn!" Mitch growled in annoyance.

"Don't worry, I'm sure you can do it later tonight?"

As the dawn crept into the sky, they noticed the debris on the streets. Usually by this time of day, the street sweepers were out, wielding their enormous palm branches to sweep the alleys and middle of the streets. The sidewalks and curb parking spaces were the province of the bowabs.

"No one sweeping today?" Barbie asked, looking around the streets.

"They are either sleeping in at home or sleeping in the square. This is a revolution for these guys for sure." Mitch sighed.

"Ahmed was usually up now, sweeping this part of the street. What will we do now?" Barbie's voice wobbled with sadness.

"Don't think we can do anything. What would we do? Who would we ask? Mohamed? 'Hey Mohamed, was your cousin, little Ahmed, involved in drugs, gambling, and underworld activities? Why would someone want to kill him like that?' Do you think I could ask him that?"

"No, Mitch, you are right. But maybe we can take up a collection for the funeral? I mean, he is probably buried now, but someone has paid out money for the shroud, for a feast, for a grave or for something, wouldn't they?" Barbie asked.

"Yeah, yeah, we should do that. Do you have any money?"

"As a matter of fact, I do. I went to the ATM just a few days ago and got 1000 pounds. I thought I was going to buy some gifts from Mr. David on Friday. It doesn't really make much difference to me at the moment. I have nothing to buy because all the shops are closed." Barbie mused.

"If you're so flush, give me 200 to give to Mohamed." Mitch demanded.

Barbie reached into her jacket pocket and pulled out a 50 pound note. "I've got it upstairs."

They walked up the stairs together, Mitch yawning, which set off Barbie. Mitch waited just inside Barbie's door as she found some more money to give to Mitch. "And don't forget, we are going to collect more for Ahmed."

As Barbie closed the door, Badboy walked up behind her and rubbed her ankles, meowing for food, attention or whatever. Barbie went back to bed.

A few hours later, Barbie became aware that her hair had grown in a bizarre manner. It was much shorter and softer. She scratched her head and a meow erupted. Badboy had wedged himself between the headboard and her head, and it was his fur that Barbie had been scratching. She breathed in deeply and felt her previous headache, aching limbs and heavy heart restored to good health. She looked at Penelope's mattress and realized that it was later than she realized. Sounds of brewing coffee, bowls pinging and silverware plonking on the table greeted her ears.

Throwing on a robe, Barbie meandered to the kitchen, hoping to snatch a cup of joe.

"I'm making eggs, which we still have, but no bread. It would be weird to eat crackers or potatoes or something," Penelope complained.

"Rice, we could do rice. The Chinese eat rice for breakfast."

"I don't. We need to get some food. Man does not live on cans alone."

Barbie protested. "Hoarding, it's <u>hoarding</u>. The only thing I feel comfortable hoarding is toilet paper."

"It's not hoarding if we eat the food. It's hoarding if we buy more than we can eat." Penelope served Barbie two fired eggs on a plate.

"Never mind, this is just perfect. I'm going off to the club to go swimming, so I don't want to eat much in any case. That is, if the club is open. The curfew isn't during the day."

"What's happening about Gamal?" Penelope asked suddenly.

Barbie looked at her with a twinge of guilt. Then she filled her in about the early morning pickup of Gamal's body. "I assume that there will be no trouble putting the body on a plane. It was obvious to me that the car was driven by US personnel and that they knew exactly what they had." Barbie paused. "And NO talking about this to anyone. Mitch's orders."

"Okay," Penelope mumbled. "But hey, what about our neighbors? Where are they? What about Llian and the new couple? I don't remember when they were supposed to be here, but here they are not, yet."

"No internet, no email, what can we do? Just wait for them to come, or not. School hasn't started yet, so no one is missing classes. And the new couple, do they even want to stay? I mean, with the Revolution, and the murders…"

"Gosh, Barbie, what are we going to say to them when they get here?" Penelope's face was animated with fear, perplexity and anxiety.

"Nothing. I'm off to swim. See you later." Barbie hadn't even changed out of her nightgown and now just slipped it off and put on her suit.

It was a ten minute walk to the pool at the Gezira Club. Barbie had discovered that when she was hired by AUE, she automatically jumped the queue for membership at the old British sporting club. Now the club was very Egyptian, and the rumor was there was a fifteen year waiting list for a new family to be accepted. When the head of a household died, his membership automatically went to his children, and did not open up new spaces. She felt lucky, although she knew she paid more than three times what Egyptians paid.

At the gate to the club, Barbie flashed her membership card. Next to an AUE ID card, this was also probably better than a passport in Egypt. A friend had described the bridge club as the place where Omar Sharif had lost so much money that they discouraged him from entering. The grounds had held international tennis tournaments and the old Polo grounds still existed. The nine hole golf course seemed an extravagance in the center of a city, but the spacious grounds, covered with 100 year old trees, was one of the few places of silence in this part of Cairo and the dominance of natural things was a welcome change.

Just inside the gate, Barbie passed one of the two grounds that was encircled with a soft walking track. Just leaving was a slender Egyptian man with the hint of a mustache. He wore a gray and dark brown jogging suit which caught the colors of his hair. He looked directly at her and Barbie looked back, a faint smile coming to her lips as a way of greeting. His eyebrows raised, but such an infinitesimal amount as to be almost unnoticeable. Barbie blinked and looked away momentarily. When she looked back, he was gone. Barbie turned around and followed his figure as he quickly walked to the gate and exited. Barbie let out a long sigh. A very handsome man. Then she smiled to herself. At least she knew she hadn't gotten too old to notice handsome men.

As Barbie entered the pool enclosure, she looked around. Normal. She went into the locker room, normal. Everything seemed normal. Although not many people were swimming this morning, everyone acted as if the world outside did not exist and that for everyone there, it was normal as well.

As she walked home, Barbie took special notice of the streets. This was Sunday, the beginning of the work week, so the traffic should have been brisk, foot traffic should have been busy, but just as at the club, it was less than normal. And those cars and pedestrians moved along at a normal pace, no anxiety could be detected. Barbie thought of afternoons during Ramadan. During the month of fasting, mornings were hectic, as were the evenings. But afternoons were quiet and the hour before breaking the fast was one of eerie silence. This reminded her of those late afternoon times. Most people went home from work or school early for a rest and only a few wandered the streets. Maybe people were sleeping late, not going to work. And as the spring semester hadn't started at schools, schoolchildren had free time.

The weather was beautiful, as befit a winter day in Cairo. The sun shone weakly through thin clouds, or was it a haze of dirt and moisture? The temperature hovered in the mid 60's so Barbie was happy she had brought her light sweater. As she neared Hatshepsut's Mansions, she saw a young woman struggling with a suitcase on wheels trying to get up the staircase into the lobby. Barbie followed her closely into the building.

Mohamed sat inside, on his usual chair, about midway from the door to the lift on one side of the lobby. He nodded to the young woman and smiled at her. She entered the lift which was sitting conveniently on the first floor. Barbie followed her.

Smiling brightly at her, Barbie asked, "Visiting?"

"Yes, I'm visiting a friend. I do hope he's here." She smiled back at Barbie. In her early twenties, with that fresh skin of youth that can easily eschew sticky make-up, she pushed back long hanks of dirty blonde hair that fell around her face. "If you live here, you must know him, Gamal McCall?"

Barbie tried desperately to keep her expression friendly and neutral, but she was caught out. The young woman looked at Barbie in alarm.

"Oh, if he's not here, it's all right. I have a key to his apartment. He gave it to me the last time I was here a month or so ago. I tried to call, but I have no money left on this little mobile phone and of course the Internet is down, so I couldn't email or skype. As I said, I hope he's here because I don't want to be around without him. I mean, I guess anyone else who knows Cairo can help, but I just don't really know what to do about all of this!"

Barbie tried to think rapidly what she needed to say in answer. Telling her Gamal was dead was not in the cards; it was too heartless and besides, it may have been dangerous. To tell her he wasn't here was easy enough, but the next questions of where he was and when he was coming back were much too delicate to answer without consultation.

"Well, did you just arrive? From…?" Barbie asked with stilted brightness.

"Oh, Gamal was busy, so I went off to Luxor and places south. Upper Egypt, I should say. I kind of got stuck there, you know the airports were really mobbed, even though Luxor was very safe and quiet. I ended up on a local train. They didn't seem to want any foreigners on the cheap night train, so a woman helped me wear a head scarf. Kind of fun, being adopted by a group of Egyptian ladies."

The lift stopped at the third floor and the young woman got off. Barbie followed. As they turned towards Gamal's apartment, Barbie thought about what state it was in. Did it smell? Was it too messy, like a dead body had been there for hours? Quickly Barbie grabbed the woman's arm and turned her around. "Come to think of it, he isn't in, I'm sure of it. He has not been seen in days. You must be thirsty. We always are, aren't we, when we travel. There is a great tradition in the desert of offering travelers something to drink. A nice cool glass of bottled water. I'm sure my friends have one, just waiting for you. And guess what? They may be able to tell you exactly where Gamal is. I'm sure they've seen him more recently than I have and know a lot more about it. You know, with all this commotion, and Gamal being Egyptian, well, half Egyptian, he has probably been involved in the demonstrations. We can ask Mitch. Mitch, Rachel," Barbie called out, knocking and ringing the bell vociferously at the same time.

"Hi Barbie, what's up?" Rachel asked as she opened the door. Mitch stood behind her, dressed in his lounge wear of sweat pants and shirt.

"Here," Barbie pushed the young woman forward. "This is a friend of Gamal's, just arrived from Luxor and she would love a glass of water. She has a key to his apartment, but I think she should come here first. Oh, I forgot to ask your name; how rude of me. I'm Barbie and this is Rachel and Mitch and you are…?"

"Tiffany."

"No, really? Well, that's nice." Rachel groaned inwardly at the choice of names this child had been cursed with. The name of a jewelry shop. "Come in, have some water, or tea or coffee?"

"No, really. Please don't trouble yourself. I have a key and I'll just let myself in. Barbie said that Gamal wasn't here, but he told me to just come on in anytime."

"Well, Gamal isn't here, he's gone back to the States," Mitch declared. "This very morning."

"Oh, I'm sorry I missed him. But I'm sure it's okay if I stay in his place. I know where everything is.' Tiffany tightened her grip on her suitcase.

"No, that is not a good idea. You can't stay there. Not alone. It's far too dangerous. No problem, we have an extra bedroom, all set up for guests and we do have some food stockpiled." Rachel picked up the string of the conversation.

"You all are soooo nice, but I'm not afraid. Gamal said it would be no problem if he wasn't here. I know the bowab and everything is fine." Tiffany gave them her best and brightest Miss America smile of confidence.

"Well, there are problems in the neighborhood. I'll go with you later. We can see about the apartment in a little while. In the meantime, sit and have some tea, or coffee?? I do a great cup of ersatz expresso." Mitch pitched in with unusual enthusiasm.

Barbie grabbed Tiffany's suitcase and parked it near the guest bedroom door, many feet from the outside door. Rachel practically pushed Tiffany into Mitch's comfy chair. "Sit, I'm sure you're tired. Want something to eat? We have some cereal or some oranges or…"

Barbie smiled brightly and encouragingly over her shoulder as she followed Mitch into the kitchen. As soon as the door shut, she hissed. "What are we going to tell her? And how? Do we trust her? Maybe she knows something about it? Maybe if she knew he was dead, she could shed some light on who did it?"

"Or maybe keeping her in the dark is the best thing we can do for her. She needs to get out of here." Mitch concluded.

"She's alive, Mitch, you can't just carry her out the door and shovel her into a car to the airport."

"We could try!"

"What are we going to tell her?" Barbie said with panic creeping into her voice.

"I think we have to tell her he's dead, but other than that, I hope maybe we can keep her in the dark as much as possible."

"But she may be able to tell us something about his life and therefore, about his death. After all, she's a 'friend' who stayed at his apartment. Did you meet her when she was here before, last month?" Barbie suddenly asked.

"No, remember, we were gone a lot, and at the end of the semester, I don't see anyone. So, I guess I missed meeting 'Gamal's lady.'"

"If she knows his other friends, maybe enemies, she could go a long ways towards telling us who killed him, and why."

"At the museum, with a knife, by revolutionaries, or perhaps by the guards."

Barbie snorted, "That's not funny!"

"That's the truth, Barbie."

"You know, I'm not so concerned about Gamal as I am about Ahmed. And I think the same people who got Ahmed, got Gamal. If we knew more about Gamal's death, we might know more about Ahmed's."

"Barbie, stop. Stop now. We are not the police, and we are not avenging angels."

"But don't you believe in Justice? Don't you believe in making this a better world? And if you do, you have to believe that Ahmed did not die in vain. And that we can do something."

"What do you mean 'we'? I don't like the sound of this."

Barbie ignored this and went on quickly. "These deaths are linked, I know it. Maybe Gamal knew something about Ahmed's death. Or maybe Ahmed found out something and told Gamal. They killed Ahmed, so they had to go find and kill Gamal."

"But why at the museum? Why didn't they kill Gamal here as well?" Mitch countered. The tea kettle whistled and Mitch grabbed it, pouring hot water in a French press coffee maker as well as into a tea pot with a tea bag.

"They killed him at the museum because of the break-in. Maybe Gamal was there protecting the antiquities, and the thieves knew he was in their way, or could recognize them, or just because there were demonstrations outside and they had weapons."

"They are not really stabbing and killing people at these demonstrations. There have been deaths, but they have been from government snipers, or someone being hit by a tear gas canister. People haven't been stabbed!"

Tiffany burst open the door. "Oh, was I interrupting? Are people being stabbed at the demonstrations now? Stabbing, that's a new one, isn't it? Who was stabbed?"

Mitch looked at Barbie with arched eyebrows, indicating that it was her turn to give news, since she started the conversation.

"Actually, you might have met him." Barbie pleaded with Mitch to help her out.

"Really? Oh my god, someone you know was killed, in the demonstrations?" Tiffany asked, startled to be so close to the violence.

"Yes, Ahmed our assistant doorman, a boy. The night before last. Near here. So that's why you simply cannot stay alone. It is not safe." Barbie concluded forcefully.

"Oh no, this is terrible. Oh my god, I met him. Was it here? Were there demonstrations here? Violence, stabbing, here?"

"Have some tea, or coffee. It's done isn't it Mitch?" Barbie took Tiffany's arm and steered her back into the lounge.

"That little boy? I met him, and now he's dead. This is just terrible." Tiffany took a tissue out of her pocket and then started hyperventilating. Barbie steered her back to the comfortable chair.

Rachel and Penelope, who had conveniently wandered down to watch TV, had heard the end of the conversation and Rachel ran to the kitchen for water, and Penelope put her arms around Tiffany, and looked around for another tissue. She helped the overwrought Tiffany to settle down.

Rachel arrived with a glass of water, setting it down within reach. She returned to fetch the tea.

Barbie looked at Mitch over Tiffany's head. She shook her head and mimed zipping her lips. Mitch nodded his understanding. If the news of Ahmed's death caused this reaction, the news of her boyfriend's death would be worse.

Mitch looked at the weeping woman and her companions. "There is more to come you know. This is just the calm before the storm."

Barbie gave Mitch an incredulous look. She thought how clueless men could be. She turned to Tiffany and in a false bright voice asked, "Well, how was Luxor, did you like it, what did you do?"

Chapter Thirteen: Bread Lines

After having a cup of tea, Barbie went upstairs to hang up her wet suit and check on the cat. "There's nothing to see but crowds in Tahrir. The 'news' isn't really new and I need to sort myself out. See you later," Barbie said, leaving the four others with their eyeballs glued to the screen.

Barbie sighed deeply. She was becoming weary of the news. She wanted to concentrate on personal things. And she worried deeply about Ahmed.

Before Barbie had straightened up her room, Penelope was back and reporting on the latest. "The judges have come to the square. They have joined the demonstrators. These are guys in suits with an education, they represent the elite." Penelope continued, "No police, just the army. They haven't really talked about the home guard stuff. I guess it is just local so far. BBC hasn't gotten ahold of the story yet. And the American Embassy is ringed with army tanks. Ditto the British Embassy. Really, really heavy duty stuff."

"We need bread," Barbie stated. "We need to go out and see if we can't find some. We could try the local stuff at the government bakery."

"What about Badboy's food, do you have enough?" Penelope asked.

"The little man will manage. Let's ask if Rachel wants to go with us to battle for bread."

Penelope used the land line instead of spending her minutes on her mobile. Seconds later, Penelope reported. "Rachel says Tiffany is asleep. That's good. She needs some time to absorb all of this and then when she finds out Gamal is dead, well… In the meantime, we are good to go. Take a nice big bag to carry the bread and another one for any groceries we find along the way."

"You sound as if we can just pick up food along the street." Barbie laughed.

"Hey, isn't that where they sell it? You saw the supermarket, crap fruit and veggies. But if the locals can get the fresh stuff from their suppliers, all the better."

Collecting Rachel as they went out, they detoured slightly to the 'entry' of the American compound in Zamalek. The barriers were not the simple ones of last week, but huge gate-like metal pipes that blocked access to everyone, even pedestrians. Not far away, men sat on the street corners, rubbing sleep from their eyes. They had obviously been part of the home guard. Barbie looked closely at the stores that sold leather jackets, designer clothes and antiques in the blocks around Hatshepsut's Mansions. All these stores had barriers over the doorways, the windows had grills, some new, and all were firmly closed.

"Remind me to call Mr. David later. The phones are back so maybe we can still do some business. At least I can look at his goods. Nothing will claim too much of my time until classes start," Barbie muttered to her companions. Silently, she wished she could try to find out what happened to Ahmed, but it seemed too difficult for her. "Maybe we could go to the Square and see what's happening?"

"Crazy woman," Penelope said. "You want to go to the other side of the river, the place where they are having demonstrations, shootings, and who knows what else. It's dangerous over there!"

"Ahmed died on our doorstep. In Zamalek. I figure we are all living dangerously."

"Let's try stopping at the Palestinian's store. I think they may have ways of getting food. Maybe they can get stuff coming from Gaza. Ha, ha," Penelope joked.

Twenty-sixth of July Street was busier than the side streets, and as they drew nearer the store, they saw the crowd outside the store and also crowding in front of the butcher shop next door.

"Oh, meat," Rachel said. "What about some fresh meat?"

"Not from that butcher. I saw him one day threatening a customer who dared complain. He had one of his giant cleavers in his hand that is missing the finger and he was shouting at the top of his lungs. Someone standing in line who knew him had to stop him from attacking the poor woman. I think he is genuinely crazy. Never buy meat from him!" Barbie added.

"In that case, never mind," Rachel demurred. "I guess we could become vegetarians for the duration. Let's see if we can even get into the Tamimi store."

The three shoved their way inside and found that the store, though crowded, wasn't impassable. They fanned out and plucked goods off the shelf that they thought might be useful and within their limited resources. Soon they had a basket full of cans, jars, boxes and packages of items that could be eaten. As Penelope tried to buy a third package of spaghetti, Barbie hissed, "No hoarding."

The one thing they didn't find was bread, so as they checked out, Barbie asked in her best Arabic, "Eish?"

"Bread? La, la, la, la (no, no, no, no)," the bearded man checking them out declared.

"Where?" Barbie replied. She figured that if he knew the word for bread, that he also knew the word for where.

An older, well-dressed man standing behind them spoke up in excellent English. "There is a government bakery just around the corner on Brazil Street. You know where that is?" He pointed across the street and crooked his finger to indicate turning. "They have bread. But buying it may take some agility. Good luck to you." He smiled pleasantly. Barbie couldn't tell whether he was enjoying himself during this civil disturbance or whether he was taking it in stride. He was of an age to have remembered wars past, much worse than this.

"I know where it is," Penelope declared.

Pushing their way through the roadblock at the door, they clutched their bags and dashed across the street. Today that was easy as the traffic was light and cars were not rushing. There were two times when it was easy to jaywalk across the street, when there was NO traffic or when it was so crowded, it was stopped. Then it was just a weave through the cars. The only drawback at that time was enduring the blast of the Egyptian cacophony of horns.

"Do you think we ought to try Metro first?" Rachel asked.

"Well, we don't have bread, and we didn't get any more eggs, but I doubt Metro will have eggs either." Penelope enumerated their purchases. "But we managed to get spaghetti, cheese, jars of tomato sauce as well as fresh tomatoes, cucumbers and carrots, muesli, jam, and even some decent apples and oranges. We aren't going to starve. But bread would be nice."

Rachel grumbled. "Yeah, but baladi bread? That stuff is nasty. It is full of bits of straw, sometimes rocks, and god knows what else. Half the time it's burnt in big places and they put their filthy dirty hands on it."

"Sounds great, let's get some!" Barbie sang out. "Rachel, we can't be too picky. We're in the middle of a revolution. And besides, what can you expect from government bread? The bakers buy the wheat from the government suppliers, then they are not allowed to sell it for whatever they want, but a fixed price. So to make the flour go further, they feel obliged to stretch it further by putting fillers in it. I mean, I don't really like the crap you find in it, but you must admit, it is tasty! And if you brush off the outside, and toast it really hot, you can get rid of most of the germ laden parts. Slather it with labne, you know the yogurt cream cheese, and some of my favorite Syrian apricot jam, and voila, I could live on that for a week."

"Hey, we might have to, so let us be nice about baladi bread. After all, eish means bread, but also life in Arabic," Penelope added. "I'm ready."

They turned the corner onto Brazil Street and ahead they saw a scrum of about 100 people. Yesterday's bread line was miniscule compared to this one. There was a semblance of a queue, but the end was not readily visible. Penelope, being the tallest, stood on tiptoe and peeked over the heads of the crowd. "I can see the hole, it's about this big," she stretched her hands to indicate a twenty-inch by twenty-inch opening. "But bread is coming out!" Just then a man walked past with two large bags full, perhaps 40 or 50 pieces of the flat brown bread. Someone else held five long baguettes over his head as he eased himself towards the street.

A young man approached them and pointed towards a second line that was substantially shorter. "Lady, lady!" he announced.

"Whoa, there's a ladies' line. Let's go," said Barbie as the three headed to the left side of the hole. "Why doesn't just one of us stand here and wait?"

As Barbie approached the end of the shorter line, one of the older women pushed a young boy aside and motioned to Barbie to stand closer. Barbie knew from experience that personal space for Egyptians was body to body in a line like this, so she moved in as far as her American sensibilities would let her. She was grabbed by the forearm and tugged closer, cutting out a young girl who tried to weasel in front of her. Her erstwhile rescuer let the young girl have it in colorful street language, only some of which Barbie understood.

"How many shall I get, ten, fifteen?" called out Barbie.

"At least twenty, there are four of us. Wait, five including Tiffany. We don't know how long she'll be staying, do we? As many as you can carry!" Rachel shouted from the edge of the crowd.

Rachel and Penelope walked further north along Brazil Street, seeing what else might be for sale. A woman often sat on the sidewalk a few blocks north of Twenty-sixth of July and sold vegetables. A small bodega stocked chips and sodas, which might come in handy as well. As there were no delivery men about today, they could only buy as much as they could carry.

After making their purchases, they meandered back to the bread line. Rachel spotted Barbie's blonde hair just a foot from the hole, waving a twenty-pound note in a hand that snaked around the shorter woman in front of her. A burly man of a dark complexion, wearing a gallabeya and a dirty turban kept back the crowd of men to let the ladies get their turn. They watched in fascination as Barbie's hand first clutched three baguettes and then a stack of brown flat bread. Another load of bread was shoved through the window, and Barbie grabbed and clutched it to her chest as she turned to leave. The women pushed and shoved to get to the window, but no one thought to cheat her by grabbing her bread. As she arrived at the curb, on the edge of the crowd, Penelope noticed that Barbie clutched her coin purse in her teeth, the only place left to hold anything.

At Rachel's apartment, they divvied up the food and bread, but decided that combining supplies at least for the next meal was good. What if they were left with no electricity or gas? What had they bought that could be eaten raw? Stored without refrigeration? Last two or more days? Could be emergency food at the airport if they had to go? They decided on cooking pasta using the last of the fresh meat that Rachel had. They worked together.

Tiffany appeared at the door to the kitchen, much brighter-eyed than before. She had taken a shower and changed clothes and declared herself ready to help. "Before I do, I'll just pop next door to Gamal's place and rescue some of my clothes."

"No!" said Rachel and Barbie at the same time. "Wait til Mitch can go with you. It really isn't safe," Rachel added.

"I'm perfectly safe, don't worry about me." Tiffany protested, digging into her purse for the key.

"No," Barbie said again. "I think Mitch is here, isn't he? He'll go with you. Really, we mean it!" Barbie walked into the living room. "Oh, thank the heavens, Mitch is here and he'll go with you. In fact, I'll go too. Gamal's apartment may not be up to snuff in the 'neat' department at the moment. Mitch, let's go, grab the key and we are off."

Mitch silently did as Barbie demanded, slithering his eyes sideways at Barbie. "She just insisted that she needed some more clothes, so I told her we'd go with her."

"I really don't need you." Tiffany protested again.

Mitch led the way, unlocking the door to Gamal's apartment. The drapes had been pulled on all the windows, so the room was gloomy. And there was a distinctly unpleasant odor wafting throughout the room. Mitch flicked on the living room light.

Papers were scattered everywhere on the floor. Boxes spilled books and copies of academic papers among newspapers and trash from the kitchen. Tiffany laughed and shook her head. "I knew Gamal wasn't a neatnik, but this is ridiculous. This is pig-like behavior, so unlike him to throw trash in the living room!"

Mitch looked sideways at Barbie again, shaking his head to indicate that this was a new development. Barbie remembered being able to negotiate the living room easily from the bedroom balcony, but this mess had been made since the removal of the body earlier in that morning. Mitch inched towards the kitchen as Tiffany wandered among the boxes and papers. Then she headed to the bedroom. Barbie followed, not remembering how the place had been left. The bed had been stripped of the bedcovers, clothes from the closet had been strewn on the floor. Tiffany yelped when she recognized a sweater that was lying on the floor as hers. "I didn't leave this like this! What a slob! Why would he do this to my things? If he wanted to make a mess with his things, he certainly had the right to, but my things? My clothes!"

Barbie let Tiffany vent and went to the balcony. At least this was clean and undisturbed. The two chairs that had been used to 'lay out' the corpse were still there, but no sign of the ice, the melted water, the ice trays or any of the plastic bags were left. Someone trashed the apartment, but cleaned up this place?

Mitch joined her briefly. "The kitchen is also a mess, the smell is coming from the garbage can." More quietly he said,

"I came back and cleaned up here, but nothing else was disturbed then. This was done in the last 5 or 6 hours."

"Oh no," screamed Tiffany from inside the apartment. Mitch and Barbie hurried towards the scream and found Tiffany, her arms full of clothes, standing in the living room, next to the desk. "I can understand leaving it messy, not cleaned up, not neat. But this is not right. Look! His computer. It's smashed, broken. He wouldn't do that, no way. What's going on here?"

Mitch approached Tiffany and gently laid a hand on her arm. "We have something to tell you. We didn't want to say it right away. After Gamal left, someone must have broken in here. It wasn't like this a few hours ago when he left."

"How do you know that? How do you know what Gamal did? When did you see him? Did you go with him to the airport? "

"Listen Tiffany, we have to tell you this. But you can't tell anyone else and you can't touch anything else here." Mitch looked into her eyes and didn't answer her questions. "Promise?"

Tiffany's eyes grew into round frightened orbs. Slowly the mound of clothes in her arms slipped to the floor, one by one. "What is it? Tell me."

Mitch looked at the floor, at Barbie, around the room, then back again to Barbie, seeking a way to tell Tiffany. Barbie rolled her eyes, but she didn't want to utter the words either.

"You see," Mitch began. "Gamal has gone home to the US. He won't be coming back, he's gone for good."

"Why didn't he tell me, something, anything, leave me a note?" Tiffany wailed.

"He couldn't." Mitch started, looking at Barbie, hoping she would pick up the announcement.

"He couldn't because he's…" Barbie started to say.

"Dead." Mitch finished.

Barbie caught Tiffany as she crumpled to the floor.

Chapter Fourteen: A Gathering of Expats II

Mitch was the last out of the apartment and indicated to Barbie that she should accompany Tiffany back to his apartment.

"I'm going to find Mohamed and settle once and for all, who had keys. This was not a break in; the lock was fine. Someone with keys has been here. Take care of her," he nodded towards Tiffany.

The smell of cooking tomato sauce with garlic, onion and seared meat greeted the two women as they entered the apartment. "Oh, I am hungry. I had forgotten," said Tiffany as she slumped onto the couch.

"I'm sure it will be ready shortly. Just sit there. You want some wine? I think we might find some." Barbie headed for the kitchen to find Rachel and Penelope happily creating a massive spaghetti dinner. The fresh baguettes had been made into garlic bread, fresh tomatoes and cucumbers had been chopped into a salad and a huge pot of noodles bubbled on the stove. "Wine here?" Barbie asked.

Penelope and Rachel both raised glasses of rich ruby liquid. "Pour one for Tiffany, would you? She's had a shock, Mitch told her." She also filled them in briefly about the apartment and especially the computer while she waited for the glass. She declined one for herself.

Barbie gave the glass to Tiffany and promised her food soon. "Tiffany, do you know anything about this mess?"

Tiffany took a gulp of wine, put it down and looked at Barbie. "I knew that there were people who were not friendly. I hesitate to call them enemies. But not enough to harm him. Just nasty enough to make sure that he didn't get any permits to dig, screwing up his chances for publication, things like that. But get rid of him? Not likely. I think it was this revolution thing. You know, he did know some really unsavory characters."

"What kind of unsavory? Egyptians or others? And what could they do to him?"

"Well, you know about his 'family' here in Egypt, don't you?" She went on quickly without waiting for Barbie to answer. "They introduced him to the 'old families', the ones that have dealt in antiquities for years. He wasn't really happy about all of this. He said that he saw marvelous things. Things that no one could, or would, tell him the provenance. He said they could have been clever fakes, or the real things. You know they have been making fakes for well over a hundred years? Some things are rare, so it is a good thing to make copies, bury them so they are well seasoned, and then dig them up 50, 60 or more years later. The one who digs it up can quite genuinely say they did not 'make' it and that the tomb or whatever where it was found is real. Gamal thought that some of the stuff being offered for sale was like this, good fakes or stolen. But he had no proof."

"Was it really his job though? Wasn't he a university professor? I mean he was an Egyptologist, but I had no idea he was involved in stolen antiquities," Barbie said with considerable alarm.

"Oh no, he wasn't involved at all, but he had met people who were. And he was unhappy about it. But he never said that he planned to do anything about it. He had ambivalent feelings about it. On the one hand, what's the harm in selling some rich American or European a fake? More money for Egyptians, right? He was on the side of poor Egyptians, that's for sure. And fakes don't really hurt the archaeologists. They usually can examine them and tell that they are fake and that's that. He was concerned about the real ones that had been stolen. For one, they would be sold to the rich, and for the most part, leave Egypt. So Egyptians would lose their patrimony. And secondly, unless they were very common types of things, they could stir up desire for them and then, more thefts, more corruption, more unpleasantness."

"Did he know who these people were?" Barbie leaned forward.

"Yeah, but like I said, he couldn't or didn't want to pin anything on anyone. He was all into avoiding unpleasantness and was worried about his permits and his career."

"A conspiracy?" Barbie inquired.

"I don't think he would go all that far. No, I just can't believe this was about the antiquities thing. Maybe it was about the revolution. He really did love Egypt, you know. He was an American, proud of it, but like lots of hyphenated Americans, he had a real fondness for the other half of himself. And I can see that he might want to join the revolution. After all, being an American, he understands free speech and democracy. Or should I say, understood. Gosh, it's hard to believe he is really dead, that I will never see him walking through a door, lighting up the very space he breathed." Tiffany stopped suddenly and looked directly at Barbie, "I completely forgot to ask. How did he die? Did he die here, in his apartment?"

"No, no, he was found at the Egyptian Museum. The night that it was broken into. He was stabbed. And they took his body, with other martyrs, to the mosque. No one knows anything, really. And this morning, his body was taken to the airport and sent to America." Barbie deliberately left out the hours that he had spent in the apartment. If Tiffany persisted anymore about going back, or staying at Gamal's apartment, Barbie could spring that on her to scare her off.

"He was murdered, you mean? Because of what he knew about thieves and antiquities dealers and stolen goods or because of the revolution?" Tiffany was becoming even more alarmed.

"Well, we don't know who came into his apartment. Mitch and I were there this morning, and it was fine, everything in place. So we don't know who has a key and why things were messed up like that. And the computer. What a terrible thing to do! An academic has his life on that thing and to mess with it is just cruel and potentially dangerous to one's career."

"That creep, the head of the department." Tiffany declared.

"But Parker Hampton was the one who brought him here. I know that for a fact, he told me so. And Gamal praised Parker all the time."

"Then that woman! I can't tell you much about her either, but I know Gamal, or rather I knew him," Tiffany went on quickly.

"How well did you know him?" Barbie asked offhandedly.

"Just friends, believe me, just friends. He was not going to get tied down until he was sure and had made his name and had the blessings of his family and had enough money to support a family and, and, and. And believe me, I was not into that. I was looking for some passion maybe, but settled for friendship. He was a very good friend. Was."

"So you were just visiting. And you said that you had been here before, a few weeks ago?"

"Yeah, I arrived just at the end of the semester and he said he was too busy to take me places, so he suggested I go to Upper Egypt and do the things there. It was a bit crowded, but I went to Aswan and found a little hotel and had such a wonderful time. Then I meandered up to Luxor and ditto. Just a cute little place on the west bank. Just sat and read books and sunbathed. This whole revolution thing was quite a surprise."

"How come we didn't meet you when you were here before? I mean, not that I was really close to Gamal or anything, but we have a tendency to run into everyone's guests. You know, living an expat lifestyle means that your friends and acquaintances become your 'family.'"

"Oh, I arrived late one night, just stayed for a day, went out once I think, then went to Upper Egypt the next day. I wasn't here very long. I didn't meet anyone, except I ran into the 'woman' and was introduced. You should have seen her face. I am sure that Gamal knew her better than he let on. I could tell. I have met former girlfriends of his and it was the same expression. He was a ladies' man." Tiffany frowned.

"Oh, I didn't get that impression. Well, not really. Well, maybe because I'm older, or not his type." Barbie felt deflated that she had not passed muster with the great lover.

"I don't know about age, he liked older women. He told me so. He said he learned a lot from them about relationships, about sex…"

"You discussed sex with him? Sex with his lovers?"

"Not exactly at my inquiry. But he was a great lover and he had lots of female friends. I was never quite sure with him, whether I was a special friend, or a real friend because we weren't in love. In any case, if I were you, I'd look into that other woman. She lives here in this building, I'm sure of it."

Barbie's mind raced to the women in the building. It wasn't her or Penelope, not Rachel, but who else? There were the couples, the English teachers and then, no. It couldn't be Mary Bell! 'Older' may have described her, but Gamal wasn't yet 30 and Mary was well over 60, nearer 70. Oh no, this was tooooo much. Barbie smiled back at Tiffany. She thought that she needed to keep Tiffany talking, spilling more. She was just a gold mine of information. Nothing specific at all, but lots of ideas.

"Yeah, well, when you see her again, let me know, won't you? And tell me more about his academic enemies. You said that some people were against him, trying to keep him from publishing academic papers?"

"Well, he didn't mention any one specifically you know. I know that you think he got along with the head of his department, but I think you are wrong. He never mentioned him by name, but he was sure that unless this person, or persons, left, he would never get tenure and the reason why was because of the papers. I think the department was in turmoil."

"Wow, I didn't know that. It is not at all unusual for departments, especially academic ones, to have a lot of competition. When a group of people are all doing the same thing, publishing in the same journals and maybe even collaborating together, then there is jealousy. But could that lead to murder? I guess that it could. But I really don't believe that could happen here."

Tiffany looked wide-eyed at Barbie as she speculated on murder because of academic jealousy. She was silent for a few moments and then burst out, "I've got to leave. I've got to get out of here. I think that it is not safe for me here."

Barbie looked startled and felt as though Tiffany had information that could lead to solving the mystery of Gamal's demise, and by extension, Ahmed. She couldn't leave now.

"Wait until you've had some food. I'm sure that you'll feel better and besides, how are you going to 'leave'?"

"I haven't even told my family where I am. Certain members couldn't care, but I think my mother may be worried. Aren't all mothers worried about us?"

Barbie laughed. "I guess. Well, you're lucky because the mobile phones work now and we've been able to call at least. Do you have a phone?"

"Gamal lent me one and said I could return it. I don't know who signed for it, but I've been using it. But I ran out of money on it and then couldn't buy any more minutes. I tried to call Gamal before I had nothing left, but I couldn't get through. Now I know why. But how is it getting out? Easy? I hope so. I have a ticket, so all I need to do to change the date."

Barbie looked at Tiffany and sighed. "If only it were that easy. You know about the chaos at the airport? It's good you have a ticket, but I'm not so sure that will help too much." Barbie filled her in on the 'three days food and water' requirement.

"Food," called out Rachel and Penelope as they entered the dining room and set dishes on the table. Before they were ready to eat, Mitch returned and they all fell on the food, escaping into tourist talk instead of the current crisis.

"Oh, by the way, Jack and Markie called. They are leaving and are having a party tonight, eating all the food, drinking all the drinks in preparation for being away for the duration." Rachel said.

"I didn't even know they were back!" Barbie said.

"Yeah, they got back last night, found the airport in chaos, got a ride into the city this morning and within an hour decided that they were leaving again. They are talking about not coming back until the fall semester. They are really freaking out. Apparently, they have transport for tomorrow morning, so they are good to go."

"Well, there you go Tiffany, get a ride to the airport with them and sort it all out there." Turning to the others, Barbie told them of Tiffany's decision to leave as soon as she could.

"Good choice, Tiffany," Mitch said.

"So, the party. They've invited all the expats and I guess we'll see everyone there. Even those who don't particularly like going to parties. It's a way to catch up on the news." Rachel handed round the food and urged all to eat.

After eating they all turned to the TV. The same old shots of the crowd in the square, the same talking heads, some looking much the worse for wear. "They are probably not getting much sleep," Barbie said rising. "Which is my problem as well. I'm off to take a nap." Barbie excused herself and left. She wanted to talk with Mitch about the mess in Gamal's apartment, but the events in the square, and all over Egypt, made it seem petty at the moment. There would be time later when her head was clear.

When she got to her own apartment, she felt more awake, but also as if she wanted some 'action'. She moved from room to room, desultorily dragging her feet, and not being able to settle on doing anything. The cat followed her, frequently tripping her up. She checked her computer just in case the Internet had come back on. It hadn't.

"David," she said aloud. "I can call David and see if I can do the visit tomorrow. The only thing he can say is 'no', right?" She looked at Badboy for confirmation.

The phone rang four times before there was an answer. "Alo?"

"Hello, is this David? This is Barbie. I had planned to come to your store on Friday, and well, I couldn't make it."

"No problem, or rather there was a problem, but it was not your fault," came the answer. "I hope you are well and safe?"

"Yes, very well and safe. I was wondering if I could redo the appointment. I know that this might not be the best time, but if nothing is happening, could I come tomorrow? Is that going to be okay?"

"Oh, yes, I think so. You know nothing is happening here at the Khan. We are all waiting for our customers, and our customers have gone home, or are trying to. So, I would welcome your visit. Ten am, Hatshepsut's' Mansions. I will have my driver pick you up," he purred into the phone.

"Thank you very much. This is wonderful. See you tomorrow." Barbie pushed the off button and sat down, a smile on her face. A ride, she thought, and his car, so I will not get lost. What service! Then her smile faded. But how did he know that I live in Hatshepsut's Mansions? Barbie became a little irritated. She was not used to strangers knowing her business, her address and everything about her. Some things are private, she thought. But not where you live, if you are a foreigner in Cairo. She started planning on who she needed to buy things for, how much she could spend and what various people might like. She really didn't know for sure what David had for sale, just that he was highly recommended. By whom, she had now forgotten, although it was Mary Bell who had given her the phone number. Maybe by more than one person. Maybe she had told David who had recommended him and so he knew, or suspected he knew, where she lived. It had been only five days ago that she had made the appointment, but now that seemed like a weird fairytale life she had pretended to live in. The revolution was more real to her now. Now she felt tired and laid down to rest.

The twilight coming into the room told her that she had slept. She chided herself for bad sleeping habits. But then she remembered the reason for this. She heard some rattling in the kitchen and followed the sound. Penelope was making tea. They shared a pot and talked about the latest news on the troubles and what Tiffany was planning to do. She had contacted Jack and Markie and had gotten a promise of a ride. They had promised Tiffany they would not take all their stuff, so that there would be room in the car for her suitcase. Tiffany was now trying to go through her clothes and things to determine what she could leave. Penelope laughed, "We could just leave all of it if our lives depended on it. It hasn't come to that, but stuff is not as important as our lives."

"Well, are we ready to party?" Barbie asked. She thought that she wanted to have a little bit of lightheartedness for a bit, the last few days had been unrelenting chaos, crisis and nothing had gone smoothly.

As they exited the apartment, they ran into Rachel, Mitch and Tiffany coming up the stairs. Penelope stopped at the door to say hello and Badboy ran between her legs and down the stairs. Barbie, with a forced smile at Penelope said, "You can lock the door, can't you, while I go chase my cat that so inconveniently got out?"

Barbie dashed down the stairs after the cat. Badboy had the temerity to look over his shoulder to see if Barbie was following to rescue him. He had done this before, so Barbie wasn't really worried about whether she would catch him or not. But scenes flashed in her head of a small body in a dark space and a cat that meowed. At the foot of the stairs, Badboy stopped and seemed to wait for Barbie, who scooped him up and held him tightly. Mohamed stepped out of the shadows and greeted her.

She greeted him and then asked, "Ahmed's family, his mother, father, are they okay?"

Mohamed jerked his head to indicate that the situation was 'okay'. "But no happy. New boy will come. Wait," he said, disappearing in the direction of his lair under the stairs.

He returned quickly and handed Barbie two bags filled with books and notebooks. She gripped Badboy with one arm and slipped the bags' handles over her other shoulder. They were heavy and Barbie involuntarily grunted. Mohamed reached over and pushed the lift button.

As they waited, Barbie turned to Mohamed. "I'm so sorry about Ahmed. Why did they kill Ahmed?"

"Ahmed bad boy. All time, looking, waiting. No his business. Trouble too much. But he funny boy, happy boy." Tears welled up in Mohamed's eyes and inched down his cheeks.

"I'm so sorry, Mohamed. We all liked him. We are all very sorry." Barbie had no trouble putting the emotion she felt into the words.

"He Badboy," Mohamed said, stroking the cat's head. Badboy responded with a rumbling purr.

At Jack and Markie's apartment, the party was in full swing. Cornelius sat in the center of a sofa with a young student on either side. Although Barbie was 99% sure he didn't 'like' girls, he certainly would have fooled the casual observer. Maybe that's why she liked Cornelius. He could be outrageous, but he never took himself seriously. Life was a series of interesting events to him and the players and the audience were the same. His job was to observe and comment, usually in a jocular style, in order to garner as much attention as he wanted. At the moment, he had a whiskey bottle in his hand and he waved it in Barbie direction as a greeting. "My dear girl, please come and join me."

"The couch is crowded and whiskey is not my drink. I'll get something else and be right back," Barbie promised, hoping that she could avoid him for at least a few minutes. She wandered to the kitchen where she found Markie trying to cope with all the food donations that others had brought.

"We were trying to get rid of our own leftovers, but everyone thought that they had to 'bring something', so I think there will be leftovers. Professor Smythe brought his own whiskey, you notice, but I also think he brought wine as well." Markie was busy cutting up more cheese and putting it on a plate.

Mercedes was also in the kitchen, directing the cheese arrangements. She had an ear cocked, listening to Cornelius pontificate in the living room. Barbie remembered that she, too, was from Boston, but her accent was entirely different from Professor Smythe's Brahmin accent. His was full of British vowel sounds and the classic soft 'r's of Boston. Barbie thought they probably had little in common, came from different social classes, or perhaps… Perhaps Cornelius' accent was a little too thick, put on a bit too much. Barbie promised herself to listen carefully as the night wore on, and Cornelius got drunker. She offered to help Markie, but was refused.

Barbie then wandered into the other public room. The dining room table had been pushed against the wall, laden with food and drink, and the rest of the room arranged so that the chairs created conversation groups, rather than sitting around the table. The TV has been placed in this room for the party and was now on. Mitch was translating an Arabic station. Tiffany and Rachel sat in a quiet dark corner. Tiffany did not know anyone at the party and seemingly didn't want to bother socializing. Barbie could see her point.

Just then, Tiffany looked up at Barbie and her eyes opened in surprise. She seemed to squeeze back into the shadows even more, putting her head down and letting her hair fall over her face. Barbie looked at her quizzically, but could not catch her eye.

"Where do you think I can put this plate," said a voice behind Barbie.

Twirling around, Barbie saw that Mercedes had come into the room with a plate of cheese and was trying to find a place on the table for it. When she had moved a number of plates and was satisfied, she moved off, wandering into the living room. Barbie whirled back to find Tiffany looking at her again.

Tiffany mouthed something and pointed towards the departing Mercedes. Barbie's eyebrows went up and she mouthed back, "Her?" Tiffany nodded yes and tried to make herself even smaller and less noticeable. Barbie took this to mean that the woman that Tiffany had met, who she suspected had been having an affair with Gamal, was Mercedes. Barbie's mouth squinched into an 'O'.

At the TV, Mitch was busy switching the channel and calling for all to hear. "El Baradei is in the square. He has talked with the reporters," he announced to all.

"But I thought he was under house arrest?" someone said from the rear.

"Here he is," Mitch said, turning the sound up. The darkness in the square did not obscure the thousands who gathered there. In a motley group, reporters stuck microphones in the famous man's face. Someone knocked against him, momentarily dislodging the famous round eyeglasses that were his trademark. He spoke in Arabic, but a simultaneous translation made it clear that the famous former UN Nuclear Energy Inspector's words would be listened to. Mingling with the crowds in the square was statement enough whose side he was on. The words were directly translated from the Arabic, and as such, seem stilted to the group of expats. But one phrase was unmistakable in its clarity of partisanship. "…what we have begun cannot go back." The 'we' made it clear that this was no longer a fight about one class against another, but a fight for freedom, democracy and inclusiveness.

Barbie was stunned and heartened by the news of such a man, a darling of a certain sector of the intelligentsia, who was willing to be seen in the square surrounded by the masses. Maybe this revolution was going to be won by the little people. She wandered from room to room, taking note that all the expats in the building were there. She waved to Mary Bell and nodded to Parker Hampton who was in close conversation with W.B., Mercedes husband. She briefly took the place of one of the students next to Cornelius and had a short conversation with him. She listened to the ever-thickening accent as he succumbed to the liquor. At least, she thought, he doesn't have far to go home.

Even though she had napped, Barbie felt exhausted. She had wanted to speak to Tiffany again, but did not want to broach the subject at the party. She had gotten the message about Mercedes, she thought, so what else could Tiffany tell her about Ahmed's death? The death of Gamal was not of as much concern to her and she now felt less certain they were connected. She reminded herself to concentrate on Ahmed. As she and Badboy snuggled in bed, her eyes fell on the bags given to her by Mohamed. When she got them, she had recognized one of the books that she and Ahmed were using in their English lessons, so she had not even asked what the bags were. She knew. Now, she reached over and pulled one bag onto the bed. She pulled out books, large notebooks and loose papers that Barbie had given to Ahmed to work with. As well, there were a number of small notebooks, like the ones that she had sometimes used to write a travel diary. They were of the cheapest kind, but when she opened them, she realized that Ahmed had been one very busy boy. There were at least six of the small notebooks that she had never seen. They were dated, Arabic style, and it took a few minutes for Barbie to figure out what order they would be in.

Her own words drifted back to her as she tried to remember what she had said to Ahmed about keeping a diary. She recalled showing him her own small notebooks and how she had dated each page, or set of pages and wrote freely. She could hear her teacher's voice, "Keeping a diary is really good for you. It makes you use the words you learn and because it is what you see and think about things; you will want to write it down. It is an important thing to learn how to do, to write. When you are ready, you can write a diary too."

Barbie felt a thrill that one of her students had really done what she had suggested. She opened the first one. Although the dates were in Arabic, the writing was mostly in English. The first diary had a mish-mash of both English and Arabic, so much so, that Barbie could not make out much of what Ahmed was trying to say. She opened the second one. She saw more English and less Arabic and things were beginning to become clearer. He had written about what he did every day. He included what he bought at the store and Barbie could see her own answers to his questions, written in his cramped hand, in pencil. 'A loaf of bread.' Barbie remembered the day they had discussed that a whole bread was a loaf. And then the next day when he bought one, he had recorded it. He had also noted the price.

As she skimmed through the later notebooks, she realized that he was truly a 'badboy'. He had spied on the inhabitants of Hatshepsut's Mansions. Barbie had nothing to hide and laughed at the notations about her own comings and goings, what she had bought, who she talked to and what she talked about. But it was with growing annoyance that she read about others in the building. He had nicknames for the tenants, rather than using their own names, and some of the things seemed to be unkind. Cornelius was called 'K' and was described as 'fat,' or 'very fat' and there was a note about a man who had visited his apartment. And a note about a fight with his manservant later in the day. Another glance at the next to the last notebook revealed notes on 'my friend G'. 'Blond girl' seemed to describe Tiffany and the date seemed about the time that Tiffany said she had visited. Barbie flipped through the diary and saw an entry, just days before Tiffany's visit, which was extremely explicit. 'My friend G fuk Lady M.'

Barbie drew breath in with a hiss. She could not have said whether she was shocked at the information, the knowledge that Ahmed knew that English word, or that she was glad he had not learned it from her. If she was going to teach a word, she always made sure her students learned the correct spelling.

Tiffany had been right, Gamal had been having an affair with Mercedes.

Chapter Fifteen: A Visit to Mr. David's

"Listen, I'll move my mattress back to my own bedroom. I would have done it last night, but you and the cat were all tucked in. Nothing is happening, so I think I'll be able to sleep." Penelope greeted Barbie in the kitchen.

"Day Seven of the Revolution. And we have bread!" Barbie slathered a piece with cream cheese and jam and bit in. "It's here, it's fresh and we need to eat it all before it goes stale."

"I can freeze any that is going stale and microwave it later. It's not the same thing, but… Hey, no swimming today?"

"No, I am off to Mr. David's and I slept too late. By the way, Mohamed is saying that a new boy is coming. I am assuming to replace Ahmed, although he was one of a kind, so hard to replace. He also returned the books and notebooks I gave Ahmed. It was really sad to see them." Barbie went back to her bread. If asked, she would not have been able to say why she didn't tell Penelope about what she had learned about Gamal and Mercedes. As far as she knew, Tiffany would have been glad to tell anyone, as she had Barbie. But then again, maybe it was too private to blab all around. Expat communities were like that. They could quite easily badmouth each other, but if someone from the outside tried to cast aspersions, the in-group stuck together. Barbie thought it was the way of the world. But she did NOT tell Penelope. Was it because she felt let down by Gamal? She didn't think much of wandering husbands and wives, but acknowledged it was a fact of life. And Tiffany herself had made it clear that she had no hold on Gamal, so why did he wander? And Mercedes was married to W.B. Barbie had never liked W.B., but was unable to pinpoint why. In that case, why should she worry about the affair? It had nothing to do with her and nothing to do with Ahmed's death. That was her major concern: what happened to Ahmed.

Unless Ahmed, knowing what he knew, documenting everything, was seen as trespassing into private territory. What if W.B. found out, and found out that Ahmed knew about it, and then decided to do something about it? What if Ahmed, foolish child, had tried to use his knowledge for gain? Blackmail? What an ugly thing blackmail is, Barbie thought. What if Ahmed had approached Mercedes and… Stop, she told herself. These are incredibly foolish ideas. She shook her head.

"Barbie, Barbie," Penelope was practically shouting. "What time are you going? When will you be back? I mean, I really don't care, but we need to be a bit protective of each other. Not wander off and then get lost and stuck somewhere. So?"

"Oh, sorry. I know what you mean. What are you doing today?" Barbie turned the tables on Penelope.

"We're doing good deeds. Rachel and I are going to visit everyone and check on them. Professor Smythe is giving us the names and addresses of all the faculty and staff that live in Zamalek and we'll try to track them all down. Sort of like the old Warden's List that the university had during the last civil disturbance. Funny how they did away with the list because they thought they didn't need it. Professor Smythe was told that if something happened, we now had Internet and we could just email each other. What a joke that was, huh? We will be part of a team, a way of trying to know if someone is ill or wants to evacuate or needs anything, whatever."

"Sounds like a great idea. Are you sure that the two of you are going to be okay? Do you need some more help? Maybe I could come later?" Barbie felt selfish, going shopping when her friends were doing something important for the community.

"Naw, we're going together and Mitch will be here with a phone in case we need anything. So, help me move the mattress and then we are off. By the way, you didn't say how late you'd be," Penelope tenaciously pressed her.

"Before dark, before the curfew, in case anything happens. And I am only planning to go to David's shop in the Khan el Khalili. Everyone knows it and he said it was very quiet there. So, no demonstrations there. And he said he'd send his car, so I won't get stuck with no transport."

Twenty minutes later, Barbie was downstairs and when she appeared at the top of the outside stairs, a car pulled up. It was not a new car, but a very nice car. It was not a flashy car, but the seats were covered with real leather. It was not a conspicuous car on the outside, but when the driver closed the door with a solid 'chunk', Barbie felt as though she were in the lap of luxury. But not conspicuously so. She smiled to herself. She was liking Mr. David more and more. She waved to Mohamed who stood in the broad entryway and watched her go.

Barbie sat and looked out the window as they made their way to the Khan. The route was not direct, as that would lead them through Tahrir Square, which was occupied today. They went south and crossed the Nile near Cairo University. Sticking to the alleyways, they encountered no crowds. Army tanks sat at crucial junctions, but no one was being stopped from going where they wanted. A quiet, well-behaved car was not the target of attention from the army. The driver made a quiet phone call which alerted Barbie to their imminent arrival. The car stopped at the entry to the parking lot in front of the al-Hussein Mosque. A young man, obviously waiting for them, leapt to open the door. The driver indicated to Barbie with his hand to go. "Walid, go!"

Barbie felt afraid, for a moment, until the 'boy', actually a young man, said, "Good morning, Miss Barbie. Mr. Dawood is waiting for you. Come with me."

Running and skipping to stay up with the young man, Barbie plunged into the Khan. More than a thousand years old, the narrow stone-paved streets embraced her. Shoppers had been coming here for eons. The slippery stones were worn smooth and the ground was not level, so Barbie had to watch her step lest she slip. Most of the shops were shut and those that were manned exuded watchfulness and silence. Her guide was able to deflect the usual cries of 'Madam, madam, only looking' that was usual for this place at this time of day. Eyes followed her form as she scrambled behind her guide. He turned, then turned again and yet again. Barbie found herself in a dead end alley that she did not recognize. She turned around and tried to see back the way she had come, but her view was blocked by t-shirts, leather jackets, metal lanterns and unknown bric-a-brac hanging off the corners. The light here was dim as the buildings were two stories and the upper story hung over the narrow street. Of course, no car could get here, that was why she was dropped off many yards away. She turned back to where the 'boy' stood.

A large plate glass window greeted her. The contents were eclectic, some jewelry, some pots, some ushabtis (pottery figurines from tombs), a wooden chair, and a series of small wooden boxes inlaid with mother of pearl. A sign above the window and door read, 'Mr. David's Antique Shop'. Under this was the name in Arabic in which Barbie could make out the Arabic equivalent to David, Dawood. A man had appeared in the doorway while Barbie had been looking around and at the sign. The boy had faded away, so only the two of them stood in the street.

He wore a black business suit, a light blue shirt, a deep blue tie, and shiny black leather shoes. It was the perfect picture of a banker. His black hair was combed back and a small mustache decorated his upper lip. His deeply tanned skin, or rather, his natural tan colored skin, was smooth, with tiny crow's feet at his eyes. His slim figure spoke of a middle aged man who took care of himself. It was as Barbie was thinking of this that she recognized him, the man from the Gezira Club that she had seen yesterday morning. He smiled broadly at her as he recognized her as well. "Welcome to Mr. David's Antiques!" He held the door open and motioned for Barbie to enter.

The shop window was a microcosm of the shop itself. The shelves were crowded with small pottery and wooden items, a long glass counter held more jewelry fashioned after pharaonic styles of 3500 years ago and the walls held excellent papyrus paintings, wall hangings of woven wool and cotton. It was a combination of the new, copies of the old and styles like those of antiquity. A mish-mash, but a fascinating and good quality mish-mash.

"What may I serve you? Tea? Coffee?" Mr. David offered with a smooth smile.

Barbie peeked over his shoulder and saw a small water caddy that gave hot and cold water. She also saw, tucked behind this, a small hotplate and a Turkish coffee maker.

"Coffee, real coffee, but not Nescafe. Do you have that?" Barbie replied hopefully. As a guest, she felt that she shouldn't be so quick to declare her preference so bluntly, but the sight of the coffee maker made her bold with anticipation. "Sorry, I don't want to put you to any trouble."

"It is no trouble for my guest. And besides, 'real' coffee as you put it, is exactly what I want. I usually indulge in a small cup at this time of day. Please be seated and I shall make it."

Barbie took the proffered seat. It was a low stool with a soft cushion on it and was surprisingly comfortable without being ostentatiously so. It was also traditional and this pleased Barbie to sit in it and be treated to refreshments and draw out the process of shopping in a time honored tradition. The aroma of freshly ground coffee with cardamom wafted and filled the air. Barbie's shoulders relaxed and she breathed a sigh of contentment. She peeked at the preparations and saw a tiny bag emblazoned with the logo of the Yemeni Coffee Company. "Ah," she commented. "Cairo's best. I also get my coffee from there."

"I'm glad you approve," Mr. David said without taking his eyes off the now boiling coffee, taking it off and letting it stop boiling, only to return it to the hotplate for three short boils. He set the copper coffee maker aside to let the coffee grounds settle while he reached for two matching coffee cups. "A gift, from

Turkey. Ottoman style painting from one of the nicer pottery workshops."

Barbie admired the delicately hand painted flowers with gold outlines. As Mr. David poured the coffee, Barbie breathed deeply and once more commented on the hospitality. "Oh, I'm afraid I have made a terrible faux-pas by accepting immediately. I should have refused politely, and forced you to ask again."

He leaned his head back and laughed. It was the first real emotion that he had displayed and Barbie was charmed. "If you had refused, I would never have asked again. You are American, and if you want something, you had better say so immediately. If not, you will get nothing from me."

"But," Barbie sputtered, "Doesn't custom demand a polite tango of offer and refusal?"

"American customs certainly do not, and you are American. When presented with a Roman, act the part of a Roman. If I may so boldly mangle the old expression!" he laughed again.

Then began a dance of conversation, debate, offering of opinions, counteroffering opinions and being bewitched by the other. Barbie felt alive, challenged, and engaged as she had not been in many years. She had honed her argumentative skills by debating just like this with her father. One occasionally took the Devil's Advocate position, then they switched. It was effortless, good natured, and at times, deeply personal. They displayed for each other, at one time arguing for the preeminence of the individual, then for the orderly running of society that does not always care about the wishes of individuals.

The topics skittered about the cosmos. American society and it's acclamation of individualism above all, Egyptian society's emphasis on orderliness and a tight control on the population, lest chaos reign. Personal stories about where these ideas came from, Barbie's experience with Catholic nuns, David's with Catholic brothers, "though I am not a Catholic myself." David gave a brief history of this shop, that he had inherited from his father, also named David, who had inherited it from his father, David, and so on for many generations past. He said the name 'Dawood' with the Arabic pronunciation, yet his English was flawless, with colors of British English and Arabic. His voice was deep, musical and soothing. When he forgot himself, his enthusiasm for a point showing through, his body leaned forward and his voice took on a heavy vibrancy that reached to the edge of passion. Barbie responded in kind, her hands taking to the air, creating ideas with wings.

They had another round of coffee and plunged even deeper into their conversation. They laughed, they sat thoughtfully, even in silence after David spoke of his older brother's early death and how it had affected him, as it was then that he knew he would be expected to take over the business. But even in sadness, they reached out to lighter topics, falling again into laughter and light-hearted play. At 2pm, David sat up, looked at his watch and declared it lunchtime. He asked Barbie what she wanted to eat, and then he rattled off a list of her favorite Egyptian foods. "Or all of them?" he asked.

Barbie laughed and admitted, "I'm hungry, very. Talking takes such energy."

David pulled out his phone and within a minute had ordered lunch to be delivered. "It may take a while, would you like a tour of my little empire?" With that he began a gentle tour, following Barbie's eyes, explaining where the goods came from, and a little about those of the finest quality.

"So you don't just have antiques, you have contemporary carpets, old carpets, new papyrus, which is certainly not antique."

David laughed. "No, antique papyrus would fall apart too easily. It is for archaeologists and museums, not for sale."

"But you also have this tourist stuff, nice, but just for tourists!?"

"What can I say? I need to make a living, and the store cannot exist on the few genuine antiques I am allowed to sell. Here, for example, are fine copies of ancient scarabs." He picked up a small one and handed it to Barbie. "Even experts cannot always tell whether these are ancient or very good modern copies. Here, try this." He picked up a silver bracelet with a row of scarabs set in silver. Barbie took the proffered piece and tried it on her wrist, twisting and turning it in the light in admiration.

"Sorry about this, but do you have a restroom, or do I have to go outside and look?" Barbie asked with a pained look on her face.

David laughed. "You are so cute! Yes, I have facilities, but they are very, very basic. Follow me." David led Barbie further into the bowels of the shop and opened a narrow door.

"Thank you," she murmured, thinking to herself, basic but adequate. After her business was completed, she let herself out. In front of her was a curtained space that she felt sure led to further treasures. She pulled aside the curtain to peer into a gloomy space that was obviously a storeroom. In the darkness, she saw rows of shelves piled high with old things, musty old things. She stepped into the room further and approached a long shelf. It contained hundreds of small clay scarabs. Barbie knew instinctively that these were old, unlike the copies she had seen in the front room. Stepping back, she tried to see more of the stock, but it was very dark. Suddenly, a fever gripped here. She needed to try out her 'voice' in this room. What should she choose that would be appropriate? A mouse? Mice?

Barbie had practiced for years throwing her voice with her father as coach. Her father, the hippie, the alternative job seeker, had practiced magic tricks: pulling coins out of little boys' ears, beans out of little girls' noses, and hidden cards out of nowhere. He made balloon animals and perfected his ventriloquism. When her parents realized that Barbie had a voice, a beautiful singing voice as well as a powerful set of lungs and the ability to throw it, their friends urged them to send Barbie to a special school or at least capitalize on their daughter's gift. They had demurred, not wanting to make Barbie a 'party toy' or a 'pet'. They didn't see her as a child prodigy so much as a small girl with an unusual talent. So her father had taught her to throw her voice. They had played tricks on their friends, and Barbie had enjoyed the small notoriety, but was glad it had gone no further.

With an experienced eye, she chose a corner and began with a whisper, a pattering of tiny feet. She made the sound move along the ceiling, by creating echoes in the small pockets in the corners. She paused, then started again with an entire army of whisking, sniffing, squeaking mice.

"Ahhhh," came David's soft voice behind her. "You have found the treasure house."

Barbie jumped back, embarrassed at her intemperate invasion of space. She wondered how much he had heard or seen of her intrusions. "Oh, I'm sorry, this must be the storeroom."

"It is. It is where I have my antiques." He looked Barbie in the face with narrowed eyes. "These, you understand, are treasures of great worth, that I sell for outrageous sums. You were not meant to see them, as they are out of your price range. But now that you know they are here, I must have your silence, as perhaps they are of questionable provenance. If you betray me, I must kill you."

Taken aback, Barbie held her breath and slowly let it out with a 'hiss' into the silence. David smiled and chuckled at her.

Suddenly Barbie did not feel so comfortable with David. Was he joking or not? Were these things truly illegal antiques, stolen from tombs and archaeological digs? Barbie looked at David with enormous frightened eyes. "Kill me? Really?"

"But you would never betray me, so you will live. Our food has arrived sooner than expected. Perhaps there were no customers today." He went into the front room and Barbie followed.

The boy who had met her at the car carried a large silver tray, covered with a cloth. She could immediately smell the tang of grilled meat and sauces and her stomach rumbled involuntarily. The tray was set down and two plates appeared from under the numerous small plates that held two or three small servings of all the things that David had mentioned. Rounds of soft white bread that gave off steam completed the spread. "Lunch." David announced. After placing the tray against a stack of carpets, the 'boy' melted away.

They used their hands, scooping fuul (fava beans) and babaghanoush (eggplant salad) into torn pieces of bread, delicately chomping on crispy taamiyya (fava bean patties) and stuffed vine leaves, popping bite sized pieces of grilled chicken and lamb into their mouths after dipping them in chili-spiced tomato sauce, stuffing in their mouths cut pieces of ripe tomatoes and cucumbers to soften the spicy flavors and savoring the sweet dessert 'Umm Ali' (bread pudding).

"Ah, I am so full, it was all so delicious, thank you very, very much. But no molokhiya?" Barbie expressed her appreciation.

"Ah, do you like molokhiya? I am so sorry not to have gotten some for you," David said, a smile twitching at his lips.

"I loathe molokhiya, that gelatinous pea green soup with a wicked flavor, but it is very Egyptian," Barbie replied.

"I, too, loathe molokhiya and I do not think that most foreigners like it, so I didn't order it." David replied. "And now, mint tea. It will help us digest the food."

Barbie stacked the dishes, most now empty, while David made the tea. He was right, it was the perfect end to the meal.

Their conversation started again, seemingly where it had left off before their lunch. "Tell me about your shop and the Khan el Khalili," Barbie urged.

David began his story in the mists of time, with Davids that were traders in the antiques business in the early nineteenth century. "We are not Muslims, you know, so we were outsiders. In some ways, this makes it easier, and many ways more difficult. In the early days, grave robbing was known by other names, such as 'digging up one's dinner,' from the ground under your feet. Some people were farmers, growing wheat, cotton, sugar cane, vegetables. But others used the land like a treasure house. There were no laws against it, and over the years, families, whose houses sat on tomb sites, or knew where burials could be found in the mountains, earned their living from unearthing these ancient Egyptian artifacts. When laws were made, what were these families to do? Suddenly, their livelihood was criminal. Who wants to call their father, their grandfather, or their uncle a criminal? They had worked hard, digging things up and making relationships with the dealers in Cairo. And so, they went underground, or somewhat so, and many in the families tried to escape into other trades. And my family? Well, they were traders, and all of a sudden, certain parts of their stock were now illegal. What could they do? Become carpet sellers, sell cheap papyrus copies, deal in fake jewelry and bad copies of Bastet, the cat god? They did all of this, but they had stock, and they had contacts and so they were forced by circumstances to walk the maze between demand from rich tourists, the availability of legal antiques, government regulations, crooked inspectors, and the poor families who needed the work of digging into their basements where the tombs of the ancients lay. Bribes were ubiquitous, thugs made sure of that. I and my family had to learn to be a friend to everybody but trust no one. So, in that sense, I too, am deemed untrustworthy." He stopped and looked at Barbie, his eyes hard, his mouth with the trace of a smile and the demeanor of a badboy.

"Surely, you aren't a crook as well!" Barbie interjected.

"Naïve must be your middle name, Ms. Barbie."

"So, you and the archaeologists must not get along very well? On opposite sides, so to speak."

"Ha, the archeologists? The fine figures who lord over the departments at universities, the puppets who play in the antiquities department of the 'pharaoh' president? Crooks? All of them. They play on all sides, and they are some of my best customers, my suppliers, my competitors, my blackmailers…"

Barbie sat still as she listened to this tirade. She was shocked, amused, taken aback and her intellect forced her to believe every word of what David said. His hands tightened on the arms of the chair he sat in, the heat of his passion radiating into the room. The muscles around his mouth grew taut and his smile, that ever-present smile, now looked sinister.

"So I guess you know the professors at AUE? A lot of them live in my building. I don't really know them well, but Professor Cornelius Smythe, and the head of the department, Parker Hampton and…"

"Yes, among others. Over the years, I have known them all." The mood lightened as he began to tell stories of the venerable archaeologists of the fifties and sixties, who discovered so many antiquities and who were partly responsible for the current massive numbers of temples, houses, and especially tombs that had been uncovered, renovated and opened to the public. These were the backbone of the tourist trade of Egypt and it had made them all rich. He mentioned the National Geographic photographers and journalists that were personal friends. "But I am not well known, although I too, have a degree in Egyptology. I prefer to stay in the background and protect my investments and my suppliers."

"Oh, where is your degree from?" Barbie asked politely.

"I attended your esteemed university, but I also went abroad. Egyptians need to see the rest of the world, otherwise we would be clueless in what the world wants from us and what we can do for the world. My two brothers never returned, so I am the sole David here. Unfortunately, I have no son to inherit, so I will be the last Dawood."

"Meow," came a cry from the back room.

"Ah, my Mishmish must be hungry." David got up and called to the cat, who sauntered out from the back room, under the curtain that hung over the doorway. He picked up the large ginger cat and stroked him, releasing a series of deep throaty purrs.

"'Mishmish' is…" Barbie tried to recall what the word meant.

"Apricot" supplied David. "Because of his color. Don't you think he is a big apricot?"

Barbie smile broadly and hugged herself. A man who likes cats, what kind of man is that? Sensitive, sensual, her kind of man. And she thought of her wicked little trick with the mice sounds. Had Mishmish been around? What had he thought of hundreds of mice? Would he recognize that they weren't really mice, but only the play of a human? It's hard to fool animals, Barbie thought.

"So, we both have connections to AUE and we both belong to the Gezira Club. You have been a member much longer than I have, I'm sure," said Barbie.

"Yes, I inherited my membership. But we are happy to have people such as you as a foreigner to give us all some diversity. And AUE professors also give us a little 'class'," he added.

"I am hardly a professor with class. My parents were hippies!" Barbie said with a laugh. She might have added that her father sported a pigtail and lived in Santa Cruz, but thought better of revealing that information to this well-dressed man.

The cat had only nibbled a few kibbles and then had sauntered to Barbie and began to purr and rub against her legs.

"How do you like living in Hatshepsut's Mansions? I know that Professor Smythe lives there, as I have visited his apartment."

"It is convenient. And living in Zamalek is interesting and fun. The Mansions are convenient to restaurants and to the university. And yes, we both know Professor Smythe and of course, Professor Mary Bell, although she is not an archaeologist, she is just as well-known in her field of politics of the Middle East."

"Yes, she is the one that Professor Smythe calls Gertrude after the very famous Gertrude Bell. There is no connection is there?"

Barbie laughed, "None that I know of, he is just being silly and poking fun of her, I think."

"I have heard that our Professor Gamal McCall has left us?" David looked at her with an open face and waited.

Barbie returned his look as a cold finger of fear ran up her spine. To herself she thought, how do I answer that one? What does he know? What does he know that I know? Is he testing me? Does he want information from me? What is his game? What does…?"

A banging on the front door made both of them turn. The cat ran into the back room in fright. In the afternoon's deepening gloom in the dead-end alley, Barbie could see a shadow at the front door. David quickly stepped to the front of the shop and opened the door. Within seconds, the shadow was gone and David was reaching out for the metal grill that he pulled shut with a loud clang. He pulled the door to, turned a lock in it and then turned to Barbie. She heard running footsteps in the streets outside and then a shout, accompanied by the sound of breaking glass.

Chapter Sixteen: Caught in the Crossfire

David grabbed Barbie's arm and pulled her towards the back of the store, dousing the lights as he went. He yanked open a door to what appeared to be a small closet and he thrust her inside. A loud 'thunk' was followed by the tinkle of breaking glass very close. Barbie's sight was blocked by David's head, but it took her only a few seconds to realize that the thunk had broken the front window of the shop. It must have been heavy to dent and then break the glass as the grill was sturdy and had small openings. Barbie felt herself being pushed further inside and then David squeezed himself in beside her, pulling the door closed behind him.

"Sorry, it is very small," he whispered unnecessarily as Barbie had realized this already. Her thigh pressed up against what might have been a filing cabinet, while her face felt squashed against a glass, perhaps a picture with glass, or a mirror. Darkness, complete darkness enveloped them. "Not too claustrophobic, I hope." David whispered again.

Another missile hit the front window and Barbie tried to answer, but was met with a soft, "Shhh, quiet."

They remained still in the closet as they listened to the noise from outside, muffled by the closed door. Shouts were heard from multiple voices; more rocks, bricks or heavy objects rained down on the front window. The group of men scuffled, shouted, and threw objects in the alleyway outside as well as assaulting David's store. Anger in their voices reverberated and once a long, loud scream of anguish erupted.

Barbie felt cramped and tried to hold her body so as not to touch David's, but realized that she already was thigh to thigh with him. She thought that he, too, was frightened of the mob. Who could they be? She thought that as he was an outsider, they may be anyone who resented his position as a merchant in the Khan, and a man of substance and position. They could be Muslim extremists, the young men of the football clubs, or just a group of lower-class citizens fighting back against those they saw as privileged. Barbie wanted to ask who they were, but also wanted to remain silent. Obviously, turning off the lights, hiding themselves and making no noise was one way to avoid more mayhem directed towards David, or her.

A small meow alerted David to his cat, who had approached the door. Perhaps Mishmish was frightened as well. David slowly pushed back the door and Barbie could feel soft cat fur slide in through the crack and wind around her feet. He tickled her ankles and caused her to giggle, which she stifled. She could not laugh at a time like this, not when David thought they may be in danger. She relaxed and thought that she might bend down to stroke the animal, but found herself wedged in too tightly. She tried to breathe and bumped her elbow.

"Shh," came the warning. "No noise." They both strained to hear as the mob seemed to move away and take their anger to some other shop or some other street. David moved slightly to ease his arm, which he now placed against the door, next to Barbie's arm. He stiffened and then Barbie heard it too, the mob returning. New noises bubbled up as a small crowd came closer. They could hear the sound of metal scraping on the street cobbles. Then more shouts from a distance, and the closer group dropped their weapons and fled.

The cat shifted, Barbie shifted and David shifted. They relaxed and found a better stance to wait out the would-be intruders. Barbie then realized just how very, very close this man stood to her. His arm wrapped around hers, his thigh pressed against the back of her leg, and his other arm was raised to press against the back wall, in an attempt to create a hollow space for Barbie. She felt his breath on her neck and the faint smell of kofta spices, coffee, the sharp tang of sweat mixed with cologne, and pheromones… Barbie felt his taut muscles protectively around her and began to feel the magnetic pull between them. It had been a very long time since she had been this close to a handsome man.

Like lovers, they stood pressed together. Danger swirled outside, but inside they were safe in each other's arms. Barbie felt herself melting as she thought of the closeness of this new man in her life. He had captivated her mind, and now, as he stood so close to her, he was captivating her body. She softly sighed and relaxed into the awkward space, creating softer, considerably less tense muscles and flesh. As the silence continued outside, she felt him also relax and melt against her. Barbie breathed deeply and let out air fraught with tension, releasing the terror of the gang in the alleyway. A response, a relaxation of his body, matched hers. They stood together, bodies touching like lovers in a deserted, moonlit garden. Barbie felt his breath on her neck, and then it became closer and warmer. She felt his lips touch her earlobe and she knew that this was no accident. Her breath came in shallower and shallower gulps as lust filled her brain and then her body. She felt as though she wanted to turn around and embrace him front to front, press her sensitive body parts against his, feel his manhood press against…

"Meow!" Mishmish said impatiently.

"Oh dear," said David, slowly opening the door. He paused while the cat extracted himself from their legs and squeezed out. Then he too moved to exit the cramped closet, gently pushing Barbie out of the door. He stepped out and motioned for Barbie to follow him. "We need to get out of here."

"But the door, the glass," Barbie sputtered.

"We will go out the back way." He took her arm tightly in his as they moved the few feet to the curtained back room. When David had safely negotiated their way there, he reached for a light switch.

"Ahhhh," escaped from Barbie's mouth as she got a good look at the back room. Although the shelves around the outside were stacked from floor to ceiling with an unholy abundance of 'stuff', the real treasures sat in a row of glass cases that were arranged down the middle of the room, also from floor to ceiling. Strong steel girders reinforced the shelves and the glass was distinctly dusty, as most things of its nature became in a week of non-dusting maintenance. Barbie involuntarily walked closer and peered into the nearest glass case. It was difficult to identify the objects in the dim light through the dusty glass, but she thought she recognized a basalt cat, standing tall, with gold paint rimming the eyes and a blue and green encrusted metal ring through its nose. The Cat God Bastet. In the next case sat a bronze lamp from a mosque or house, seemingly from a very different era. "Ohhhh," Barbie said again in awe.

"You did not see this!" David said again sternly, dragging her to the back of the room and another door. He slipped his key into the lock and the door popped open. Mishmish dashed from between their legs and out into the narrow space. David doused the lights and they were left with the fading light of the day. David pulled the door to behind them and locked it.

The space could hardly be called an alleyway as it was more cramped than the narrow alleys of the Khan el Khalili. Pinched in by brick walls painted with ocher-colored wash, the space was punctuated with small doors like David's and Barbie wondered where it began and ended. Warned to keep quiet, Barbie stuck close to David as he stepped gingerly into the tiny space. Grabbing her arm and pulling it towards him, he inched along the alley, listening carefully for any noise. When he came to another small doorway, like the one in the back of his shop, he gingerly tried the doorknob. It yielded gently to his grip and soundlessly swung inwards.

A dark space met them and David pulled out a tiny flashlight and shone it around the interior. It was a storeroom, half the size of the one in David's store, and used for carpets, clothes and cloth of all kinds. They squirmed around the piles and stacks until Barbie thought they were halfway through the maze. Then David called out quietly, "Mahmud?" They inched forward again. When they arrived at a fabric-draped doorway that mimicked the one in David's shop, David whispered again, "Mahmud?"

This time he was answered with a grunt and the couple moved out into the dim light of the shop. Mahmud was ancient with white hair and very large ears. He sat in a chair behind the counter where he could not be seen from the front of the shop, let alone the street. David whispered briefly and then led Barbie to the front of the shop, holding tightly to her hand. The grate was up on this shop, but the alleyway seemed deserted. David let them out and as he did, he handed Barbie a headscarf, like the ones that local women wore.

"Here, wrap this around your beautiful blonde hair. Do you have any sunglasses?"

"Yes,' Barbie answered, digging deep into her purse and extracting a pair. She slipped them on as David arranged her scarf. Barbie had seen many women wrap their headscarves on very quickly, but David was all fingers. "Let me," she offered. It was not in the proper style, but it covered. "Where did you get this?" Barbie asked suddenly, realizing that David had not carried this on his person.

He nodded towards the shop they had just exited and as she turned, she saw Mahmud's face framed by a display of bright scarves. David tugged at her arm again. "Let's go."

As they scurried down alleyways, David listened for any noise that might indicate someone was once again looking for him or his shop. At one point, they hesitated while David pulled out his phone. The exchange was terse, quiet and before she knew it, they had once more arrived at the parking lot in front of the Mosque of al Husayn.

"We must meet again and talk about the gifts you wish to buy. I will call you. We will meet." He gripped her hand tightly and a wistful smile played around his lips.

Before she could react, the door closed on Barbie with a 'clunk'. The darkened windows prevented her from seeing David's face clearly as he backed away, giving the car room to turn and leave. He was not one to let emotions show on his face, she thought. But his words, 'I will call you. We will meet,' echoed in her head. He had said that, unprompted by anything she said. This was a new one on Barbie, a man reaching out to her.

The car edged through the traffic easily, not being a large vehicle, and as they neared the newer areas of downtown, where traffic was sparser, they went faster. Barbie noted that there were fewer women than normal on the streets, and those that were there wore headscarves, cast their eyes down modestly and walked quickly and purposefully. Few were alone, they clumped together in twos and threes and held tightly to one another. Their bags of groceries or packages of goods were clutched tightly in sturdy fingers. Gangs of young men hung together on the street corners in more organized groups than she had ever seen before. Their eyes glanced around, wary of everything and everyone. Many had their phones clamped to their ears and Barbie wondered if they were wealthy enough to have unlimited minutes, or if they knew where to top up the phone minutes. An air of menace lay on the streets of Cairo, so unlike the city that Barbie had known. She was very glad that she could not be easily seen behind the tinted glass.

As they came close to downtown, the driver swung the car around in some back streets, and soon Barbie realized they were on the elevated roadway that would take them directly to Barbie's apartment in Zamalek, but would also take them behind the Egyptian Museum, and not far from Tahrir. They were slowed by the traffic as they neared Tahrir Square.

As they closed in on that crucial point, Barbie pressed her nose against the window, anxious to see for herself the chaos that was reported in the square. Just south of their trajectory, lay the pink hulk of the Museum, and below that she could see army vehicles moving slowly towards Tahrir. She was familiar with the black police vans, but these were tanks, army tanks, with gigantic treads that tore at the street surfaces, leaving pinked scars in their wake.

As they slowly moved forward, the driver gripped the steering wheel tightly and Barbie could see sweat on the back of his neck. He had taken her the long way around when she went, but now, Barbie wondered why they were heading into the fray, instead of away from it. Was it because David told the driver to take her home, immediately? It was more direct and presumably faster, but this seemed scary.

She heard 'pops' in the distance and saw puffs of smoke. Tear gas? Gunshots? They stopped. The traffic was solid in both directions and soldiers in their camouflage uniforms stood an equidistance apart on the bridge. Helicopters flew overhead. The 'whup whup whup' of their rotors preceded them and made Barbie think of the Vietnam era movies in which helicopters were a prominent feature. Were these helicopters friend or foe? Were they now shooting at the demonstrators from the air? No sound of shots followed their appearance, but Barbie's stomach churned and she then regretted she had eaten so much.

"Madam," the driver said politely, pointing to the clock, it read 3:30pm. "Curfew madam."

Barbie looked out the window and could see streams of people moving towards the square from just below her. Despite, or because of, the puffs of tear gas, the army tanks, the helicopters, the soldiers, the demonstrators were drawn to 'Liberation' Square.

"No," she shrugged. "I don't think there is any curfew today."

Chapter Seventeen: A Visit to Professor Bell

Barbie arrived home to a quiet apartment. Badboy was sleeping on her bed, but Penelope was nowhere to be found or heard. Barbie realized that she must be downstairs watching TV and felt guilty for not making sure the TV had been properly restored to usefulness after they had returned from winter break. It was embarrassing to have to traipse down the stairs to find the news. She sat on the bed, then collapsed backwards and soon she was asleep.

She woke with a start as Badboy jumped off the bed and ran to greet Penelope. The cat has changed allegiances, she thought, as she too went to greet Penelope. "What's new?" she demanded

"Oh, same old, same old as far as I can see. Army tanks in the square, helicopters overhead…"

"I saw them," Barbie declared.

"You saw them. How close were you? I thought you went to the Khan? Instead you went to Tahrir?"

"No, just when I was being brought back, we passed close to the square and I saw the helicopters and the army. Don't look at me like that, I was perfectly safe. In fact, it looks like everyone is perfectly safe," Barbie said, picking up her cat and stroking him.

"That's what I saw on TV. Nothing much happening in the square, just more and more people and more and more staying."

"Let me tell you about my visit with David, or Dawood, as he refers to himself." Barbie launched into a recitation of the conversation, the coffee, the lunch. "And then hooligans outside tried to break the window and he shoved me into a closet, and he got in too. It was a very, very small closet. Ten minutes, or was it a half hour, thigh to thigh, his chest to my back, stuck there, while a crowd outside tried to break in! Oh my!?" Barbie looked at Penelope's face and laughed. "Not to worry, nothing happened, not a single part of my body was violated, nor was I hurt," she finished triumphantly.

"I don't care; it is dangerous out. There are bodies; dead people out there."

"There's a curfew; who's out there?" Barbie asked with a sneer.

"There might be a curfew, but everyone is ignoring it." Penelope sat down. "Tea, I want some tea, but I have done nothing but drink tea all day and I feel like I will float down the Nile if I have anymore."

"There was one really interesting thing he said. It scared me at the time, but it was just then that the door incident occurred, you know, throwing rocks and things, and then there was no time to talk about it. He said that he had heard that Gamal went home. We were talking about all the archaeologists here and how they all knew each other and he knew them because basically they were in the same trade and we started naming names and the he said, 'I heard that our Professor Gamal McCall has left us.' It felt funny that he said 'our' Gamal, as if he knew him quite well and that as a mutual acquaintance we should both be concerned about his departure. It was as if he knew all about it, that Gamal was dead and his body shipped out. And I keep wondering who he knows and how he knows these things. Scary. And I was about to formulate a question of how he knew this when the banging and breaking started. Now that I think about it, whoa. I wonder if I want to know."

"The way he said it, and I don't know him at all and how he might phrase something like this, but it sounds like he knew a lot more than he let on. And if he knows, and we don't know him from Adam, who else knows?" Penelope offered advice, "You might talk to Mitch, he knows more than any of us and he might know how the message got around. Funny thing about Tiffany. She just went back into that apartment sometime, cleaned up a lot of things and apparently took Gamal's computer. I mean, it might tell who it was who wanted to murder him. I didn't think it was a smart thing to do, but who am I to tell others what to do? Actually, Tiffany was telling everyone that Gamal went home on the plane and that she was going too. And she went this morning, with Jack and Markie, at least to the airport. I hope they get on a plane. Apparently, there are a lot of cancelled flights, as most of the tourists left late last week. But now, some of the scheduled ones are coming here full; full of Egyptians coming home to be part of the Revolution. So, there are still plenty of flights out. Egypt Air isn't running, but a lot of others are. So, we may not have missed our last chance to leave. You don't want to leave, do you?"

"No, good heavens, no! This is too interesting, and although I felt scared of that little mob today, I don't really feel threatened by anyone, I mean, we are on the side of the Egyptians, aren't we? Stand with the people, don't we?" Barbie declared.

"By the way, Professor Bell has invited us after dinner this evening. Just us, just a little soiree for the three of us. Maybe some others, but a very small party! This Revolution is fun in a way. Drinks, she said come for drinks." Penelope added.

"Great, we can ask her a few more things about politics in Egypt, of which she knows a great deal." Barbie fell into a quiet spell.

"Penny for your thoughts?!"

"A Penelope for my thoughts, huh? I understand why you never wanted to be 'Penny'. Yeah, well, I told you that David practically accused all of the archaeologists in Egypt of being in on the antiquities trade. In one way or another. And he accused the AUE staff and even himself of not being straight. Our archeologists! Our precious professors. And of course from the fellaheen who find the loot all the way to the rich people who buy it and take it out of the country. The police, the dealers, everyone is in on it."

Barbie stopped again and began speaking as much to herself as to Penelope. "And maybe that's it. Maybe that is why someone killed Gamal. Maybe it was someone who saw him stealing and killed him for it. Not necessarily because what Gamal was doing was bad, but because he wanted it. Or maybe it was the other way around. Maybe Gamal was cleaner than the rest; maybe he was the one who objected to the theft and so was silenced. Or maybe he was just at the wrong place at the wrong time. Maybe he was defending King Tut's treasures, gave his life to keep them from being stolen. Oh, all of these ideas sound so pitiful." She looked at Penelope. "And no one must know what I've been thinking. These are dangerous ideas. I don't know if I am or could be in danger, but I am beginning to think that in this case, too much knowledge is a very bad thing."

"I see your point. Mums the word. Nothing will pass my lips. You just remember what YOU said. You can blab too much as well. I am really looking forward to Mary's little party tonight. 'Gertrude' as Cornelius Smythe calls her. I think she is a lovely lady and the name Mary suits her just fine."

"I'm going to get a little quiet time, just me and the cat. David has a cat too. Its name is Mishmish. Isn't that cute?" Barbie saw Penelope's puzzled face. "Apricot, for his color."

Barbie stepped out onto the balcony and Badboy followed. He would have loved to have been a wild cat, but Barbie knew that he wouldn't live very long that way, so she tried to keep him in. "Beautiful evening, huh, cat of mine?" A grey mist had descended that was beginning to turn pink with the setting sun. Even though she could not see the sun, it was behind the building, she knew from experience that the sun was now just an orangish-red ball slowly moving through the goop of air pollution and moisture that was the atmosphere of this part of Egypt. It smelled as well, a rancid, acrid, oily miasma that reflected the conglomeration of twenty million souls and their effluence. If there were laws about pollution, Barbie didn't know about them, and if there were controls, they were ignored and certainly not enforced. And not this week.

Barbie thought of the small villages of Egypt, where the pollution could be just as bad, what with burning in the fields, car exhaust and fires for cooking. And that made her think of Ahmed, the little boy from the village up the river, who had come to Cairo. He was loving the Revolution and he would have loved it all even more these past few days. But maybe that was his downfall, loving it too much. Spying too much. Playing the game of intrigue too well. Knowing too much.

Barbie sat on her bed and picked up one of Ahmed's notebooks, the ones that she was familiar with as she had directed his writing. On many pages, she found her own handwriting, where she had written words that he had asked for. Every page was noted with the date and Barbie found herself amazed at how many days Ahmed had studied English. He had begged for at least an hour long lesson, sucking up every word, and every bit of grammar that Barbie taught him. And he had begged for a lesson every day. Sometimes she declined, especially on evenings when she was busy, but by looking though the books, she realized that he had had an average of 5 hours a week for 15 weeks. That added up to a semester worth of English lessons, one on one, with copious practice in between. No wonder he spoke so well. Barbie had noted that after she had returned from her winter break at home. He had been a little sponge, who had asked everyone to speak with him, to correct his grammar and his pronunciation. She thought back to a day when she found Gamal speaking to Ahmed, gently teaching him the correct pronunciation and spelling of a new word. Ahmed had parroted it back, trying different pronunciations and inflections until he had gotten it right. And it wasn't only with Barbie or Gamal, but with everyone. He had hounded them all with 'What mean?' which gently changed a week later to 'What does it mean?' Barbie thought of the 'f' word she had read in his diary. Who taught him that? Anyone could have, most probably male, most probably as a joke. But he knew what it meant all right.

Barbie tossed aside the notebook and reached for the stack of diaries. Plunging in wouldn't give her the whole story, and starting at the beginning, when most of the entries were in atrocious English with numerous entries in Arabic, would not tell her much. She should go through them, one by one, thoroughly, as she might find a clue to why someone thought he needed to die.

The first volume flew by easily as she was unable to read much beyond the date. By the end of that small book, she was beginning to feel out his style. She recognized more words, and more thoughts. He wrote about what he knew. 'M' as a person figured large in his thoughts and 'M's' actions and words were duly noted. 'M' was obviously his cousin Mohamed. In the second volume, she began to see animal names ascribed to what obviously were people. Barbie thought back to the day when she taught animals. She had a sheet from an internet website to teach children their animals. Ahmed had taken to it immediately. Within a day, he had the whole sheet down. And now she found him using coded names for the inhabitants of Hatshepsut's Mansions. Gamal was 'Lion', 'Donkey' was used for what could be Parker Hampton, W.B. was 'Pig' and his wife, Mercedes was 'Pig Wife', although later she got her own name 'Mercy Lady'. How little Ahmed thought of W.B. to give him the moniker of 'Pig'. As a Muslim, he would have abhorred the animal, so a Muslim to call someone a 'pig' was a sign of great disrespect or hatred. What had W.B. done to Ahmed? Not long after the entry that had the use of animal names for people, Barbie ran across a reference to herself as a teacher, she was 'Blondy', an obvious reference to her blonde hair. But the diminutive Blondie? Where had he heard that? She closed her eyes and saw Cornelius referring to her as Blondie, the ditzy blonde. What an incredible ear he had, as well as recall of a short conversation. Maybe he had later asked Cornelius about it. What a little sneak!

Getting tired and not finding anything more of great importance, she was about to close the diary, when she came across the day after she had taught '…ing'. What a collection of words: giving, carrying, bringing, walking, and then there was a reference to 'head' and 'long stick'. These things made no sense to her, but she had no doubt they had meant much to Ahmed.

Penelope yelled out, "Soup for dinner!" The two of them ate a small, quiet meal in companionable silence.

"When can we go to Mary's?" Barbie asked.

"Just about any time after 7. You know she is an American and she is inviting Americans. So we know that we all eat early. Let's go as soon as we're ready.

Twenty minutes later, they knocked on Professor Mary Bell's door.

"Come in, come in. So wonderful of you to come. I would have invited you for dinner, but I am afraid that the kitchen and the house are in a state. My maid hasn't been able to come for days, and although I clean up, I am just never up to the job," Mary apologized. She was a petite woman with a firm voice, and decided opinions. Her determined walk had been slowed in recent years, though she was still full of energy, ideas and opinions. Her steel-gray hair was cut in a simple bob and her deep blue eyes crinkled at the edges when she smiled, which she was prone to do at any time, followed by a merry laugh.

"Never mind, we brought some cookies. We are not sure who bought them or when, or how old they are, but they will cheer us all up. They are chocolate chip. American, so maybe someone brought them back from home." Penelope offered the box to Mary, who found a plate to put them on.

"Tea? Or wine?" Mary asked.

Penelope's eyebrows went up at the 'wine' suggestion and Mary reached for the elegant long-stemmed glasses from her over-sized buffet. When they were cozily sipping wine, Barbie tried to think of a polite way to ask this silly question and talk about that other famous Bell. She couldn't, so she blurted out, "Why does Cornelius Smythe call you 'Gertrude'?"

"He not only calls me Gertrude, but he often gives me the full name, Gertrude Bell, which of course is utter nonsense. I am absolutely no relation to THE Gertrude Bell, and I'm not even sure I want to be allied with her brand of thinking." Mary looked thoughtful.

"I think what we were wondering is more about who Gertrude Bell was and why he is stuck on that name for you, other than the fact that you are both women with the last name Bell." Penelope added.

"For one, I am very much in the American tradition of scholarship. I have my degrees, including a doctorate in Political Science, not in archeology, or travel writing or nation-building, all of which are more Gertrude than Mary. And I was not unhappy in love, I married and was happy for a number of years. I have my life, my friends, and my work. No, no, we are not even alike."

"But Cornelius called you the 'Gertrude Bell of Egypt' or perhaps it was 'the modern-day Gertrude Bell," Penelope went on. "And thus you are identified and the name sticks. Besides, Gertrude is so much more memorable than Mary."

"Maybe I'd like to remain 'unmemorable.' I think he says that because we are both interested in the Middle East. I have done more work in Lebanon and Jordan that in Egypt, and of course, Gertrude is inextricably linked to Iraq. Here, read for yourself." Mary jumped up and ran to her bookshelf and pulled down the recent biography of Gertrude Bell, Queen of the Desert. "Please, please return it. It was a gift and I would despair if it was misplaced. Stolen, shanghaied, nicked, whatever you want to call it, I do want it back. But please read it and then decide if Cornelius is right, that old goat."

"But you are an expert on the Middle East and you have lived in Egypt for years. So, tell us, what will happen with this revolution?" Barbie said leaning forward with intensity. "If it is a revolution."

"Only time will tell whether Mubarak will go and stay gone. This all happened because of his dictatorship, corruption, leaving the little people out. Even college graduates have no jobs. The Tunisian president left, and maybe so will Mubarak. But there is one thing that I am sure of, that Mubarak is right about at least one vital thing."

Barbie and Penelope leaned forward, anxious to hear what the expert had to say.

"If Mubarak leaves, he says there will be chaos. And I believe he is right!"

"But the people, they are all so excited and energized, so confident in what they want…" Barbie said.

"The people are lovely, but they cannot control themselves or run their little Tahrir demonstration, how can they run a country?"

There was a lull and they sipped more wine.

Barbie was anxious to tell Mary just a little about her adventure of the day. "I went to see Mr. David today."

Mary's eyes narrowed. "And how did you find him? Well, I hope?"

Barbie noted Mary's tone, but had no way to judge it. She plunged on, playing the game with Mary, who most likely knew a great deal more than Barbie about the man and his business. "Yes, he is well. His store is very interesting and he has such a wide variety of things. Do you think his prices are fair?"

"Oh, I'm sure his tourist prices are fair and if he gives you a discount, he will still earn money. And even his prices for his 'antiquities' are fair, although I would not want to believe the provenance he tells you."

"And why do you say that?" Barbie went on.

"He has a reputation."

"He told me that he knew everyone."

"I'm sure he does. I am not an Egyptologist, but of course I know most of the players." Mary sighed.

"And is he one of the players?"

"Yes, he is, definitely."

"How well do you know him?" Barbie began to become more and more curious.

"I met him as a young man. His father had a business, and he was a David too. He is either the third or the fourth David. A true family legacy."

"And what do you know about his background? What is their family name? Where did they come from? He told me that he was not a Muslim and so was an outsider, but I didn't ask, or feared to ask more."

Mary shrugged, "I really don't know much. As you said, his family is not Muslim, but no one would ever say what they are. I'm sure there is Jewish, and so they have many reasons to hide or not say where the name 'David' or 'Dawood' comes from. But he could be Coptic, Armenian, or Greek, maybe some Italian, or all of the above. They have a shadowy past."

"He mentioned two brothers, who live abroad, but what about a wife, and children?" Barbie asked, eyes wide in innocence.

"No family here. No wife or children that I know of. But that is not to say that he doesn't have a wife somewhere…."

Barbie smiled to herself and hoped that her amusement or interest in David's marital status was not noted. Frankly, she thought, if he has a wife, I hope she is definitely elsewhere.

Penelope began talking of Tiffany, Gamal's 'girlfriend' and how she had left this morning. "You do know about Gamal, don't you?" Penelope asked Mary.

"Yes, my dears, Cornelius told me everything. And I mean all the details!"

Barbie was taken aback at this information. What is everything, she thought. Do I know everything? What is there to know and what is to find out? Did Cornelius learn something else? What? And most importantly, could she ask?

Chapter Eighteen: Stuck in Cairo

Penelope and Barbie slept late. When Barbie looked at her bedside clock, she almost panicked at the lateness. Then she thought that there was nothing to get up for. It seemed as though it was going to be more of the same.

When she had some coffee in her stomach, she called Rachel. "What's up?"

"Mitch just got back from guard duty," she whispered. "He's still sleeping. I've got the TV on, if you were wondering, and it is more of the same. The army is firmly in place, it looks like, and they are urging everyone to go home. As if. And they are saying that this was all the fault of hooligans, not the people of Egypt. Well, hooligans or not, no one is budging."

"Are we sure that Markie and Jack and Tiffany got off safely?" Barbie asked.

"Well, they went in a car to the airport yesterday, Mitch told me he saw them just as he was going off duty. But whether or not they are safely on a plane, stuck at the airport, or if they even made it, not sure about any of that. I'd call them to check, but I am hoarding my phone minutes. As far as I know, no one has been able to get ahold of any more minutes, although I've heard rumors, if you have the right phone service. So, I'm not calling anyone willy-nilly. Oh, and Mitch said he tried every ATM in Zamalek that he could think of and they are all down now. So, I hope you have some money stashed."

"Well, I don't want to spread this around, but I do have quite a bit. So if you really neeeeeeed some…"

"Not right now. I'm trying to read a book as a way of passing the time when I'm not glued to the TV. But it is so thrilling; what a life! I'll call back later when Mitch is up and company is to be welcomed."

Barbie filled the time when she could politely return to the TV screen. She tried the internet, just in case she might be able to send messages to family and friends. She wondered if they were aware of the seriousness of the situation or if they were panicking at not being able to communicate. How distance makes one blasé, Barbie thought.

The phone rang and Penelope jumped to answer it. "It's Rachel, we can come down now," she said to Barbie.

The revolution was one week old today and the commentators continually remarked on this. There was euphoria in Tahrir Square. International leaders were now beginning to weigh in, seeing as how the crowds had been well behaved, there was no looting and rioting, just continued insistent protests asking for freedom and democracy. How could foreign leaders reject that honest call? Not that they would countenance it for their own population, Barbie thought, but it sure sounded good to Westernized ears.

"Whoa, look at this one," Mitch sat up. "A tear gas cannister that says quite clearly, 'made in USA'. Whoops, Obama probably doesn't like that one, even though he may not have given it to Egypt in the first place, he is continuing to do so, and supporting Mubarak. How does that make you feel, my fellow Americans?"

Penelope looked closely at the screen. "Are they going to blame us for that 'made in USA' stuff? I mean, we represent the US, sort of, we work at the AUE, the American University. Gosh, I wonder if I can deny it?"

Rachel leaned in to join the conversation. "I think we ought to say that Americans support Egypt, and that these things were for foreign warfare and so if Mubarak wants to use them on his own people, Mubarak is to blame, not us. We're pro-Egyptian people. Aren't we?"

It was one of the first times that the group had to stop and think about the political ramifications of who they were and what they represented. Of course, they wanted freedom and democracy everywhere, especially where they lived, but they also knew that true freedom and democracy was rare, even in their own country. "What can we do?" Barbie asked. "Can we go and join them? I mean, we want democracy for them, but they have to get it for themselves, we can't give it to them. So even if we went to Tahrir, what could we do?"

"Well, Cornelius said that the last time it was this bad, it was the Israeli…" Rachel told the rest the stories that Professor Smythe had told her of evacuations the last time. Barbie asked Mitch to help her find some dishes in the kitchen. Reluctantly he got up to join her. When they were behind the closed door, Barbie leaned in to whisper her questions.

"What does Cornelius know about Gamal? What did he tell Mary? Everything, some, what?"

Mitch said slowly in his low voice, "Everything, I think. You know, Cornelius may know a lot more than we do. I think he had a definite hand in spiriting the body out. It went too smoothly. And he does know everyone. And possibly the family too. They were all archeologists and antiquities people. Often the archeologists were as bad or worse than the Egyptian thieves. And I think that Gamal's family may have been in the thick of things. Ask your friend Dawood about him."

"David, what could David know about all this?" Barbie became quieter then, and began to think that she might be better off keeping her own counsel about her friend David.

She continued, "Cornelius, if he knows about Gamal, he knows about Ahmed too. And the knife? What does he think about the deaths of two on the same night, with the same kind of weapon, and two who knew each other as well? I mean, you do think they are connected, don't you?"

Mitch snorted, "Maybe the Egyptian mafia, an old Egyptian assassination method?"

"Hey," Rachel called from the living room, "the airport, look at the airport."

Mitch and Barbie ended their conversation and quickly placed themselves in front of the TV again. Although the background seemed familiar, the vast airport terminal for international flights, the crowds and chaos were new to them. Individuals and small groups milled about the terminal; pulling suitcases, small children and even an ice cooler on wheels. The talking head told them that the airport had been fully opened now, protected from demonstrators and gangs of hooligans, and flights were proceeding apace. A few tourists who had not been able to get out in the first panicked wave were now in queues for the many flights that were arriving, surprisingly full. The Egyptians from overseas were flocking back to their homeland. One young woman was interviewed and in perfect British English said, "I had to come back, how could I stay away? This is the most wonderful thing that has happened in my life. I knew that I wanted to be part of it. Although I have abandoned my studies in the UK, I must be here. I must be here for my friends, my family and for the wonderful, brave, strong Egyptian people!"

Penelope piped up. "She looks exhausted, I wonder how long it took her. I wonder if she will go straight to the Square? Wow, what an amazing thing."

They watched as more Egyptians poured out of the arrivals area, laden with luggage and courage. Occasionally an obvious Western journalist was seen, khaki vest, camera and notebooks overflowing pockets. "Do they really dress like that?" Rachel asked. "Really?"

Then the pretty blonde reporter spied three young people looking tired, disoriented and perhaps unsure of what the next move would be. "Sir, ma'm, ma'm, are you leaving Egypt?"

"Yes," volunteered Tiffany, more sure of herself now that she was at least partially on her way home. "I've been touristing and my friends here were teaching. Now, we are all heading home. We wish the Egyptian people well, but we must leave now."

"And what have you thought of the events of the last week?" the reporter probed.

"Exciting, interesting, a little scary for us," Tiffany continued to answer.

Jack, however, felt compelled to join the discussion. "We think it is wonderful that the Egyptian people are finally standing up for themselves. We've been here for a year and a half, and we have never heard anyone say anything good about Mubarak, except the media. We sincerely hope that the people can have what they are fighting for." He raised his clenched fist in the air for the camera.

Markie could be seen in the background trying to pull him along.

The group watching the TV burst into laughter. "I think Markie wants to come back some day and Jack's remarks might not go down too well." Barbie remarked.

"At least we know they got to the airport," Rachel remarked. "They left here yesterday morning!"

"And wow, if flights are still coming in, what about Llian and the other teachers, do you think they will be coming back soon?" Penelope asked.

The others shrugged and gave no opinion, turning back to the chaotic scenes at the airport. Soon the scene changed and returned to Tahrir Square, the center of it all. The overhead TV shots made it appear as though there was no room left to squeeze another body into the heaving mass of humanity. However, the reporters on the Square itself seemed to be able to move quite easily, belying the sense of packed sardinity of other views.

"Wow, Tiffany and Jack are famous now. I feel so bad, just sitting here, pretending to be scared, or being perceived as indifferent. I want to go there, I want to be seen and see what's there. Let's go, let's join the 'March of the Million'!!" Penelope said, standing and holding her head aloft.

"Yes, this is history. This is history being made on our doorstep and we just sit here. Penelope is right, we should go, join the people, be part of history," Rachel added.

"If Ahmed died because of this, maybe even Gamal, then I for one want to go too. I need to feel as though I am doing something. Even if it is only supporting all these Egyptians, I want to go too." Barbie added.

The three women looked at Mitch. He lifted his head and stared back at them, "What?"

"Of all the people here, you know best about Egyptian society and how it treats women. You know that it would be a bad, bad idea for us to go alone. You have to go with us. We need our masculine escort," Barbie said.

"Okay, I don't know how you think going to Tahrir will help Ahmed or Gamal, but I think the same. It is history being made and I guess I want to be part of it. I want to experience this revolution too. Staying up all night watching little sticks being fed into the tiny fire kept alive by the bowab next door is not exactly exciting. All he wants to do is to talk about sex. You know, how American women will have sex with just anybody and he wants to know how to get some of that. So, if you ladies will dress appropriately, I'll escort you."

A flurry of activity ensued. Discussions of the appropriate time to go were settled. After noon prayers seemed the most appropriate. The demonstrators, not usually very devout, had taken to more effusive and public demonstrations of their faith and more men could be seen kneeling in prayer, even on a Tuesday. Therefore, afternoon, before the official curfew came into effect, was selected.

"Do we know anyone who has been? Maybe we can get a better idea of what to do?" Barbie asked.

Rachel piped up, "Yeah, I talked with one of the teachers in Maadi last night. I could actually hear the gunfire on the phone. Scary. But she said it was only at night and far away, not really near them. And that is in Maadi. She said they had been to the Square, and I think she took as little as possible."

The discussion continued as to the selection of what to take. Passports were rejected as being 'American' and therefore dangerous to themselves, but that their AUE ID cards would substitute. Everyone knew the university and possession of an ID card didn't necessarily label one as an American.

"Should we take food and water?" Penelope asked. "I'm afraid I'll get hungry."

"Eat before you go, but don't drink too much. I don't think nice toilets are likely." Rachel added.

"Toilets, nice or otherwise, are a problem," said Mitch.

"Money?" queried Barbie.

In the end, they elected to take only a small amount of money. They didn't want to be seen flashing wads of bills, even though they discussed the idea of donating some to the first aid station. Mitch would carry that.

Barbie lingered in the living room with Mitch as the other two went to prepare. "Mitch," she started timidly. "Can you tell me exactly where Gamal's body was found?"

"Barbie, why do you need to know? What does it have to do with you?"

"It has to do with Ahmed, you know it does. So, do you know?"

"No, only that his body was found at the Museum. I don't know if it was inside or outside."

"Was he dead already? When he was found. And when was he found?" Barbie pressed.

"Dead or dying, don't know. Time, midnight, early morning, don't know. I wasn't told much at all," Mitch snorted in frustration.

"But what if you went there and asked?"

"Barbie, I can't do that! Under what pretext? I probably couldn't get in, for one thing, and as for information about someone who died days ago, really??!!"

"But how can we find out? I just know there is a connection. And I think others know too. I think David knows. He knows everyone, he can find out, maybe."

Mitch's head whipped up. "Barbie, I warn you, be careful about that man."

Barbie's breath swooped into her lungs, then slowly she let it out. This warning shook bells in her head. "What? What do you know about David? Why are you warning me?"

"Careful."

Chapter Nineteen: Joining the March of the Million

'Doing' something had galvanized the group. They called a few friends, but no one else wanted to go with them. They had already been to the Square or were still unsure of the safety or advisability of the endeavor. In the end, Barbie, Penelope, Rachel and Mitch, their escort, walked the mile to the Kasr el Nile Bridge by themselves. They had no backpacks, but their pockets were full.

At the Lions' Bridge, which was not its official name but called this because of the two enormous lions that guarded either end, the throngs became thick. Only a few cars and motorcycles were being allowed through as pedestrians took up most of the roadway. Egyptians, mostly male, but a few women and children sprinkled in between, marched resolutely towards Tahrir Square, immediately across the bridge. Stairs on either end led to boat landings and walkways under the bridge; the haunt of prostitutes, lowlifes and small boat owners trying to entice passengers onto small party boats that plied the waters, mostly in the early evening. On this day, the general populace mingled together in a sense of purpose bigger than social class, occupation or lack thereof. A horse drawn caliche came by; the skinny horse rapidly pounding the pavement as the owner whipped the beast across the bridge. Mitch grabbed at the nearest female of his entourage and pulled her and his small herd back out of the way. Barbie thought she could smell the sweat, the feces, and the general smell of stables as the horse galloped by. They have no business here, Barbie thought, there are just too many people.

The excitement grew as they neared the Square. Today was the one week anniversary of the start of the revolution and the mood of the people reflected that milestone. Never before had so many stayed so long, fought so long, for a cause. There was no consensus of the cause, except for the departure of the elected president, but that small thing was enough for the long-suffering populace of Egypt.

The weather was sunny, but cool with streaking light clouds. The sky was not blue, it seldom was in Cairo, one of the most polluted cities Barbie had ever lived in. In the desert, it was blue, without the daily smoke from car exhaust, cooking fires and industrial waste. Barbie wondered if it was too much for them to want a little rain. Probably not, as there were so many camping out in Tahrir that it would not do the people or the mood any good. Luckily it rarely rained in Cairo, the average rainfall was just one inch per year. As they walked, Barbie looked out over the Nile River. Brown, disgusting and in many places smelly, the Nile was the source of their water as well as the irrigation source for the whole country. Egypt was truly the 'gift of the Nile' and it was a foolish or misinformed person who thought otherwise. Egypt would not exist without this river. This vast human spectacle before them would not be there.

"Barbie, what are you looking at?" Penelope called from a few feet away, but she had to shout to be heard. "Let's go lady, don't want to miss the parade!"

Barbie looked down at her jeans and sweatshirt. She had tucked a scarf into a pocket, but she didn't feel as though it would disguise anything. She was a blonde foreigner. Around her was the mix of costumes that comprised the modern fashion sense of Egypt. Today there were no high-heel-wearing socialites in their Paris fashions, but the women reflected the range of clothes worn in Cairo of 2011. The older women of the lower classes wore voluminous floor length dresses of dull colors topped with a simple head scarf demurely tied over their heads. The sandal choice was slip on plastic with the average age of a few months. Poor people had few clothes to choose from and when one garment became too tattered to wear outside the house, it stayed inside. Some had only the clothes on their backs. Younger women of the lower classes wore skirts and blouses that had a tendency to reveal more of their figure, having more of a figure to show. Hijabs (headscarves) were in brighter colors and often tied in imaginative ways. As one went up the social class ladder, the more freedom in dress, the more revealing the clothes, the more wisps of hair were to be seen under the head covering. The upper class young women who attended the AUE wore jeans and skimpy tops, the tresses flowing free. A few like that were seen here, but all women in Egypt knew that to avoid harassment by men, the more one covered, the better. It did not avert all sexual harassment, but it gave the wearer a false sense of being modest in a conservative country.

The men were also divided between young and old, upper and lower classes. Older men of the lower and working classes wore flowing gallabeyas in earth tones, their heads wrapped in untidy turbans. These 'rags' had become useful as emergency bandages and coverings for the mouth and nose during tear gas attacks. The young men favored jeans. Barbie felt that she could count on the young men to be wearing the world-wide ubiquitous blue denim trousers. If a young man wore anything else, he was 'religious' or a business man on his way to an office. The young football fans favored jeans and shirts with their team's name or logo. If the desired shirt was too expensive, or being saved for football matches, then a shirt of the appropriate color could substitute. Young men rarely wore hats, even in the burning heat of summer in Egypt. Shoes were the plastic slip-ons of the lower classes, flip-flops or cheap leather, many made in Egypt. Expensive running shoes were only for the rich or the flash. As the weather was cool, light weight jackets were worn by all. The feeling was that the clothing choices of the myriad groups of Egyptians that met in Tahrir was one of diversity, color and personal choice. Just as in the old days of revolution against the British, what one wore designated his political and religious leanings, turbans for conservative and religious, tarboush (fez) for the modern and progressive. So too, one's choice of clothing in modern Egypt labeled one as to social class, political leaning and religious conservatism. But today they all mixed, all devoted to a single purpose, united at least temporarily for the greater good.

As the expat group moved closer to the Square, they saw orderly queues snaking back from barriers that had been erected between the League of Arab States building and the towering blocks of the Semiramis Hotel. They were orderly and seemingly managed by someone. As the group joined one, a man came by, talking to the people. When he saw the three women, he stopped and pointed towards another line nearby. "Ladies, ladies," he said. Figuring they could wait for Mitch on the other side, they happily went off to the ladies line: shorter, more efficient and more polite. The young women 'manning' the barrier only asked, in very good English, if they had any weapons. The three laughed and raised their arms to be frisked by the serious women warriors. "Have a nice day," one called as the three wandered into the Square. They waited, but not for long, for Mitch. He reported that he was warmly welcomed, especially when he greeted them all in Arabic.

"It's not as crowded as it looks in the TV cameras. Those cameras make it look as if there is no place to flap your arms, but look," Rachel exclaimed, raising both arms out to her sides. Just as she said that, a tall young man came by in a hurry and ducked to avoid the outstretched right arm. "Oh, more crowded than I thought," she commented.

Penelope had volunteered to take her camera and as they walked, she snapped. They saw signs, many in English, some rude, others funny, many extraordinarily creative and all handmade. Some were simple scribbles, "Irhal" (leave) and others were long exhortations or lists of Mubarak's crimes. Themes on the place of emerging technology and the role of social networking were common. Twitter was being credited with mobilizing the population. Facebook was the hero of the crowd for its place as a rallying cry and indeed, the seminal social networking site was the Facebook page, "We are all

Khaled Said." The general populace may not have been computer literate, but enough knew about Facebook to give credit to this emerging technology and to embrace its potential.

The small group gravitated towards the central circle. Groups of men wandered in wide circles, arms locked, chanting and carrying signs. Family groups also stuck together, especially the women and daughters, sisters and mothers. At the traffic circle, they turned north and headed for the Egyptian Museum, its distinctive pink walls and central dome unmistakable in this section of the Maidan. As they neared the museum, they could see the army tanks in a gentle circle near the museum. They could also see the Party Headquarters of Mubarak's party heavily damaged by fire. Smoke stains smeared the walls above every window, all of which gaped open, black inside.

As they tried to get nearer the museum, a heavily muscled, crew-cut young man, casually dressed all in black, approached them. Mitch stepped forward, greeting him in very polite Arabic. A flicker of surprise crossed the man's face, but he answered authoritatively and pointed back towards the demonstrators. Mitch answered the man and turned back to the ladies. Shrugging his shoulders and rolling his eyes, he told them he had been told that there was nothing to see and to go back towards the demonstrations.

"Then, we do know there is something to see, or to find out," Barbie surmised. She turned back to look at the serene gardens, now strewn with trash. She tried to imagine the chaotic scene a few nights before. Where had they breached security? It would be easy enough to lean a ladder against the fence, or bribe a guard to unlock the gates. Although there was security, it was inside and not very thorough. Tourists were supposed to check all cameras in a special room near the entrance gate, long before they entered the museum. But Barbie had seen the 'camera room' full and was told to hang onto her camera, but not to take photos. She didn't, but hordes of other tourists lifted their phones and blasted away at Tutankhamen's golden mask. In the small room, no one could stop them. Security Egyptian style, she thought. And now, she saw how easy it would be to climb the walls and get inside. The massive entry staircase was not the only way in. The news reports said that on the night of the break-in, last Friday, the thieves were frightened off and dropped some of the loot in the grounds. But that was also the night that the phones were down, the internet was out, the notoriously corrupt Egyptian 'police' (as opposed to the army) were in charge. And where was Gamal? Where did he go? Who was he with? What was he doing here? Whose side was he on? Barbie knew that no one here could answer her questions.

"Mitch, can you go back to the mosque and ask some questions?" Barbie asked quietly.

"I can try, but they told me little when I got there. I don't see why they should tell me any more now.

"Go left, go!" said Rachel. She had answered her phone and was informed that a number of other AUE teachers had changed their minds and were even now in the square. "Join the gang," she called out. "And they even have signs! They are on the other side, in front of the Mogamma."

The group walked towards the Mogamma, the huge Soviet-style government office building, just opposite the mosque on Omar Makram Street. This was the place Mitch had been directed to find Gamal's body on Saturday morning. As the other two women went in search of the AUE teachers, Barbie and Mitch approached the mosque door, but the way was barred by a large turbaned guard. Mitch greeted him in fluent Arabic, but was turned back. Barbie waited for Mitch as the others found the AUE group and the signs.

"Mitch, won't they let you in? I guess it's because you are not in disguise today." Barbie commiserated.

"Barbie, what is that you want to know? I can't just barge in there, they won't let me in any case, but what is it that you think is there?"

"Information. I am looking for information that will tell me what happened. Gamal's family need to know and I need to know because I am certain that these two murders are connected. Ahmed deserves better than he is getting."

"Barbie, no. I can't go there today. Maybe I can come back sometime, dressed incognito again. But it may not be safe. Let me ask someone else, my way, my contacts. For now, let's go demonstrate!"

He grabbed her arm and shoved her gently towards the large group of Americans standing in the middle of the street. Large hand lettered signs were being passed out. Barbie took one and slipped it over her head by the string knotted through it. It read, "Obama, support the Egyptian people, not the dictator who is terrorizing them." Barbie wasn't sure those would have been her own words, but they were good enough.

They posed for photos as a group, then individually. Penelope grinned the whole time. "I'm part of history," she whispered to Barbie. "I'm thrilled. This is the most important thing I've ever done. "

"Get a life," mumbled Mitch as he declined a sign in favor of being the photographer. Foreign news photographers gathered around, even a BBC camera crew jumped in and tried to interview some of the participants. A CNN reporter discreetly hung in the background, staying close to her male photographer as he filmed the foreigners demonstrating.

Barbie broke loose, gave back her sign and wandered a few steps away, glancing at the Museum. She felt a presence at her shoulder and she whipped around. "Ah," she said.

It was the CNN reporter, young, blonde and looking scared. "You should be careful you know. You shouldn't wander here by yourself, it is NOT safe."

"Well, I live here and this looks safe to me," Barbie retorted. "I know how to deal with the men. And besides, my friends are over there." She pointed.

"Well, you need to be careful," she said, turning to her camera man.

Barbie watched her walk away and analyzed her clothes, her walk, her ability to stand out in even an enormous crowd. Clothes too tight, too revealing, a wiggle in her hips as she sashayed away with the confidence of a good-looking woman. Barbie wondered how many times she had been harassed. She lived in a different, American, world and did not understand this one.

A low hum in the sky forced Barbie to look up. A flock of helicopters made their way in a ragged formation from the north to the south of the Square. After clearing the bridge that loomed over the Egyptian Museum, they decelerated their pace, hovering and sweeping past the crowd. Barbie stared transfixed. There was no sign of aggression, other than being helicopters flying in a strange place and thereby threatening. Calls from the crowd indicated approval, although Barbie felt unable to follow their logic. As the copters flew off, a higher, swifter and larger airborne flock passed over, this time from the south to north. Planes, military jets, left faint contrails in their wake. They turned over what Barbie thought was Heliopolis and returned, this time lower and louder. In the background, a series of 'pops' could be heard. Barbie turned her head, trying to place where they came from.

Barbie found the others standing in an agitated clump. "Hey guys, we can go now!" she called out. "Been here, saw all of the demonstrators, saw the planes, heard the gunshots, now time to go home."

"Oh God, what are we going to do?" Penelope began to seize up with tears. Penelope infected all of them and they began to walk quickly, then into a slow jog as the planes returned. They squeezed through the blockade and regrouped near the lions. Penelope had tears running down her face and was hyperventilating. Rachel wore a frown and Mitch twitched his shoulders in a nervous gesture that Barbie read as 'I'm not going to panic, but could we please just get out of here.' Barbie felt her heart pounding as the noise of the planes receded. She looked back to the Square.

She watched as a man walked up to the queue to get into the square. She took in his height, his gait and the way he carried himself. She knew he was not an Egyptian; he was an American. She smiled to herself thinking about the things we know, that we are not sure why we know, but that we know. Just as she turned to head home, he looked over his shoulder and Barbie whipped her head back. He had again turned his head and Barbie could not see his face, but she had recognized him. Professor Parker Hampton was another one who could not stay away. His companion, an Egyptian, was talking with him animatedly, using his hands in gestures that Barbie recognized as 'engaged Egyptian man'. Barbie thought that he should be warned about the helicopters and planes and the sound of guns. Then, she scoffed at herself. Parker had lived in Egypt for years and he knew how to negotiate things. He was obviously with someone he knew, he probably had somewhere to go, something to do. He didn't need a warning about anything from Barbie.

But what was he doing there and who was he with?

Chapter Twenty: A Party at Professor Smythe's or A Gathering of Expats III

The visit to Tahrir had drained them all and the four had gone aground, each to his own bed. Barbie found Badboy sleeping on her pillow and shoved him over. She closed her eyes, but her mind raced, attempting to put together all the information she had gathered that day.

Parker Hampton, she thought, was he one of the 'antiquities specialists' that David accused of being involved in the antiquities trade? David did not mention him by name, but he really didn't mention anyone specifically, with the exception of accusing himself. Professor Hampton had been in Egypt for years. She had little knowledge of his personal situation, but he was well-known, even in American Egyptologist circles. She knew that he had written several books and had starred in at least one National Geographic special. Googling him would result in academic as well as popular articles. She knew he was single, but whether he was divorced, never married, widowed or 'other' she did not know. He lived alone and she had never heard anyone refer to a companion. At least his academic career was well-known. But was he one of David's 'thieves'? David was full of innuendos and vague accusations, so tarring him with the same brush as the others was not a definite. His presence at Tahrir was not that unusual, she thought, even though it was strange that she saw him there.

And she thought of Gamal's and Ahmed's deaths. At first of course, there did not seem to be any connection, but as the days went by, Barbie began to see the connections more and more. The same method was used, the same type of knife, the same type of wound. In the dark, not expecting it, a man could grab from behind and sink a stiletto blade between the ribs and into the heart. Instant death. It couldn't be two assassins with the same method? Or could it? But even then, if two different people did it exactly the same way, then the killers must be related. Assassins, such a good term for these killers, maybe someone paid them, or they, like the original assassins, were under the influence of hashish, or other drugs?

And the timing. She found Ahmed's body about 11 or thereabouts. She had no idea and she was sure no one else could remember either. Too many other things going on. Gamal's body was found 'during the night'. What time? This was crucial because if they were serially, then there could be a stronger connection between the two. One was killed because of the other. If they were targeted by someone, some gang for example, would they have gone out of their way to kill them in such different places? Why not catch them together and do them both in?

A new idea sprang into Barbie's head. What if they had been together? What if one was killed and the other got away? Wouldn't that mean that the assassin(s) would hunt down the other? Immediately, before they spoke with anyone? Gamal wouldn't hesitate to speak out against a murder, but Ahmed might hesitate. He might not cry out immediately, but return home and find a trusted friend or confidante to tell what happened. He was a low-class boy and he might feel as though no one would believe him if he shouted for help, or tried to tell an authority figure that he had witnessed a murder. Who would believe anyone on a day like last Friday? Who would believe a small boy? But Gamal, he would know who to approach, who to tell, who to alert to a murder, even if it was a small boy who had been murdered, or injured. Besides, it was Barbie who found the body, or rather Badboy, so if Gamal knew who and where Ahmed was killed, why was the body left there? So it stood to reason that it was Gamal who was killed and Ahmed saw the deed done. Then he escaped, but was followed and killed for his knowledge.

Oh, Barbie thought, too pat, too easy to spin webs of ideas. But if someone knew their relationship, that Gamal and Ahmed were acquaintances and that Ahmed often ran errands for Gamal, could they think that Ahmed knew something, or that Gamal knew something that the other needed to be killed for?

Stop, stop Barbie, she told herself. Then she remembered the diaries, Ahmed's English lessons, but full of interesting comments on life as seen through his eyes (and using his spelling and grammar…). She reached for the stack of them, now lying on the floor next to the bed. She sought the last entry she had read, about Mercedes and Gamal. As she skimmed the pages, ignoring the descriptions of errands run for Cornelius or Mary, she looked for any kind of comments about anything interesting. Then she spied it.

"Stairs walking." This phrase was repeated a number of times in among a series of adjectives. "Small stairs, little stairs, big stairs." And then there were dates, from last November and December. And then who was walking. "Mercee Lady go up little stairs. 15.05 Dec 10." This was the most specific of a number of entries that were about the little stairs. Other entries, about one every other day, were similar. He had noted Tiffany's arrival and departure. No name was attached, but he gave a fair description of her. She went up the 'big stairs', in other words, the main staircase. This was a coming and going that Barbie and Penelope had both missed; they knew nothing about Tiffany until she had arrived back from a side trip to Luxor. But nothing escaped the eyes of Ahmed. How could he be in all those places at once, to see as much as he did?

But he did know that Gamal and Mercedes were having an affair. She read more and then she spotted something in a chronological order. "Pig go out." Then there was a garbled description of going up the big stairs and waiting in a darkened corner. "Place no see." Then he noted that "Mercee Lady stairs walking small stairs. Go Gamal." The Pig was W.B. and Mercee Lady was Mercedes and when W.B. went out, Mercedes went up the 'small' stairs and visited Gamal. And Ahmed had to hide in a place where no one would see him, so that he could spy on people? But where were these small stairs? A fire escape? Another set of stairs, like a servants' set of stairs, in the back? Barbie had been alerted to such stairs in other buildings in Cairo, as the lifts were all so unreliable. Barbie tried to look back and a little forward from this entry to see if Ahmed would give her more clues.

She heard the telephone ring and Penelope answer it. She heard some mumbles and a delighted "Oh yes, of course we'll be there." Soon after this, Penelope poked her nose in the room. "Party tonight! Hosted by Parker Hampton, but at Prof Smythe's apartment as it is bigger. This revolution brings out the best in the party animals around here. Party! Party!"

"Yeah, great. Now, can you tell me where the small stairs are?" Barbie asked.

"Small stairs? As in miniature, or just not the main staircase? Why do you want to know?"

"Long story, but apparently Ahmed was spying on people who were using the small stairs. Obviously another way of getting up and down in here. Maybe it's a fire escape or something?"

"If Ahmed was talking about small stairs, maybe he was talking about the internal staircase that is supposed to be an alternate fire escape. It's at the end of the hallway on every floor. I think someone told me about it, maybe Mohamed, when we got here. But it's all locked up, I think. If you go to the north end of the building, this way," Penelope pointed to the opposite end of the building from theirs. "You can see a locked door. It's not well-lit there and I'm sure they are all locked."

"Hah, someone must have a key. And I'll bet little Ahmed knew who did."

"I'll show you on the way downstairs. Come on, get ready. Party starts whenever we get there!"

Barbie showered and tried to find some casual clothes to wear. She dug into the dirty laundry bag and realized that all of her casual clothes were dirty. She had worn nothing but causal the last few days as there was no 'work' to go to. She chose a shirt that she thought of as her 'work blouse' and a pair of jeans that were not 'dirty', just worn. She examined her face in the mirror for a few minutes. Did she look tired? Anxious? There were no extra lines on her face and her color was good. The last few days had been hectic, full of adventure and uncertainty. But she had plenty of time to sleep and she was constantly surrounded by friends, so why should she be anxious? Dead friends, maybe?

"Let's go," Penelope advised. They locked the door and Penelope crept down the hallway to the darkest corner beyond the last flat. The doors to the apartments were somewhat close to the main stairwell and the lift. The lights were dim, always. However, the light at the far end of the corridor was particularly dim. "Here," Penelope pointed. A door, common, small, possessing a door knob, was tucked into the corner. Barbie now understood why she had never seen it. It was too far and too dim to see. She reached out to the door knob and grasped it.

She turned, but the handle just slipped. She took it with both hands and held tight. She gripped it and tried again. Locked, or stuck; it would not open. "Ahmed talked about this door, or at least these stairs, so it means that someone had a key."

"Maybe the door downstairs, next to Gamal's apartment. Could that be the one he wrote about? He wouldn't have sat here and watched. If Gamal was coming and going, then it would have been from his floor, not from here." Penelope led them out of the gloom and down to the next level.

Passing Gamal's doorway was nerve-wracking for Barbie. The door itself gave off an odor or a miasma that frightened her. Not too long ago, behind that door lay his dead body. Barbie felt her hands tremble and moisten. When they arrived at the same small hidden doorway, Barbie just stuck out her hand and grabbed the knob. She tried to turn it, but it did not budge. "That's it. This is too much for me. I will just let the matter lie. Someone had a key, I guess. It doesn't matter, let's go party." She turned quickly and walked to the lighted part of the floor.

Penelope ran to catch up. "We could try the other doors, maybe they were the ones?"

"No, I'm sure they're locked as well. It doesn't matter. He saw what he saw or he didn't. Locked doors or no. That's it for that." Barbie raced ahead and down the last two flights of stairs to Professor Smythe's apartment.

The door was open and the cool night air rushed into the crowded rooms. The noise level was already high as the expats voiced their concerns, experiences, opinions or just talked for the sake of having something to do. Bored, anxious or just high on life, they drank, they ate and they talked, loudly.

Barbie and Penelope first tried to find their host, who sat in his grand armchair in the middle of the largest living room, his usual place. They said hello and gladly headed to the food and drinks table that Cornelius waved them towards. After they had taken a plate of food and drinks, they wandered around the rooms. They noticed that the usual crowd was there and they waved to Mitch and Rachel, as well as other friends they recognized. Barbie wandered back to the front room and Cornelius waved her over.

"Sit, sit my lovely lady." He indicated a low pouf set conveniently next to his chair. Barbie sat down happily. Professor Smythe always had something interesting to say, some juicy morsel of gossip, some snide putdown of a colleague and he phrased it all so well. Even when drunk. He leaned forward conspiratorially. "Tell me, how did your visit to Dawood's turn out? Tell all, now!"

Barbie blushed. How much did he know? Then she realized, he could know little, but perhaps he did know David, the handsome, suave salesman of antiques. Perhaps he assumed that Barbie would be flirted with and perhaps she would be captivated by him. She could tell him about the antiques, the flirt, but she needn't mention her captivation. He could just guess at that!

Barbie told about the visit, the antiques, the lunch, and the final dash through the streets.

"Ah yes, that is what I heard. An unfortunate experience with the lower classes. We do not yet know who they were.

There are speculations. One is that they are thugs hired by the dictator, another is that they were thugs hired by Dawood's competitors and enemies. The other possibility is that they are Islamic extremists. The Muslim Brotherhood and their more extreme allies, the Salafis, are also not happy with our friend. Oh, the man has many enemies, that is for sure."

"How did you know about the attack? You must have ears everywhere." Barbie said in a conspiratorial whisper.

"Indeed I do! Yes, years of experience have given me insights. I have made friends, and a few enemies. I have 'ears' as you call them, waiting and watching. Knowledge is power."

Barbie nodded her understanding. She was beginning to learn about the ubiquitous 'eyes and ears' that appeared everywhere, employed by everyone. This kind of cloak-and-dagger world was one she had thought existed only in spy novels and found on conspiracy websites. But here in Egypt, she began to understand the pervasive nature of information gathering. Sometimes it appeared that it was done 'just because' and other times it was used to keep ahead of one's enemies, or friends.

She watched Cornelius as he began a chat with another younger woman, a new teacher at AUE. How much information did he have about people? For example, did he know about Mercedes and Gamal and their affair? And who else knew? It was certainly not public and Barbie was at first completely baffled about it. But she now thought that it was perhaps more common knowledge than she originally thought. What did Gamal and Mercedes see in each other? Mercedes was horsey about the face and body, her hair was thin and stringy and she was years older than Gamal. And what did he want with her? Tiffany was much younger and prettier, although obviously not as available as Mercedes. She wanted to ask Cornelius if he knew about the affair, but certainly not within earshot of anyone here. It would have to wait until another time.

Then she saw them, the couple at the heart of her question. They had just arrived and a number of people turned to greet them. Barbie closely watched the body language. W.B. put his arm protectively around Mercedes' waist and she just as effortlessly slipped out of his embrace and headed for the food and drinks. Barbie had never paid attention before this, but now she watched them interact, or fail to. Then she realized that she had not often met them together. She had been on Saturday faculty trips with Mercedes, who was passionately interested in architecture, and that she had often encountered W.B. on the campus or around the Mansions, but she was struck with the fact that she had seldom encountered them together. She had never been inside their apartment, but she was fairly certain she knew the layout of the flat and the furnishings which were all provided by the university. She had not been friendly with them beyond knowing who they were. But now, just minutes after they had arrived, they were circulating separately. A couple? Or just married to each other?

Sitting on the small stool next to Cornelius, Barbie understood why he chose this spot for 'his' chair. There were excellent views to all parts of the main room and a good view into the dining room and beyond to the kitchen.

Parker Hampton arrived and everyone gave him a cheer for hosting the party. He approached Cornelius and asked how he was getting along and if anything more were needed. He was directed to Cornelius' manservant who slithered in and out of the kitchen. Parker Hampton glanced at Barbie and gave a slight acknowledgement of her presence. He went to find the man in charge of the food and drinks.

Barbie sat in silence, watching the swirl of people and conversation around her. W.B. and Mercedes, could either of them have killed Ahmed and Gamal? Being in the same room with a murderer was a scary thought, but Barbie watched them and thought they might be capable. W.B. by all accounts was ruthless as an academic. He apparently had used a student's research and called it his own, so the grapevine had said. But many professors did that; it was a common enough practice and to use that bit of information to label him 'ruthless' was stretching the term. And Mercedes? Was she capable of murder? What was her motive? Covering up an affair? That seemed unlikely, really? W.B., was he getting revenge? Love, sex, revenge? Could people kill for this?

Parker Hampton appeared suddenly in the archway leading to the dining room. His lanky frame leaned against the wall and he surveyed the room, as a king might survey his courtiers. His eyes landed on Barbie. She looked at him and his eyes narrowed as he stared openly and pointedly at her.

Barbie's phone rang. She broke off the eye contact and lunged for her purse. She moved some things aside and the ring tone became louder. She flipped it open. "Hello."

"This is David. Tomorrow."

Chapter Twenty-one: The Stairs

Barbie woke with a headache and took a huge gulp of water from the glass on her bedside table. She sat up and took another long drink. A bit of a hangover, she thought. Why did I do that, drink too much? Why can't I learn to limit myself, save some for later? Then she thought some more. Nothing to do, boredom. Is that the answer? Then she thought of her trip today to see David. All in all, the Revolution was a little boring. Tense, yes, producing moments of anxiety, yes. But the in between times were without excitement, hence the drinking and overindulgence in food. She finished the water in her glass. Badboy curled up next to her.

Then the smell of coffee wafted to her and she jumped from bed.

Penelope stood in the kitchen, waiting for the machine to stop dripping. "Funny, I can call, but I can't text. It's cheaper, so I thought I could contact people, but…"

"It's the way the demonstrators contact each other. Everyone knows that the phone cards are not available anymore and so they curtail their use or they have no minutes at all. But if the phone companies, or rather the phone companies at the instigation of the government, shut off texting, that means they 'own' the airwaves a little bit more, without cutting out all communications," Barbie explained.

The land line rang. Penelope ran to answer. A one-sided conversation ensued, so Barbie felt left in the dark. What can a person learn from a series of 'yes,' 'uh-huh', 'no way!' and 'wow'. Barbie waited until Penelope hung up before she asked who it was from.

"A friend in Maadi, you remember Ann? Well, the last time I called, I could hardly hear clearly for the gunshots in the background. That was late yesterday, just after dusk. The scariest time supposedly. I wanted to call again, but not use minutes. She used the land lines, which seem to be working just fine. She said that everyone in Maadi had run out of phone card minutes and couldn't get anymore, every place was sold out. They exchanged phone numbers, if they had land lines, and who knew whom and where people lived. There used to be a phone tree where all the foreigners were listed by neighborhood. I can't believe the university abandoned that. Wow, were they ever wrong! So, they are constructing their own, like we did."

Barbie's phone rang. It was David. The conversation was almost as brief as last evening's, but he said the car would come by at noon and this time they would go to the Café Riche. It would be easier and safer. Barbie agreed. He hung up quickly as if he had other calls to make, or like a criminal, didn't want to be traced.

"I'm off to the Gezira club for a walk. Somehow or other, swimming seems a little too decadent." She threw on her walking sweatshirt and shoes. She was out the door before Penelope could ask any questions about David and the trip to the Café Riche.

Barbie looked around for David, but she did not see him. He was probably here much earlier in the day, as a proper exercise enthusiast would be. She put her head down and purposefully walked five times around the small oval and twice around the big one. With the walk to the club and back, it was a good forty-five-minute workout.

As Barbie and Penelope sat over coffee, bread donated by the ever vigilant and resourceful Rachel, and yogurt, Barbie broached the subject. "Well, Watson, Penelope Watson and ever faithful sounding board, please help me with this case."

"Barbie, this is not a case; you are not a sleuth. This is real, this is murder, and our friends are gone. How can you make a joke of it?" Penelope protested.

Barbie ignored her and pulled out a piece of paper and a pencil. "I always think better with the ideas and the facts in front of me, written down. And I know that this is not a joke. That's why I'm doing this. No one else seems to think it is at all necessary. Ahmed was a throw-away kid, and NO one cared about him. Gamal was a treasured son, but his death will be put down to the Revolution. He will become a martyr. I don't know how many people know or care, but it is damn few. If no one else cares, I do. And I want to know. Maybe I can't do anything, I hope I can, but I NEED to know. And do what I can. I think these two deaths are connected. Do you?"

Barbie wrote Ahmed's name and Gamal's name on the paper, as if they were headings for two lists.

"I can't really think with this Revolution hanging over our heads. But I think the revolution is part of all of it. There is something about the fact that these murders were done in the midst of so much chaos. It's as if the chaos and the revolution are an integral part of the murders. Don't you think so, Watson?"

Penelope agreed. "It's almost a distraction, but then part of it. I can't really see what it is all about. I don't know Egypt well enough. I can see the revolt of the little people against the big rich people. I can see the youth rebelling against the system, the old people, the entrenched. But I can't see where the murder of these two fits. I mean, you are right, Ahmed was a country boy. He was precious to us, but not at all precious to this society. Gamal, on the other hand, was one of the privileged elite. It's a wonder that his death has not caused more concern, among all of us."

Barbie responded heatedly, "But lots of people don't even know that he is dead. They think he left and went home. I guess his death will come out eventually, but for now, we need to go on the assumption that only a few know about his death. To others, it is a 'going away', a vacation, a 'he's not here'. And another thing, I feel the concept of revenge keeps coming up."

"It's a distraction, I don't see how it involves our friends' murders." Penelope said.

"Obfuscates things." Barbie laughed. "I've always wanted to use that word. Before this, I don't think I've ever had a chance. And Ahmed's diaries, that's another obfuscation. I keep reading and I keep finding things. It's like a crossword puzzle; clues and things are not always what they seem to be. It's like the 'affair'. I know that they were seeing each other, Gamal and Mercedes, and Ahmed said they used the stairs and Tiffany said she knew that there were sparks when she met her, but is that important? Am I barking up the wrong tree?"

"Well, there is a motive there, both for Mercedes, a cover up, blackmail maybe, and for W.B., revenge (there's your word again), but what about Ahmed? What place did Ahmed have in a murder about sexual jealousy?"

Barbie said, "He knew. About the affair and maybe he was the one doing the blackmail. I hate to say this, but he was so entrepreneurial, that maybe he saw it as a way to make money. Look at it from his point of view. If he slyly approaches Mercedes with the idea that for a few pounds, he will remain quiet about what he knows, or even offer to be a lookout for their trysts, then what's the harm in that? It's a little like 'I'll watch your car for you and make sure those other kids don't steal your hubcaps. And, by the way, I won't steal your hubcaps either. But only if you pay me.'"

"But Tiffany knew about this affair too. You remember what she said? She said that when she met Mercedes, she knew that this woman had been doing it with her man. She was positive."

"But," Barbie countered. "Tiffany arrived after Gamal and Ahmed were dead. She couldn't have done it. And no one bothered her. She was in and out of here like a flash. She really didn't talk to anyone but us four, and we are in on all of it. I don't think she was involved in this thing, except tangentially. And another thing. Do you really think anyone is going to be upset about an affair? I mean, this is the twenty-first century and some people might get upset, but normal people don't bother about it. They just say, 'oh hell' and get on with their lives. Divorce or not, who cares anymore?"

"Hell hath no fury like a woman scorned," Penelope quoted, "especially if she is an older one. Or what about a man who's been cuckolded? So where does Ahmed fit in all this? Someone may have had it in for Gamal in all this 'affair' business, but he was a harmless kid."

"You are so right about that! But remember, if he was blackmailing someone, they may have felt as though he needed to be out of the way. Blackmailers can't always be trusted. Maybe he would tell the other party, for money, to get into his good graces. Don't forget, he was a kid and maybe had some problem keeping his priorities straight." Barbie hummed with annoyance. There was nothing written on her sheet of paper. They had simply been talking in circles. "Okay, let's get to real work. "Motive, means, opportunity. Who had them?

"Motive," answered Penelope. "Well, for whom? I think you need to fill in those two columns. You keep insisting they go together, but they may not."

"Ok, for Ahmed? If we say that getting rid of him as a blackmailer, then Mercedes and W.B. If we say that he saw something, then, well, it depends on what he saw."

"Barbie, you have no idea who you are looking for, because we really don't have a motive. If we say that the motive was to get rid of a love rival, then W.B. has a motive for killing Gamal."

"And Mercedes had revenge for a lover who betrayed her. But then, does she have the means and the opportunity? I can't quite see Mercedes skulking through the night at the museum to kill Gamal."

"She could have had an accomplice, or hired someone? Could she have hired Ahmed?"

"Ahmed would never have killed Gamal. Never! Get that thought out of your head Penelope Watson."

"Just speculating; I thought that is what we were doing here."

"Skip motive, let's go to opportunity and means. Opportunity is a bit sketchy because we don't know when they were killed. Gamal was killed sometime during the night and Ahmed was between dusk and 11pm. I mean, who was the last one to see Ahmed; when was he definitely still alive?"

"If we look at opportunity, then it is just wide open. Even if we say that someone was tucked up in bed, who can really vouch for that? Mohamed might know if someone went out at night, but he didn't even know about Ahmed. You, dear Barbie, were the one that found him."

"Badboy found him. Let's move on then, means. Who would know how to kill someone in that manner? Remember, it was the same in both cases, so that is one of the prime ways that I think these are related cases. Other than the fact that Ahmed and Gamal knew each other and could be linked in myriad ways, the method of murder is the same. Stabbed from behind, presumably by a right-handed person, needn't be tall, but that would have helped." Barbie stood and pretended to grab someone from behind, first lifting her right arm over the right shoulder of the victim and then mimicking an upward thrust to the left side of the chest. She squatted down and tried it again, pretending that she was reaching under the right arm. "Both are possible."

"Mercedes is tall. Taller than W.B.," Penelope pointed out.

"I thought I just demonstrated that a person needn't be tall. But they did need to know anatomy. Do you know where your heart is? Do you know how to 'get to it'?"

Penelope wavered. "All I know is when my uncle had open heart surgery, he said they 'cracked his chest open' and that it hurt like hell. I guess that the rib cage protects the heart and that if you want to stab it, you have to get past the ribs. But what you did, that 'thrust' thing you just did, under the ribs, upward to the heart is a real tricky thing to do. And you really have to know where the heart is and that you can get it. I don't think I could do that."

"I'm not sure I could, but I do know where the ribs are, where the heart is and that it is possible, though tricky, like you said. And the reason I know this is because I studied anatomy."

"When did you study anatomy, Barbie? I thought you were an English teacher!"

"You forget, I majored in Anthropology. And Anthropology is a very eclectic group of subjects. There is archaeology, linguistics, cultural and physical anthropology. I studied bones, and muscle attachments and how humans and monkeys and apes are the same and different. Grey's Anatomy was my textbook for the course. And anyone else who has a foundation in Anthropology, or any of those fields, must have studied some anatomy, maybe a lot. Archaeologists know a lot about skeletons, and bones and ribcages and hearts. Any of our archeologists could have known this."

Penelope had no answer for this, but to start a list of all the archaeologists that she knew. "Professor Smythe, W.B., Parker Hampton, David, Mercedes…"

"Wait, Mercedes is only an amateur. She doesn't have the background."

"She's married to the background. She could find out, easily. Gamal (but he's dead), Zahi Hawass."

"Okay, that's enough! The head of antiquities for the government? And of course, the graduate students, the other Profs who aren't back from vacation yet. And did I hear you add David to the list? What does an antiquities dealer have to do with this?"

"Barbie, didn't you say that he had an education in archeology? Need to add what there is to add."

"He didn't do it."

"How do you know? Are you just a bit taken with him? A little prejudiced?"

"No, and you know who else would know about how to kill someone like that? Military, spies, Green Berets or Special Ops or whatever they call them these days. This list is getting us nowhere."

"Let's go back to motive. That's the key here. Let's say that the motive has something to do with antiquities. You said that David talked about a conspiracy among the antique dealers, the archeologists and the locals, perhaps we can throw in the local mafia? If Gamal was on the wrong side of them, or him…"

"Or her" added Barbie. "Let's not be sexist here.'

"If Gamal, along with Ahmed, got on the wrong side of these rascals, they might very well want him, or them, out of the way. The Revolution is just a smokescreen for the murder. They hoped that it would go unnoticed, blurred in with all the others. And they silence the opposition."

"Brilliant, Watson. But where does Ahmed fit in? An accomplice? Of whom? Did he know too much? Did he see too much? Transactions? Money changing hands? Even though he knew about and wrote about the Gamal and Mercedes affair, maybe that is just a red herring?"

"Or not." Penelope threw a wet blanket on Barbie's enthusiasm.

"I need to get back to Ahmed's diaries and see what else is in there. He wrote about everything. And maybe he left some clues about the antiquities trade. I wasn't looking for that. And, wow, look at the time. I'm expecting a car at noon." Barbie jumped up, leaving the pad of paper, with nothing but two names written on it, to flutter to the floor.

Barbie found herself at 11:45 ready to go. She called out gaily to Penelope that she'd see her later and nipped out the door. She walked quietly down the stairs and surreptitiously tried the narrow doors again on each floor. She tiptoed past W.B. and Mercedes' door and cautiously tried the door hidden in the corner of the second floor. She grabbed the doorknob and twisted.

With little resistance and no noise, the catch drew back and Barbie opened the door. She slipped in, cautiously wadded up a slip of paper from her notebook and jammed it into the hole of the lock. She thought that it might close on her and that she would be stuck in here without a key. As the door swung to, she realized that it was extremely dark. Tiny light bulbs gave just enough light to make out the steps. Barbie thought that ten watt light bulbs were obsolete, but these could not have been more than that.

She cautiously walked up the stairs. On the third floor landing, she reached for the door and turned the knob. It swung back and Barbie pushed the door open just a fraction of an inch, before letting it slowly slip back into the door jamb. She let go of the knob and she heard it click shut. A one-sided door. It could be opened from the inside but not the outside. Slowly she turned and returned the way she had come. She could have left from this door, but she felt she needed to return and retrieve her wad of paper.

As she neared the door, she heard some commotion in the room or corridor. Voices penetrated the walls or the door. As she came closer to the door, they receded and she was just about to open the door, when they returned, with a bang and a locking of the door to the apartment just beyond this wall. Barbie froze.

She heard the two of them, Mercedes and W.B., their voices raised and unmistakably angry.

"I told you, he's gone, it's finished." Mercedes' vitriolic voice penetrated the door.

"But the next one, where and when…" returned W.B., his voice wobbly and angry.

Barbie stopped and let them go. She heard their footsteps recede. She cautiously opened the door and pulled out the paper. She didn't want to go out from here, but where?

Barbie chose to go down, maybe the ground floor door would work like the others and W.B. and Mercedes would have gone out by then and not see her. She went down two flights, and then another. She lost track of where she was. Where was the door for the first floor? She vaguely remembered that the ground floor ceilings were higher than those above and so there might be more flights of stairs. Barbie continued until she reached a door. She felt something was wrong as this door seemed to be on the other side of the building, placed at a different orientation. She opened the door and looked out.

She was in the basement of Hatshepsut's Mansions. The room that the door led into was a storage room, full of discarded furniture, but included a small bed and a row of hooks. A lamp sat by the bed, plugged into the wall. Light came from windows set high in the wall to her left. A doorway also shed light and when Barbie approached it, she saw him standing in another doorway.

Mohamed's face was inscrutable, totally unreadable. Barbie could not tell if he was angry, embarrassed or totally unmoved. She walked towards him as if he held a magnet. She noted a small bathroom, a corner of the room with a stove, a stack of pots and pans, and a simple wooden table. Another bed sat against the outside wall, near the open door. Barbie had stumbled into the living quarters of Mohamed and Ahmed. It was clean, neat and spoke desperately of poverty and lack of money for 'nice' furnishings.

As Barbie opened her mouth to apologize, Mohamed intercepted her. "Car, wait." His eyes slid towards the front of the Mansions. He stepped back as Barbie gingerly inched by him and headed out into the brightly lit lobby, which was now deserted.

Chapter Twenty-two: A Visit to the Café Riche

Barbie stood on the top step as the car pulled up gently at the precise bottom of the stairs. Barbie raced down and got in. She never stopped to think it was anything other than her car, precisely on time. Her heart raced as she sat and shivered. She looked at her hands, dusty from the unused stairs and she sought a clean wipe from a package kept permanently in her large purse. She scrubbed her hands and thought of Lady Macbeth. What was she cleaning from her hands, dirt or a guilty conscience, snooping in the bowels of the Mansions?

Even though the Café Riche was only two blocks from Tahrir, the neighborhood and the surrounding streets were surprisingly quiet. Again, the driver took a circuitous route to get there, and stopped directly in front of the door which was set at an angle to compensate for the nonlinear location on a rounded street corner. Barbie got out, closed the car door and immediately proceeded to the front door. Barbie had heard it referred to the 'the old man's hangout', being the historic site of previous gatherings of rebels, but that now it was just an old man's place for coffee and tea. Few women entered here. She hesitated at the entrance.

She had seen the Café Riche once before on a walking tour of downtown Cairo, given by the historian of the university as part of her orientation. That day, the place was closed and they had peeked into the windows, seeing the pictures on the dark wood-paneled walls, the wooden tables and chairs emblazoned with 'Café Riche' on the back. They had been lectured on the historic importance of the café, but couldn't quite believe it was true. Umm Kalthoum singing in the garden, young military officers plotting coups, Naguib Mafouz holding court at 6pm every day.

At the door sat a large man with a cheap fly swatter, dressed in shabby old man's pants and a stained sweater. He looked at her and waved her in with his swatter. She had passed the first test of entrance to the fabled café. Barbie had chosen her wardrobe more carefully today. She wore wider, looser pants, a turtleneck and a long blouse that covered her arms and came halfway to her knees, obliterating her figure. She had wound a scarf around her neck, handy for slipping over her blonde curly locks if necessary to blend in.

She stopped inside the door, her eyes swept the interior, looking for David. The tables were all full, mostly older men, but a healthy sprinkling of young, had gathered at the tables, coffee cups scattered. They were dressed in suits, or what passed for more formal attire in modern times when few men wore suits, even to work. The noise consisted of a low hum and over that, the intense, sharp passionate sounds of political debate. Cigarette smoke hovered. She spotted him in a corner, alone at a small table, a coffee cup in front of him, but deep in conversation with a man at a neighboring table.

Barbie wended her way through the tables, excusing herself with the French 'pardon' as a substitute for an appropriate Arabic phrase. She was ignored. Did she feel happy to be ignored, or was this a good sign of acceptance? Acceptance, no, but if she was tolerated, that was sufficient to be in this place at this time. David greeted her with a double-cheeked air kiss. She returned it enthusiastically, as this was truly the sign of acceptance in modern Egypt, to be greeted as a friend with a kiss.

"Coffee?" David asked.

"Yes, please," Barbie answered.

"Mas boot?" David asked as he quickly raised his hand, snapped his fingers at a waiter and pointed to his own coffee cup and indicated 'two'. 'Mas boot' was the first phrase that Barbie learned in Arabic and it was how she liked her coffee, with just a cube of sugar, a little sweet, but not too much. She had never bothered to look up the word in a dictionary, but assumed it meant just that, sweet.

Barbie sat in the small wooden chair, none too solid, that appeared at the tableside and looked around. In front of her was the portrait of the famous singer, Umm Kalthoum, beloved of Egyptians of all ages. Barbie had listened to her songs and appreciated them for the artistry and ability to capture passion and nuance, although she readily admitted that she preferred to listen to something else. To her left was the entrance to a second room, smaller than the big room, but equally full with tables and chairs, with photos and yellowing political cartoons of decades past. The tables were littered with coffee cups, small plates with bits of pastry, now being devoured by flies, glasses with amber dregs and ashtrays spilling over. One waiter prowled the room and customers waited their turn to order and waited for their order to arrive. Time was not a premium here.

"Ah, it is nice to see you again, my customer who had no time to buy anything. Have you had any more thoughts as to what you might like?"

"Sadly, no. It's this Revolution thing. It takes all our time just to shop for food, find out the latest gossip and party. There was another party last night at Cornelius' place. Way too much to eat and drink. Is it always like this during civil disturbances?"

David gave a throaty chuckle, showing his even white teeth, in appreciation of Barbie's facetious question. "Yes, I'm afraid so. Even here, you see", he gave a minute head gesture towards two men at a table, both leaning forward and speaking heatedly at the same time. "A judge and a lawyer, a proponent of law and order and the other, of democracy, freedom and Western values. Egyptian nationalists both, and we never know which side they will be on which day. They are the best of friends."

Barbie watched the interchange and shook her head, "The best of enemies it looks like."

"Sometimes they are joined by other strong, imaginative debaters."

"Only men?" Barbie asked. "No women?"

"Few." And then, as if on a cue prompted by Barbie and David's conversation, a woman burst into the café. She wore her halo of white hair in a badly cut circle around her head, no headscarf for this Egyptian woman. A long-sleeved blouse and baggy trousers were her only nod to local visions of what a woman should wear. She had coffee colored skin that contrasted sharply with the color of her hair and her eyes were small, dark and she now squinted them to an ominous narrowness. She walked in, her head held high in a queen-like gesture that was also one of defiance. Would any man here dare to tell her to leave? To take her ideas elsewhere? To belittle her assumed status of the right to be here? She was one who would not be talked down to, ever.

A few men in one corner clapped and gestured her to join them. Others simply grinned and waved their greetings as she passed by.

"As I was saying," David continued. "Few women come and now you are blessed with the presence of one of the most important feminists in Egypt."

"Who is she?" Barbie asked. "I've met her, or rather I've encountered her, in the ladies' locker room at the Gezira Club. She was absolutely naked, walking around after her swim and I was really taken aback. Most Egyptian women are rather modest and here was one who was not. Bold, loud, I was quite taken with her attitude. She talked of a new business that had just been opened by a woman. She seemed so happy, so proud of the businesswoman and her accomplishments. For that reason, I thought she must be important, and perhaps a rich woman entrepreneur, even though she is up there in years, isn't she? So, who is she?"

"Nawal el Saadawi, our treasure! And I am not surprised to see her here today. She has been out there, marching, talking, and making her ideas even better known. She is a novelist, writer, doctor, psychiatrist, inhabitant of jail on occasion. She has been in government, in high positions, and been kicked out.

She has fled Egypt, but she is here now, with us for the Revolution."

"Wow, I think I've read some of her essays. I feel very, very privileged."

"These small rooms are historic, you know! It is not just this revolution, but the revolution of 1919, and the revolution of 1952. This revolution will join them. Those who care deeply about Egypt will always gather at the Café Riche."

Barbie stared at David, not sure whether he was joking, making fun of the plotters of previous revolutions, or whether he included himself in this august company.

Before she could ask him, he continued, "But we are old now, and I am not sure that we can do much to help the youngsters. They are doing a god job of tweaking Mubarak's nose."

"But you are not old. Maybe these others are old, but you are young!" she cried.

"Ah, you are young, or at least not old. I asked you here today because I thought it safer than the shop. The others here, these 'old men' may protect me, and us. So, what shall we talk about today?"

Barbie leaned in to speak quietly to David and he complied by leaning in as well. "I wanted to know what you meant by saying that you had heard that Gamal had left. What did you mean by that?"

He stared directly into her eyes. "I heard that he had died and that his friends had managed to get his body out of the country. Is this true?"

"Yes. What else do you know?"

"Why do you ask, my sweet Barbie? What do you know?" His eyebrows arched at the question.

It flashed through Barbie's mind that David's name was on the 'list' of suspects. But if he had killed Gamal, would he tell her anything? Even this bit of information that was not common knowledge? Or was it?

Just then, the waiter approached with their coffee. As the waiter fussed with placing the cups of coffee down and removing the old cup, Barbie glanced around the shop. Nawal was deep in conversation with another group at a neighboring table, the lawyer and judge had been joined by another well-dressed man and their conversation heated up again.

Barbie took the opportunity to think if she felt comfortable giving out information about Gamal's death. Was it even her 'information' to give out? But then again, she thought, two can play at this game. "I know little more than you do. He lived in my building, so I became acquainted with the broad outlines of this, but the details are really not known. But what concerns me is what you said before about the antiquities trade, if this could have been involved in his death." Barbie's voice drop to a whisper at this final word.

"Gamal McCall was a very interesting young man. I heard that he had a way with the ladies. Isn't that so?" He smiled at her in a way that Barbie found intimidating, lascivious, but ultimately neither of these, just knowingly.

Barbie would never have said that Gamal was one for the ladies until the last few days. He had always been polite with her, friendly, but never, never flirty or had the least interest in her. He obviously liked older women, so perhaps Barbie could say that he didn't care for blondes or that he was just not taken with her. Should she feel dismissed by him? "I never thought of him that way, but perhaps he was, yes, I think maybe he liked a number of women."

"Is this perhaps a reason for his demise? But, please, I do not wish to speak ill of the dead. He is gone, but he is not forgotten; his talents as an archaeologist will be missed." David smiled as he said this.

"'And as an antiquities dealer, one who perhaps made extra money from his archaeology?" Barbie thought herself bold and clever to ask this.

David stared at her but did not answer.

Suddenly Nawal stood and began to harangue the gathered crowd. She shouted and shook her fist. She looked around at the gathered company and challenged them. Barbie heard the word 'irhal' many times. Nawal threw in words in English and French, and Barbie realized that she was speaking loudly and insistently about the demonstrations and the 'Revolution.'

"What is she saying?" Barbie asked David. "She doesn't seem happy with the patrons of the Café Riche."

"No, she is not. She has just been at the Square, where she joined with the demonstrators. She is demanding that the patrons here put their money where their mouth is, as you Americans say, and go to the Square. Walk the talk, she says. She asks us why we are so lazy, or are we spies or cronies of the Pharaoh Mubarak. Ah, she is so bold, so honest. I wish to jump up and join her."

"And leave me here?"

David laughed again, a throaty, cautiously joyful chuckle. "No, I shall not abandon you. And perhaps we have already been to the Square and are finished with our demonstrations for the day. Now we wish to have a quiet cup of coffee."

Nawal continued to harangue the customers as noise came from outside the café. The doorway began to fill with the sight of hundreds of young men and a few women, running and shouting as they fled up Talat Harb Street, away from Tahrir Square. In the distance, the sound of gunshots mingled with the cries of people, the sound of running and the 'pop pop' of tear gas canisters. Faint white wisps of smoke began to float eerily in the street outside.

Then three men fell into the café. They were linked with hands and arms over their shoulders and immediately the smell and sight of blood blended with the acrid overwhelming stench of tear gas. The man in the middle of the three held up his hand to his ear and took it away covered in rich red fresh blood. "Doctor!" one of his companions called out.

A man in the rear of the café stood and pushed his way forward. Nawal stepped aside for him, but then followed him forward. The front door was slammed shut and then reopened, the shutters being pulled down and fastened. Barbie and David sat at their seats for a few seconds, but when the distant sounds of gunfire began to come closer, David stood and grabbed Barbie's arm.

"Déjà vu," Barbie said as she was pulled along by the arm. In the smaller second room, a small door opened that led to a dim flight of stairs down into the basement.

Chapter Twenty-three: The Battle of the Camels

In the cellar of the Café Riche, two sets of hands were hastily emptying a cupboard of glasses, unceremoniously setting them aside on a discarded rickety table. Barbie thought it strange that it didn't appear to be dusty down here. The floor, the small stacks of old tables and chairs, seemed remarkably free of the ubiquitous stuff that could create a layer of filth in her own apartment in a matter of days. Someone had been down here recently and cleaned everything.

David whispered to the waiter and a dusty gallabeya appeared. David slipped it over his clothes. Barbie unwound the scarf from her neck and draped it decorously over her curls. A set of hands snatched it off Barbie and rewound it tightly against her head and then tucked the end into the side of her head. Barbie caught a glimpse of the 'newly veiled' Barbie. She hardly recognized herself. David snatched her bag and slipped it beneath his own voluminous skirts. A flashlight was shoved into David's hands and whispered instructions were given. Behind the two, another group of men prepared their exit from the Café Riche from this back exit rather than risking the front door, or remaining inside the closed restaurant. One older man fussed, but his companions were insistent that he exit through the back of the glass cabinet, which was even now beginning to swing open. Barbie still heard the booming voice of Nawal haranguing the Café customers above the continuing noise from outside.

David whispered to her, "It is only one minute through here to the basement of another shop on the back street, much quieter." He switched on the dim light and grabbed her arm. They ducked their heads to enter the tunnel. The walls were concrete, no electricity and no lights were seen, but the way was clear, just as the basement had been cleared and dusted of debris. Barbie heard a few men behind her, also entering the tunnel.

Before she had time to become scared or disoriented, they came to another door, pushed it open and emerged into another storehouse, this time for a shoe store. High stacks of cheap shoe boxes surrounded them, and only a narrow aisle was left for them to move through. As soon as they could, Barbie and David crunched themselves into an aisle at right angles to the one they were negotiating, letting three men pass them by. A few others could be heard behind them, but David pulled Barbie along with him as they proceeded to a narrow staircase. Boxes toppled behind them, but David pulled Barbie along without stopping. A small door at the top of the staircase opened and emerged into a crowded shoe store. Crowded with shoes, that is, not customers.

They stopped in the back of the shop and breathed deeply of clear air. The narrow street in front of the shop was almost empty and the sounds of clashes far away. David whispered again to Barbie. "That tunnel is almost a 100 years old. It's been used before, not by me, but perhaps even during these troubles. Let us go out and then together we can lose ourselves in the Square. Apparently, the Square is quiet today, unlike the surrounding streets."

Together they scurried past the shop assistant and out into the small alleyway. David pushed her onwards and Barbie had trouble keeping up with him while watching her step in the garbage strewn back streets. Soon, she could make out the streets, as she had wandered them in her months teaching at the University. They burst into Bustan Square from a narrow street between high buildings. Barbie recognized a few familiar stores, one was where she and David bought their coffee, the Yemeni Coffee store. A large parking lot was full of cars, and black-clad men stood on the street corners, armed with sticks and perhaps guns underneath their shirts. David slowed to a stroll and motioned Barbie to walk beside and slightly behind him. He shielded her from the eyes of the men in black.

They wound their way through the parking lot and entered the Bab el Luk market through the main entrance on El Bustan Street. Most stalls were open, though many were half-staffed or looked as if they might shut down any minute. Gunny sacks were pulled over piles of fruit and vegetables. The stench of the meat and fish market wafted to them from the rear. They wandered through the market, and then left by the small exit on the east side. The street was deserted here, narrow, lined with parked cars, and today lacked the bustle of its usual busy commerce. The wives and maids of upper-class Egyptians had stayed at home and only men appeared, doing the limited shopping necessary. Also, it was now afternoon and housewives were at home, preparing the midafternoon main meal.

Suddenly, Barbie found they were on Mohamed Mahmoud Street, which led directly to Tahrir Square. David again motioned her to stick close to him as they walked down the sidewalks, although the street had no traffic, being blocked at the end where it debouched into the Square. The silence was eerie as they hurried towards the noise, the excitement, the ACTION in front of them.

When they neared the Square, Barbie recognized the now shuttered McDonald's and just a few steps further on, the KFC that sat on the corner. She could see white flags with a Red Crescent on them flying in the air above the white and red neon signs emblazoned with KFC and a silhouette of the colonel. She had heard the news reports of this makeshift hospital, but was surprised that they were true. They separated briefly for the security check, David handing her back her bag. "You are less likely to be hassled about it. Just a simple open and close. With such a large bag, I may be suspected of trying to smuggle weapons. Besides, it looks too feminine for me."

Barbie lined up, trying to keep David in her sights. She felt vulnerable without him. She was not good at trying to 'pass' as an Egyptian. She felt no one would believe her if she opened her mouth. The two young women who manned the checkpoint barely looked at her. One did a cursory pat down, while the other looked through Barbie's bag and asked for ID. When she saw Barbie's AUE ID card, the woman looked at her face and especially at her eyes. "Oh," she said quietly, recognizing Barbie as a foreign employee of the university that everyone in Egypt recognized. When she spotted the phone, her eyes gleamed. "Please, one phone call, you have minutes, yes?"

Barbie couldn't say no and waited patiently while the revolutionary guard made her phone call. She quickly punched in a number and waited only seconds before it was answered. "Magdy," she cooed. She turned and Barbie heard no more of the conversation. A boyfriend? A phone call away from prying ears of a mother? Let her have her half minute, thought Barbie.

David appeared at her side and waited impatiently for the love call to finish. The caller turned and saw Barbie's companion and the phone snapped shut quickly. "Shukran," she said sweetly at Barbie as she handed the phone back.

They walked into the Square and for the first time since they were seated quietly drinking their coffee at the Café Riche, they had a chance to breathe. As they strolled casually among the demonstrators, David relaxed briefly.

"Sorry about the quick exit, but I saw someone I knew. It was one of the men in the street. He had a scarf over his face, but I recognized the eyes. Those eyes are unmistakable. Not too many Egyptians have that color of green eyes. I did not need to be found there. They know where I live of course, but I do not want them to know all about me or all about my friends. You saw the violence?"

"I saw blood."

"And maybe death. This man kills if he can. And as well, I saw others on the street corners, accomplices I am sure. Several of them wore sunglasses, did you notice? It's so that people like me cannot recognize them easily. I am sorry to take you in such a circuitous route, you did notice, didn't you?"

"Yes, this is my neighborhood in downtown Cairo, if you will. I know Zamalek, but the university is so close, and I have taken to walking the streets at lunch time just to see the sights. This seems so familiar to me." Barbie sighed deeply and let some of the tension flow from her.

"Look," she said, pointing to the atmosphere of ease, with women and children mingling with the overwhelmingly male crowd. "It just doesn't look like this on TV. Yesterday when we were here, it was also quiet, although I think there may be more people today. I just can't imagine it as a place of fear or violence." She was silent for a few minutes as they wandered aimlessly.

David had found a turban to put on during their run through the streets, but now he took it off and wrapped it around his neck. He looked more at ease than he had outside the Square, as if inside here he was anonymous and outside there, he was one of the enemies. Barbie sensed his quietness and plunged in again with her questions.

"So what else does your network of informants know about Gamal?" Barbie asked quietly.

"That he had friends in high places, who may be interested in a cover-up. You never know who you can trust."

"Cover up? Of what? His death, how it was done, what he was doing? What?" Barbie became more agitated as she felt David pulling away, obfuscating again.

"Careful," David shouted at her as a seething mass of people moved towards them, shoving against them and separating them.

When Barbie found her footing, she slipped her bag over one shoulder and clutched it tightly. "David," she called out. She tried not to be too loud, but panic began to rise in her chest. She twirled her head around in all directions, trying to spot him.

Then from the direction of the Museum, came the swiftly clopping sound of horses. Screams of the crowd mixed with the shouts of the horsemen. A space opened in front of her and Barbie began to step into it, when she felt a pull on the back of her shirt. A horse and rider suddenly loomed over her. Two sets of hand reached out and pulled the rider to the ground, the horse bucked and danced, wild with fright and confusion. The crowd swarmed in on the downed rider like flies to honey. The horse's bridle was grabbed by another man and the horse pulled to the side, away from the crowd. Barbie looked at the mass of people standing over the screaming horse rider, as abuse was hurled on his head.

Barbie stepped back and looked around again for David. She felt sure it was he who pulled her shirt, it was somehow an intimate gesture that could only have come from an acquaintance. Or maybe not. She turned and tried to walk away. It was then that she spotted the horse's companion.

Camels, as well Barbie knew, were tall. To even get to a seat on them, one had to have the camel sit on the ground, and even then, it was quite a haul up to the saddle. Three lurches later, the rider will find himself up to ten feet off the ground, master of all he surveys. Purposefully coming directly towards her was such a camel and rider. The rider was far too high up to pull off and the camel was an imposing beast. People scattered. The rider had a long switch, which he used on the crowd at his feet, lashing out at them as they tried to touch his legs, or the bridle. The camel was frightened as well and fetid foam spewed out of her open mouth. Contrary to the horse, the camel made no sound as the soft pads of her feet hit the ground.

Barbie stared at the camel's feet as they came nearer to where she stood. She felt rooted to the ground, unable to move, fascinated by the camel as it approached her. Hands pulled at her, causing the spell to break and moving her back into the crowd, out of harm's way. She was once again saved by David, "Thank god you are here," she mumbled. She turned and looked at her rescuer.

Parker Hampton loomed over her. "What are you doing here?" he demanded.

Barbie looked around for David, but only saw a seething mass of people, no obvious David. Perhaps he had put his turban back on and melted into the crowd. Perhaps he didn't want to be seen with the obviously foreign woman pretending to be Egyptian. She saw the rush and swirl of gallabeyas, signs, women screaming with their children in tow. Yes, what am I doing here, she thought. And where is David? She looked up at Parker Hampton, who looked calm, well-groomed and much like a university professor in this strange mélange. If she was not to be saved by David, at least someone had come to her rescue. Don't look a gift horse in the mouth, she reminded herself.

"Shall we get out of here?" the Professor asked.

"Yes, please. Thanks for 'saving me'. I really think it is time to go now." Barbie said as she pulled on her scarf that had slipped in the melee. She took it off and slung it around her neck. No need to pretend now. They worked their way through the crowd, still angry at the galloping horsemen and camels. They swiftly went through the exit gate near the Lion Bridge. At the foot of one of the lions, Parker found a taxi.

"I'll escort you back to Hatshepsut's Mansions," he said, holding the door for her.

Once inside, Barbie burst into tears. As she wiped her eyes, she found a layer of dust on her face that turned to mud as tears slipped down her face.

"I'm Barbie," she said. "An English teacher."

"And I'm Parker, now we are properly introduced, but I know who you are of course. All the occupants of the Mansions are known to me. I feel as though you are all in my charge, all of you who work for AUE are my colleagues, friends, and I need to make sure you are well taken care of. I have been in Egypt for thirty-two years, and more before that, as a young archeology student and…"

Barbie listened to the fascinating flow of information which was given in an intimate, warm and upbeat manner. Parker talked about his young years as an archeologist, his intense desire to come and teach at AUE, the 'only' place for him. How he made friends with the movers and shakers of the archaeology world, how he met the greats of his youth, names and places and topics that Barbie knew nothing about. It was a monologue that turned into a shaggy dog story. Barbie almost fell asleep.

"And then I met Gamal. Such a wonderful boy, his family so well placed to help AUE with the diggings, the publicity, and a little money besides. And Gamal himself, such a great scholar. I thought of him as my son, my mentee, and I supported him so much. I mourn him, I truly do. And I want to thank you so much for all your help. Mitch told me that you were helpful with the removal of the… remains. No, no, of course others don't know. We need to keep this quiet, especially now, during this time of chaos and uncertainty. I wish I had been available to help, but you know, I was called away. By the czar." He winked at Barbie, or did she imagine it?

"At the museum, you were called to the museum?"

"No, no, to the university. Which is where I was today. This you know is the very seat, the heart of all the antiquities work that goes on in Egypt. I know the Czar has his office, but the real center is at our home, at the university. You know, we have our own collection of antiquities? Well, yes, much smaller of course, and indeed, I would be a bit embarrassed to display our paltry number of finds, but some of them are so important. In terms of situating the great finds, you know. But then, do you know? Do you understand the ins and outs of the great effort we have made over the years? And of course, I am needed there, as I have been on many occasions, to protect Egypt's patrimony. From those who might steal, or destroy these magic treasures. Unscrupulous antiquities dealers for starters. Looting our museums and storerooms to sell to the highest bidder. Even our very own staff, corrupted by these crooked men, bribed to turn their heads, and not see or hear the theft that goes on. But who knows? Who knows who can be trusted and who can't? Friend or foe? Who can you trust?"

Parker gave Barbie a hearty smile that reminded her of a crocodile smile. It looked so sincere and pleasant on his face, but the proverbial teeth stuck out, fierce and sharp. The words reminded Barbie that David has used the exact words about trust.

"Ah, we have arrived. You need to go get some rest, you must be very tired." Parker leaned across Barbie and opened the door. He used his body to motion her to get out, practically expelling her from the car. Then he slammed the door shut and the car shot off.

Chapter Twenty-four: The Internet Returns

"The internet is on! We have internet!" Penelope's voice drifted through the fog and sleepiness in Barbie's brain.

Hearing this, Barbie sat up and rubbed her eyes, making sure she could see and then shouted back. "Are you sure? When?"

Penelope stood in the doorway, grinning enthusiastically. "Sometime this morning, but we didn't know it right away. Apparently Mitch, the night owl, got a funny noise and realized his Skype program had opened automatically. That's how he knew. And the speed is good. Come on, get up, time is wasting. You've been sleeping forever."

Barbie looked at her bedside clock and realized that she had been sleeping for at least ten hours, and in bed for twelve. Yesterday's adventure needed lots of processing in her sleep.

By the time she was dressed, she could smell coffee which spurred her on. Penelope sat at the breakfast table with her computer balanced on the edge opposite her bowl of cereal. "You should check out all the emails. Everyone I have ever known is now concerned about me. Of course, they have it all wrong. Some think nothing is happening, others that we are all besieged and starving. What fun would that be? And listen to this, from my mother. 'And I hope you are managing to keep warm, and don't forget to take your vitamin pills and tell Barbie to stay out of trouble.' See, she knows you. Should I tell her you were almost run over by a camel yesterday?"

"No," Barbie answered wearily. "It will probably be headline news on CNN by now. I guess I need to check my mail too. I'm sure my mother will be worried."

As she sat in the living room, she heard Penelope on the phone to Mitch and Rachel. They had been there the evening before, listening to the tale of the horsemen and the camels again and again. A few other teachers had stopped by and Barbie was relegated to telling the story over and over. Then someone mentioned that he had heard from Parker Hampton himself how he had rescued Barbie and brought her home to safety. Barbie was unable to counter this interpretation, nor did she want to say that she had been at the Café Riche with another person. No one had asked her why she had been in the Square by herself, a very foolish act in most minds. Parker had made them out both as heros, or as stupid tourists, whichever interpretation was apt for the listener. Although Barbie had hinted at a lot more goings on than just being chased by a camel, she swore Penelope to secrecy, "For your own good. Knowledge is power, be powerful for once."

"Mitch and Rachel will come up later, or we can go down. Everyone is on the internet, it will probably crash!" Penelope chose a favorite place on the sofa in the living room and Badboy jumped up beside her, settling down for a long snooze.

They read emails of interest to one another. "You can go to my brother's in Switzerland," one read. "He has lots of room for refugees." "My uncle lives on Crete, we're going there, care to join us?" read another.

Penelope's sister <u>demanded</u> that she come home immediately. "Oh, I couldn't do that," Penelope said. "I'm having too much fun. And since the internet is back on, who wants to leave?"

Mitch and Rachel came with bread. "I know that bread is the staple, and I know that a meal is not a meal without it, so I'm not surprised that the bakeries are going full blast again. I mean, who is so selfish as to withhold flour from Egyptians?" Rachel said, dividing the largesse.

After a while, Rachel called a break from the incessant self-absorption in emails. "Let's see what's new on TV, or maybe we can look at some websites."

"I've got BBC here," Penelope said. "We can trade information from the various websites."

Mitch said, "I've got some interesting information about yesterday's 'Battle of the Camel'. The horsemen and camel drivers, who normally work at the Pyramids, were bribed by Mubarak's henchmen with 'a hundred Egyptian pounds and a Kentucky meal.' I don't know whether to be offended or proud that an American fried chicken fast food meal is so noteworthy as to be part of the bribe."

"There is the Kentucky Fried Chicken restaurant right near the entrance to the Sphinx. Maybe KFC is a status symbol and to be able to eat one of their meals, the cost of which would feed a whole Egyptian family for a day, was seen as so desirable that they would attack their fellow Egyptians. KFC!" Barbie snorted in disgust. "I feel so ashamed to be an American right now." She tried to remember if she had seen any residue from their meal, telltale grease on their fingers, boxes with the Colonel's smiling face. She didn't think so. "Maybe it is one of those urban legends."

"Oh, here is some news." Mitch announced. "The Egyptian Museum was attacked again. Maybe that is why Parker Hampton was in Tahrir, gone to help. Didn't you say he was there to help?"

Barbie thought about exactly what Parker had said. "I think I was fairly certain he said he was there to help at the university, not at the museum. But you are right, he was blocks away from the university, but close to the museum. Maybe I heard him wrong, or maybe he wasn't being totally honest with me. He did say 'the czar' called on him. What would the czar care about the university treasures, whatever they may be? Strange. What else does it say?"

"No losses, the army with the help of the security staff repelled any would be thieves. Yeah, sure, the staff are the biggest thieves of all. That is well-known. Look here." Mitch turned his screen so they could all see the action. A line of protesters banged against the fence surrounding the Museum, while a shot of Molotov cocktail damage zoomed in close. A line of soldiers marched together in another quarter of the Square, as protesters pushed back. A scrum of protesters, pro and anti-Mubarak, were seen on the top of the bridge just behind the Museum. Smoke spiraled up in the background.

"I am NOT going back to Tahrir," Rachel said. "I don't care what, this is way too dangerous for me."

"But this is democracy in action!" Penelope countered. "This is the real deal, important history is being made here."

"Make it without me!"

"Liberty and freedom are too dangerous for you? I agree, it does look bad. And this stuff was happening at one end of the square and I was just a block away!" Barbie ruminated.

"Look, we've already lost Gamal and Ahmed, and almost lost Barbie, I think that is enough for one neighborhood, don't you think?" Penelope opined.

"Speaking of Gamal and Ahmed, Parker did mention Gamal. He knows." Barbie murmured.

"Of course he knows," Mitch said. "Most people in this building know and everyone in the department knows, so what? What is this all about?"

Barbie's phone rang and she lunged for it. She took it out of her purse and turned her back. Who could be calling? No one ever called these days, except…

"Hello?" she said tentatively. "David," she breathed and moved off into her own room. "I lost you yesterday."

"Sorry about that. I saw that you had been rescued and I had something to do. I'm sorry, I should have said goodbye. But you got home all right, didn't you? No more crises?"

"Yes, I got home all right, but I thought I had lost you, I was worried."

"I wasn't."

"And I had hoped that you might contact me sooner than this."

"Again, my deepest apologies. To tell you the truth, I was detained."

"By the police?"

"There are no police. No, by the enemies of freedom. My enemies, and yours too. Take care of yourself, my dear Barbie."

"But Gamal and Ahmed, they… Will we ever know?" Barbie felt desperate. She did not want him to hang up, she wanted the smooth warm voice to go on and on. She clung to the phone, mouthing silently, "Don't hang up, not yet." What was going on, she thought. Have I fallen in love? Or am I being led astray? What is my relationship with this man? Do I have a relationship? What do I know about him? Really?

"Where can I reach you?" Barbie blurted.

"I'm here, I'm here for you," came the smooth rejoinder.

"Here, at Hatshepsut's Mansions?" she asked.

Gunshots rang out in the background of his phone call. They sounded like popguns, but Barbie knew they were real. "Where are you? Who is doing the shooting?"

"Do not worry. I am here for you. If you need me, call. I will answer, or someone else will answer this phone. Also, do not worry about Gamal and little Ahmed. They are gone, but…" the line crackled.

"David, David. What's happening? Where are you? What about Gamal and Ahmed? What do you know…" The line went dead.

Penelope burst into the bedroom. "Llian is at the airport. She and two other teachers have come back. They couldn't stay away. And now they are trying to find a ride back into the city. They are crazy!"

Chapter Twenty-five: Arrivals from the Airport

A welcoming party stood on the steps of Hatshepsut's Mansions to welcome back the three teachers who had made it in from the airport. It had taken almost three hours, and many phone calls from Llian before they were finally at the door. Two of the teachers were Egyptian-Americans who had gone to visit family in the US for the winter holidays. They knew that they were not expected back, but bubbled enthusiastically to all how happy they were to be 'home' where the 'action' was.

The two teachers were helped to sort their luggage and sent off to their respective homes with the request to come back and keep in touch with their AUE colleagues. "We're in this together!" Llian declared as the broken-down taxi spewed black smoke as it left the curb. "It was like the 60's, you know, how many can you get into a Volkswagen? Squashed in there. Whew, glad to be back. Any food? Or are we eating out of old cans?"

"I'm doing a fresh chicken tonight, and you are invited, fresh tomatoes and cucumbers, bread straight from the bakery, and oodles of those little sticky dessert things…" Rachel and Penelope took Llian in hand as Mitch carried the suitcase. As usual, Mitch took the stairs, having been caught too often in the lift, while the three women crowded into the ancient lift. Barbie walked with Mitch.

They listened to the conversation as they slowly trudged up the stairs, keeping up with the slow lift. On the second floor, the door to W.B. and Mercedes flat opened and the two popped their heads out to say hello to Llian and enquire about the other teachers. Barbie tried hard not to look towards Parker Hampton's door for fear that she would see his face as well. She had no urge to meet him again. Just a feeling. Not that she was happy to see the cheerful faces of the two Lees, just not feeling spooked about them.

"Use Vodaphone if you can, it seems to be working better than the others. And there are rumors that more minutes will be released soon. No texting yet, but phone calls. They however, should be short, succinct and only when necessary. Call on your landline to the others in the building and AUE people. All of our landlines work just fine. Isn't that weird?" Penelope filled in Llian.

"And keep ahold of as much money as you have now. No frivolity! The ATMs are empty, and there is no word when they will be restored. We are in the middle of a revolution!"

Llian nodded energetically, "I found out about the ATMs at the airport. Empty, closed. I have some cash in my apartment, and of course, some with me. I really hope it is enough."

"We are not using taxis much, I mean we are not going anywhere very often, and we avoid the expensive restaurants, keeping the money for everyday food. But Moneybags there," gesturing towards Barbie, "has told us that she got a lot of money out of the ATM just before the panic, so she is lending, but at exorbitant rates, so she says!" Penelope added.

Suddenly, Barbie perceived a pair of shoes on the stairs just in front of her. She stopped. Looked up into the smiling face of Parker Hampton. He was coming down the stairs and momentarily blocked Barbie's way. Flustered, Barbie stammered, "Hello again. Uh, thanks for bringing me home yesterday."

"Ah, my damsel in distress. I was only happy to rescue you. But, now you must be very careful of Tahrir. Don't go running off there again. Dangerous is the only word for it. Careful!"

Barbie smiled but seethed inside. How dare he, she thought, tell me what to do. If someone tells me not to do something, by golly, I will do that. But inside, Barbie knew he was right. It was dangerous for her. But she had no intention of going again, at least alone. In a group, or with protection. Stop, she told herself, it is dangerous, you know he's right. She smiled at him as she passed. She couldn't think of anything else to say to him. Arrogant…

Barbie declined to help Llian settle into her apartment, but she did admit that it would be nice to have one more person on their floor. Llian was energetic, interested in everything and bold in her opinions as well as actions. She had been missed these past few days, especially by Rachel and Penelope. She however, had a tendency to keep out of their apartment as she detested cats, and Badboy seemed to sense this, rushing to the door to greet her whenever she arrived. But now, Barbie wanted to read some more of Ahmed's journals.

She had acquainted herself with Ahmed's style of writing and had deciphered much of what he wrote. She tried to remember as much Arabic grammar as she could, reasoning that he might use Arabic grammar when he didn't know English grammar. He was good at vocabulary and used the words he learned easily, but he had a tendency to be blithe with his use of grammar. For example, he chose the singular when he meant the plural, maybe because he didn't know the plural, maybe because he didn't know he was supposed to use the plural or because of just plain focus on meaning, not the form. As soon as Barbie settled into read more, she became weepy and distracted.

"Take ahold of yourself," she said aloud. She felt caught up in the Revolution and had forgotten the small boy who lost his life. She sighed and went back to the journals. She thought that she had not gotten anywhere with any other investigations, questions, or lines of inquiry. She had gotten no closer to who had killed Ahmed. Perhaps the answer was here, in these journals. Go, read them, she urged herself.

Badboy curled up with her and that made it easier for Barbie is concentrate, the hum of his purr settled her mind and helped her focus. She read one paragraph again and again. Finally, she reached for a pen and wrote it out in English that she could understand. Apparently, Ahmed had been spying on W.B and Mercedes. He described the encounter where they had been arguing and then W.B. moved closer, reaching out to touch Mercedes, who backed away. Ahmed indicated that he knew that the argument was about Gamal. Barbie looked at the date, only a week before the Revolution. What were they all doing here then? Didn't any of them go home for Christmas? And where was Tiffany in all this? She had encountered Mercedes, but what about W.B.? And were they gone at all during the holidays?

Barbie read some more. She recognized that even Ahmed knew about her appointment with David the day the internet went down. How many others in the building knew about it? Common knowledge or just gossip gone wild? But nothing else seemed relevant. Then she saw that he had made one last entry on the evening he died. It was in Arabic. Barbie struggled to read it, and had to consult her Arabic textbook to make sure. It read, "Gamal. Tahrir." That was all. What did it mean? Did it mean that he was going with Gamal to Tahrir? That he knew Gamal was going to Tahrir? That Ahmed would follow him there, knowing that he was going? When was it written, before Gamal went? Presumably. But what was so special about Gamal going to Tahrir? Lots of people were going to Tahrir, it was the thing to do, so why make a note that Gamal was going to go, or had been, to Tahrir? Did he go with Gamal, or follow him to Tahrir and to the Museum and then saw something? This was something she had thought of before, but now it seemed a lot more likely.

She looked once more at the childish writing in pencil. The last thing he wrote.

Penelope's voice floated through the apartment, "Llian's TV is working, so I'm over there, come over when you want. Rachel is doing the chicken and I guess we'll go to her house for dinner. I'll come and get you for dinner, okay?"

"Do that," Barbie murmured, looking at the notebooks once more. She had struggled through the first few, but realized that the gossip from months ago was not that relevant here. He became more coherent as he went along. He had a better idea of what he wanted to put in his notebooks. They were a gossip monger's dream: dates, times, places. She read again about the stairs and reassured herself that she was right about her interpretation of those stairs. They were the way Gamal and Mercedes visited each other. But what else about that affair? She skimmed, looking for the nicknames of Mercedes and W.B. and Gamal, who had no nickname, just Gamal.

"Look at that!" she exclaimed. "How did I miss it?" She read in bits and pieces, many items seemed incoherent to her, but the one she had spotted seemed clear enough. It was just as W.B. and Mercedes must have come back from vacation. It was two days before the notation about the husband and wife arguing. But this was about Gamal and W.B. arguing, or rather, W.B. shouting angrily at Gamal. The grammar was again tortuous and Barbie felt as though if she had an Arabic speaker read it and then back translate into English???

She quietly moved Badboy off her lap and slipped her shoes on. Not wanting to disturb Mitch again, who had quite firmly warned her off any snooping, she quietly called Mary Bell. Finding her at home and not busy, Barbie slipped out the door. She heard the TV coming from the apartment down the hall, as Penelope and Llian preferred it loud. She tiptoed downstairs. She did not want to run into Parker again. She stopped halfway down when she realized that he had been going downstairs, but he lived on the second floor. So what had he been doing upstairs? Visiting, silly, they all visited up and down stairs. She looked over her shoulder and around to see if anyone else was moving and then knocked quietly at Mary's door. A tickle at the back of her neck made her wince and turn around, and then she was aware that Mohamed the doorman had seen her. Was she never to feel safe from prying eyes? Was this 'safety,' for someone to know where she was, or was this intrusive and uncalled for? It was a cultural thing, she decided.

Mary answered her door and ushered her in quickly. It was obvious that Mary had been a bit lonely, as she had prudently not gone out much at all. She had her TV on, but turned it off as Barbie came into the living room. "What news?" Mary inquired.

"We've been busy today. Llian came back with two other teachers, Egyptians who couldn't stay away at this momentous time. I was in Tahrir yesterday, and was rescued by Parker Hampton from a rampaging camel. I guess you heard about that?"

"Yes," admitted Mary, "I have been keeping up with the Mansions' gossip. And are you all right for food, and such like?"

"Yes, we have been sharing a lot of meals and also the bread, which is difficult to get. How about yourself? Taken care of?"

"Yes, Mohamed takes care of me and Cornelius. Cornelius has his man to help and if he's going out, he makes sure I have enough as well. Egyptians are so generous like that. They know that it is the most important thing in life, to take care of others. So what is it that you wanted?"

"A quick translation." Barbie took the notebook out of her bag. "Here, I am trying to translate this. This is our Ahmed keeping a diary as I taught him. Clever he was, but it is not always easy to understand what he meant. Here," she pointed to the paragraph. "He writes in English, but I think the grammar is mostly Arabic. Can you make any sense out of it?" She allowed Mary a few minutes to peruse the text and look forward and backwards to see the context.

"Well, Pig, does he really mean a pig? That's most unusual. A man, does he mean Willie Bob?"

"Willie Bob?" asked Barbie. "W.B.? Yes, Pig is his name for him. Not flattering, huh? W.B.'s name is Willie Bob?" Barbie shook her head in amazement.

"If your name was Willie Bob, wouldn't you change it as much as you could? And I guess he does look like a pig, small eyes, and funny hair. But I don't think Ahmed liked him much to give him a nickname like Pig."

"To be fair, I was using a book that was very American and it had all the animals. Pig was cute and was a nice animal. I think I tried to tell Ahmed that Pig was a 'good' animal in

America. And that he didn't have to feel offended by pigs, just didn't have to eat them. So, maybe using Pig as a nickname for W.B. was because he looked a little like the Pig in the book. Anyway, what does Ahmed say about him?"

"This is about an argument between Gamal and Willie Bob and the topic is Mercedes. It appears that 'Pig' knew about 'it' and was angry. Gamal seems to have said nothing. Silly, reckless young man. Maybe he thought it was some coming-of-age thing, having an affair with an older woman. It was dangerous and they both knew it. But this, "she said, tapping the notebook page, "seems clear that the husband found out and was angry."

"How angry? Just a few days later Gamal is stabbed with a cheap tourist knife. And so is Ahmed, who so clearly knew about the affair. Thanks Mary, for helping with this. I couldn't have read this without the help of an Arabic speaker. But now you know. Now you need to stay safe. And I need to hide this away, and be very, very careful." Barbie retrieved the notebook and placed it deep into her bag. "Take care, Mary!"

As she mounted the stairs Barbie was summoned to dinner and lost herself in stories from the others; what they had seen on TV, what news from family, what the blogs were reporting. Wine flowed and laughter followed. In the midst of it all, Barbie's phone rang. She reached for her bag and dived into the depths to retrieve it. Her hand touched Ahmed's notebook and she felt silly to have left it here, rather than in hiding in her apartment. When she finally found the phone, she stood and moved away to answer it. She glanced at the number, but it was not on her list.

"Hello," she said tentatively.

"David here, I just wanted to call with another number. Just in case. Save this number. Take care," he crooned.

"David," she started to say, moving into the kitchen in order to hear better. "Okay, but is the other one still good, too?"

There was a silence and then David's smooth voice came again. "Yes, yes, take care." The line went dead.

Nervously, Barbie punched the keys that would save this phone number. She named it 'David 2'. What was being so wrong that he needed to have another phone number? Hacked? Someone listening in? Who were his enemies?

Penelope appeared in the doorway of the kitchen, letting the door swing to behind her. "Barbie, be careful. Was that David? You need to be careful with that man. Remember, the antiquities trade? The people who murdered Gamal and maybe Ahmed? Why are you getting wrapped up in this? And how do you know that David is a friend and not your enemy?"

"Because," Barbie stuttered.

"Because you, girl, have fallen for the man! And that makes you very stupid!"

Barbie opened her mouth to protest, but Penelope had already gone back to the party, leaving Barbie with the memory of David's dulcet tones.

Chapter Twenty-six: The Egyptian Museum

It was late. The parties had all broken up, the streets were quiet, and the night-time home security guards were at their posts, burning pieces of wood or old furniture in small fires on street corners. All of Hatshepsut's Mansions residents were in their own apartments. Muhamad had closed the front doors, but left them unlocked, in case there was a late comer, or an emergency. He retreated to his lair, but left the door open so he could hear anyone who knocked, or opened the door, which was left to squeak for this reason.

Barbie sat with Penelope, both in their nightgowns, waiting for sleep to overtake them.

"Watson, I need your advice. I have now found out information that might indicate that the murderer of Gamal and Ahmed is in this building. I'm not really afraid for myself, but I'm afraid about what I know, who else might know it, and what that evil person may do next."

"For pity's sake, tell me Barbie!" Penelope wailed.

"No," she answered. "Well, maybe I can give you some idea, but this goes absolutely no further. Knowledge may put you at risk."

"But you are at risk!"

"Ok, here goes. Mercedes and Gamal were having an affair. Ahmed knew about it. And just a few days before Gamal and Ahmed were killed, Ahmed saw Willie Bob and Gamal having an argument. He wrote it down in fractured English. Now, perhaps W.B. (for that is the name we know him by, stop laughing Penelope), saw Gamal and Ahmed take off and followed them, or maybe just Gamal, not both. Maybe Ahmed followed W.B, following Gamal and saw the murder. W.B. then found out that Ahmed knew or saw, and then killed him too."

"And who made up this story?" Penelope scoffed.

"It's in Ahmed's journal."

"No, you made it up. Look, your friend David is as likely, or more so, to be Gamal's murderer. Gamal, the czar, David, even Parker Hampton, Cornelius, all of them are tainted with real questionable behavior. Any of them could have murdered Gamal at the museum," Penelope reasoned.

"Not Cornelius, he's too old, but he could have hired someone. But I don't believe that. And why do you say David is a suspect? Don't, no we've gone over that before," Barbie held up her hand to stop Penelope's protest. "And Mercedes? Are you going to leave her out? Might as well include everyone."

"She is strong enough to do it. And perhaps mean enough. But it really appears unlikely. And you are unwilling to see the two murders as two separate events. If you look at them as having two motives, two windows of opportunity, then you might as well look at two separate murders. They weren't the only ones that night, of that I'm sure."

"But they were killed the same way." Barbie countered. "I don't believe that there was a knife-wielding maniac around. Something is not clear, not answered. Gamal and Ahmed. Too many reasons to kill Gamal, none for Ahmed. What else is there to know? Where were all these people on that night? How can we find out? Who has an alibi?"

"Barbie, I know you call me your Watson, but you are NOT Sherlock Holmes. You need to back off, take a deep breath, and let it go. Go to bed!" Penelope got up and headed for her bed, leaving Barbie sitting on the couch, clutching a cushion and shivering in the cool night air. After she got too cold, she went to bed as well.

Surprisingly, Barbie fell asleep almost immediately. The past week had been too eventful and sleep was the only escape she had. It also gave her the time to think about all the new information she had acquired that day.

The noise awakened her and she crawled out of a black hole of sleep to answer her phone. Who was calling? And then she thought it was too early, or too late, so that maybe it was her ditzy mother.

"Hello," she answered.

"I have something important. More information. I'm with the guard at the Museum. Come now, a car will be there."

"David? What are you saying? Is this the secure line? Why are you at the museum? Are you safe?" Barbie stumbled over her words.

"Yes, please come now." He hung up.

Barbie stumbled and almost fell as she pushed and pulled herself out of the bed. She dressed in simple warm clothes. She grabbed her phone, her ID card, the keys to her apartment and a few Egyptian pounds. No bag, she thought to herself, too much trouble. She quietly let herself out of the apartment and stealthily sneaked downstairs.

She saw Mohamed coming from his room as she reached the big door. He stood in the shadows, backlit by the thin stream of light from the small downstairs apartment. "La, la, la (no, no, no)," he said shaking his head.

Barbie looked outside where a car waited at the curb. At another time, she might have questioned the wisdom of plunging into the black menacing night, but Mohamed's warning set her off. She articulated her line of thinking. If some man thought that he was going to tell her what to do, she would do exactly the opposite. She did not stop to think that one man had demanded her presence and she was flying to do his bidding, while rejecting the sane advice of another man.

She pushed open the door and skittered down the stairs. She jerked open the door and jumped into the car. "Tahrir, Museum," she said unnecessarily. She leaned back and closed her eyes, letting the sway of the car through the streets soothe her anxiety. She opened them as they crossed the Twenty-sixth of July Bridge. She thought back to the revolution that created modern Egypt. It was on the Twenty-sixth of July in 1952 that the king abdicated and left the throne. And now, there was another revolution, this one to overthrow yet another strongman and dictator.

The lights in Tahrir were bright, so she could see the milling crowds and the tents that had been erected on the grass circles. The car passed the museum and took the next exit, approaching it from the rear, not from Tahrir. It was darker in this section, more shadows where plain clothes police could hide, or gangs of roving football fans, the White Knights, could squeeze into indistinctness.

The car stopped on the side of the museum, and Barbie leapt out. She stood by the car and looked around. She closed the door and started to move towards the dark hulk of the pink museum building's entrance, but the driver leaned out the window and shouted at her. What could he want, she thought. She came closer and looked at him. He was not the driver that had taken her the last two times, in fact, the car was different as well. Perhaps this driver wanted money, she thought. She rummaged in her wallet and found 20L.E. She thrust it at him. He looked aggrieved and Barbie did what she had always done when she felt she had overpaid and the driver tried to pretend to be underpaid. She turned her back, thrust her nose into the air and deliberately walked away, far from the curb and in a place where the driver could not follow with his car.

Barbie pulled her scarf over her hair, believing that advertising herself was not a good idea. She walked purposefully towards the entry gates of the museum. There were few people around, no women and no children. The aimless wandering of the men indicated that they were there for the demonstrations, but had no plan once the bulk of the population had gone. Barbie wondered what time it was. She looked at her wrist and realized she had forgotten her watch. Her phone was buried deep in her pocket. Never mind, she thought, David should be here somewhere. If she didn't meet him soon, she knew she could call.

She paused at the entry gate, now firmly locked. Two men emerged from the shadows of the garden and spoke to her, but she didn't understand. She realized that David wasn't here, inside, or he would have been waiting for her. Maybe around the back side? She continued walking, keeping the pink bulk of the Museum to her right and the Nile Hilton directly in front of her. She came to the corner, stopped and looked around. She began to feel neglected, misled and finally, slightly fearful. She backtracked towards Tahrir, keeping away from the entry gate, but scanning the neighborhood. What exactly did David say, she asked herself. Where but the museum?

"Where are you?" she asked out loud. Her phone, she thought, she should call David NOW.

She reached into her pocket and felt the content. Keys, small coin purse with a few pounds and her AUE ID card. Where was her phone? She twisted around and tried to peer into her pocket. She remembered that she had another pocket and scooped her phone out of it. She flipped the top open, but no dim glow appeared. She tried again, and this time a faint glow appeared with the battery icon empty with a flashing warning. "Damn, why now?" she demanded of her phone. She stuck the phone in her armpit in the vain hope of rejuvenating it for one short call.

Holding her arm pit closed, she walked across the street towards Mohamed Mahmoud Street, all the while trying to judge the mood in the Square. She could see lights from the small tent city, and hear desultory conversations. Maybe she could ask someone if she could use their phone. But then again, the numbers were in the phone and she hadn't written them down anywhere. Modern technology bites the dust again, she thought. She stopped momentarily at the corner of Tahrir. Across the street, the KFC Clinic had lights on and a number of people inside were busy unpacking boxes of supplies. She took the phone out of her armpit and tried it again. Nothing.

She looked at Tahrir and ducked down the street. The checkpoints here were temporarily abandoned. She hugged the high brick wall to her right as she moved eastwards, away from the Square. Was it only yesterday? The sound of the crowd screaming, the click of the metal horseshoes, the whoosh of the large camel bodies as they rushed by her. These memories drove her away from the well-lit Square towards the darker streets.

This is my territory, thought Barbie as she quickly put distance between herself and Tahrir. The university was only a few blocks away, and these streets were like home. She had been here yesterday. She turned the corner of Falaki Street. The way ahead was dark, very dark. Every streetlight was out and the only light came from the glow behind her and at the end of the block.

"Psst. Barbie."

She looked around. A dark figure on the opposite side of the narrow street stood in a shadow, but indicated the way down the street.

"David, thank god you are here. Where have you been?" Barbie crossed the street, but the figure darted away, leading down the street. She followed. She thought to herself that David was being unusually coy, or was he too, afraid of his enemies, and hers, that he needed to be so evasive? And why wasn't he at the museum, why did her meet her here? And how did he know she was here?

She should follow him, she thought, just to be safe. Emboldened by this idea, she tried to close the gap between them as she followed David as he made his way swiftly down the street.

A loud 'crack' and a burst of laughter alerted Barbie to a large group of young men ahead, at the corner of Falaki where it met Sheik Rihan. She looked up and that caused her to stumble. She reached out to the wall to steady herself, but missed, falling with a loud whimper, "David!!??"

She pulled herself up and looked around. David had disappeared, but the group of men at the end of the block had seen her in the dark, maybe they had heard her feminine voice. They had recognized 'prey' and they turned towards her.

Barbie heard the soft hissing sound of snakes on the prowl and the smacking of lips, like a naughty hungry boy contemplating an ice cream cone. She found the opening to an alleyway and ducked into it. Maybe this was where David had gone and he expected her to follow. It was even darker here and garbage filled the gutters. The stench of rotting food and human waste rose up from the ground. She slowed and watched her feet to avoid debris.

She heard the gang of young men behind her. They had seen her turn in here. Hide, she told herself. She saw a large dumpster ahead and behind it, a niche in the wall. She silently moved forward and squeezed herself into the hidey-hole. The gang turned the corner, now directly calling to her. They kicked the garbage and laughed at their own remarks.

Barbie searched her mind for the perfect foil for this group. Dogs: that is the one thing besides guns that would frighten them. She looked around the brick lined alleyway and chose a spot just beyond where she hid. She cupped her mouth, filled her lungs and then threw her voice, as she had been trained by her dad.

"RAARRRR," came the first sound, low, menacing, but big in voice. "Ruff, ruff!" the subsequent noises came in rapid succession. Snarls, growls, barks, high-pitched squeals of terror. Afraid to even look or think of how these sounds of a pack of angry, fighting dogs was being interpreted by the gang, she concentrated on having the sounds move forward, by bouncing the sounds off the brick wall in front of her.

Then she heard shouts and frightened yelps; then the sound of running feet. She did not let up, moving the sounds of her pack of dogs along the alleyway towards the opening at Falaki Street. When her vicious pack of dogs had reached a point past where she hid, she stopped and peeked out to look. She found no one in the alley. She was alone, with her amazing pack of imaginary dogs. Not wanting to stay in the alley a moment more than necessary, she quickly and quietly walked carefully towards Falaki Street once again.

The ambient light on the street seemed bright compared to the blackness in the alley and she proceeded once more in the same direction. She thought to herself, where had David gone? Why wasn't he around to chase off the gang of boys? She trusted that the gang had been sufficiently scared off and would not be waiting for her and hurried towards a better lit street. When she turned the corner, she saw the brightly lit Square, just a few hundred yards ahead of her. And no gang in the street. She hurried forward.

The checkpoints were lightly manned here and Barbie was able to slide into the Square easily. She stopped near a light and looked around. In the distance, she saw David, talking to a group of protesters. He was standing in the circle, but she recognized the clothes. Then she realized that this man was too tall for David, who was only one or two inches taller than she. This man stood almost a head above the Egyptians that he spoke with. Then he turned his head slightly and Barbie saw his profile. It was not David. But she recognized the man.

She turned her face away and pulled her scarf over it, moving quickly back towards the checkpoint. She approached one man at the checkpoint. "I need a taxi," she said.

Abruptly, another man appeared from the shadows and said to her, "Follow me. You should not be here tonight. Danger."

Fingers of cold fear clutched at her heart and she finally began to shiver with fear. Why had she come out tonight? What was she thinking? Why did she let a phone call from David make her do this stupid thing? And now, who could she trust? The young man on the street?

He had a turban wrapped around his head and partially pulled over his face to keep out the cold. Now, he lowered it slightly to speak with Barbie. He seemed somehow familiar, she had met him somewhere before, but where? She looked him over, jeans, cheap running shoes, and nondescript jacket. He had no identifying clothes. She looked back into his eyes. Kind, sorrowful and full of concern for her.

She decided to trust him, because she must. Because in the square was a man who had faked David's voice on the phone, who had lured her out on a dangerous night, and who had cajoled her into following him down a dark alley. Perhaps he had even sent the gang of young men to intimidate her. Injury, rape and maybe even worse had awaited her. She had to trust someone. She chose to trust this man, now.

The faintly familiar young man gently touched her elbow and moved with her around the Square to El Aini Street, where a car awaited late night passengers. He opened the door and watched Barbie slide in.

"Don't worry, my friend. Go home now." He gently closed the door and the driver looked at her in his rear view mirror, awaiting her instructions.

"Marriot Hotel," she said boldly, hoping the man would think she was staying there and was a tourist. Did tourists have any cachet left in Egypt? Would he do as she asked, or take her to a deserted place and… Stop it, she told herself, now is the time to trust someone.

She started to shiver halfway back to Zamalek and when the taxi pulled in front of the Marriott, she could barely open the door. She reached into her wallet and extracted all of the bills she had left and shoved them into the driver's window. It was over 60LE, at least 6 times the normal fare. She barely heard the driver's thanks as she headed into the hotel.

She meandered through the lobby and down the back stairs. She stared at the few patrons who still sat on the terrace, the pool glowing in the distance. She went out the north entrance, which was the closest to Hatshepsut's Mansions, and carefully looked over her shoulder as she headed the short two blocks home. A fire burned in the middle of the street, a number of men stood around it, the tips of their cigarettes glowing faintly.

Barbie was still shaking when Mitch stepped from the group and spoke, "Barbie, what are you doing here? Where have you been?"

Barbie looked at him and pasted a bright smile on her face. "Out and about, just coming home. Having a good time?" She tried to keep the quaver from her voice, but instead she squeaked.

"Yeah, we're having a great time. I hope you are headed home?" came the reply.

"Good night!" She rushed towards the large doors of the mansions in full view of Mitch and the home guard.

When she pushed open the door, Mohamed was there, having just risen from his chair. "Missy okay?" he asked.

"Yes, great, good," she answered, feeling more confident by the moment.

She allowed Mohamed to call the lift for once, eschewing the stairs in favor of the little cage that would take her directly to her floor.

As she passed the second floor, she peeked out at the deserted hallway. No lights shone under the doors, and Barbie hoped fervently that Parker Hampton was not yet home from Tahrir. She held her breath until she had inserted the key, pulled open the door and closed it behind her. She locked it carefully. She did not want to see Parker Hampton ever again, because it was he who had lured her tonight into that dangerous place. She knew now that he knew that she knew too much.

Chapter Twenty-seven: The Friday of Departure

Barbie went to bed, again. After all the adventures of the night, she felt sure she would be unable to sleep. However, just as the faint light of dawn crept into her room, Badboy wormed his way under the quilt and settled against her, purring a soothing tune. Barbie slept.

Smelling coffee, she woke. After a quick shower to wake herself up, she steeled herself for a grilling from Penelope.

"Whoa, lady, you are up late today! And this, they say, is the 'Friday of Departure', the day the Man will finally leave, or they will push him out. By the way, you are eating the last piece of bread and the cans in the cupboard are getting thin. No potatoes, a little rice, some old pasta, and this," she held up a can of mackerel.

"Nope, that is for the cat. It's cat food. I wouldn't touch it. Don't we have anything else in the freezer?" Barbie was amazed that Penelope was discussing their empty larder and not her escapades of the previous night. Perhaps she had slept through it all, which was just as well. Barbie smiled and discussed a shopping trip.

Penelope arranged with Rachel to hit the stores and left with a large shopping bag. Barbie wandered around the house, checking her email, unplugging and checking her phone now fully charged. She sat in the living room on the couch, staring into the blank screen of the nonworking TV. She tried to process what she had seen and done the night before. She was glad that she had said nothing to Penelope, which had given her the freedom to act as usual. Would Parker Hampton try to harm the others, if they acted normally? If they didn't know that he had murdered Gamal and Ahmed, would they be in harm's way? She was, and she had been, but that was because of what she knew.

Her phone rang. She flipped it open and looked at the caller ID. It said, 'David', which meant someone was calling on his original line. Cautiously she answered, "Hello?"

"So you did get home safely?" David's unmistakable voice asked quietly.

"Yes," Barbie whispered. She knew it was he, but still felt unsure of giving out too much information.

"I worried about you, but most Egyptian men are trustworthy. Last night you found some. Last night was particularly difficult. You know that there were street battles between the demonstrators and the pro-Mubarak supporters and…"

"David, did you call last night? Did you ask me to go to Tahrir?"

"Aha, so that was why you were there."

"David, I know who he is."

"Stop Barbie. Meet me at the Gezira Club, Children's Park. Eleven." The phone line went dead.

Barbie sat, stunned at the quick phone call. Obviously, David did not want to talk on the phone. Was he busy, near someone, afraid that the phone may be bugged? She was sure that this was David's voice. This was a true summons. Last night, the man on the phone, the man who asked her to follow him, that was not David, that was Parker Hampton, the killer.

Quickly she dressed in a long flowing skirt and a long blouse that hung loosely along her arms and kissed the back of her knuckles. She wound a scarf tightly around her head. Except for her blue eyes, she could pass for a local girl. This time, she packed her large bag and slung it over her shoulder. She quietly descended the stairs, not daring to look at Parker Hampton's door as she passed.

Mohamed smiled broadly at her as she passed: he probably thought that this was the best outfit she had ever worn, that she had finally come to her senses and decided to dress properly. He nodded as she let herself out. Today was a day in which she really missed Ahmed. If he were here, she would request his presence walking on the streets of Zamalek. He would come with her, maybe even holding her arm as they walked along, the man accompanying his female relative, duty-bound to protect her.

The Gezira Club was only a few blocks away and the streets were quiet as they usually were on a Friday morning. She kept her head down and within minutes was at the gate near the Children's Yard. She quickly showed her pass, daring the young guard to question her. She entered and immediately spied David, lounging against a tree at the edge of the playground. He wore an exercise suit of light gray with a red stripe down the leg of his pants and red edging on the jacket. Smart and expensive looking, perfect for the club. When he knew that she had seen him, he raised his eyebrows in recognition and ducked off into the bushes, finding a quiet corner to chat. A bench sat in the shade, a private bower for the rendezvous.

"Sabah al kheer," he quietly said in Arabic, extending the common Egyptian greeting for 'Good morning'.

"Sabah al fuul," she answered, emphasizing the beauty of the morning and the person she greeted.

They sat companionably side by side on the small bench and David casually crossed his legs and leaned towards her. "Now tell me about this adventure you had."

Barbie recounted the phone call, the waiting car, the futile search for David at the museum, the odyssey through the back streets, and the encounter with the gang of thugs. David laughed uproariously at the tale of the pack of dogs advancing down the alleyway. "This is one thing I wish I had not missed. But go on, tell the ending."

Barbie tried hard to be linear and chronological in her telling, but that was contrary to her nature. Several times he had to backtrack, but she finally arrived at the recognition of Parker

Hampton in the Square. David questioned her about the reason for her going so late, at only a phone call, supposedly from him. "Do I have such power over you?"

"I came today, didn't I?" She retorted.

"But this is daylight and in such a quiet, peaceful place. Nothing can happen to you here."

"Parker Hampton lives in my apartment building. And now he knows that I suspect him. He knows that because he lured me out last night. I don't know if he saw me when I got to Tahrir, I am assuming that he did. He let me go, why? Was he afraid of showing his hand to too many people? I know that he will try to get to me again. It was scary for me to come here today, to pass his apartment door on the way out of the building, and then to walk the streets. Maybe he's watching me even now!?"

"Barbie, Barbie!" David took her hand in both of his. "Don't worry so much. We can solve this, we must solve this. The time has come." He looked away from her, his face filled with a pensive but anguished look. "The time has come," he continued. "I guess I always knew that at some point in my life, I needed to make some decisions. Well, now I need to. I have always been an outsider here, but at the same time, I am nothing BUT an Egyptian, what else could I be? And I have not always been on the right side of her, or her people. I have perhaps cheated more than was good for her, even though it was good for me. I have not always kept the best company, but I lied to myself about what life is, how I couldn't change anything; that I just had to live life as it was given to me. But now is the time to admit that I have been wrong, I have been selfish and now I need to do something. For Egypt, for my country and for myself. I am not sure I believe in God, but I do not want to live the rest of my life outside of the right way to live. I must choose and I must do it now."

All this time he had been holding Barbie's hand, but not looking at her. Now he turned to her. "I have many things to do. I do not know when I will see you again. Do not be afraid for me. I will make sure that you are safe."

He took out his phone and chose a number from a long list of numbers. "Mohamed?" He gave rapid fire instructions in Arabic. Another call was similarly short and decisive. "Go home, Barbie. Watch your TV, visit with your friends, and say nothing. Today is a big day in Tahrir: they think Mubarak will leave and so they will all be there, strong, determined and perhaps there will be more violence. You stay away. Stay safe at home."

He let go of her hand and gripped both shoulders in his strong hands. His voice trembled with emotion. "I do not know when I shall see you again. I have many enemies and I am sure that my actions will make more for me. But you have been a delightful friend! You are such a brave, courageous and…energetic person. I will miss our talks, and I will miss your lovely face, your laugh, your…" He bent forward and kissed her gently on the lips.

"Maasalama, may God go with you," he said, rising and disappearing quickly through the foliage. Barbie sat stunned.

As she returned to the Mansions, she heard the Friday call to prayer around her. Usually the mosques in Zamalek had quiet loudspeakers, only a whisper in the distance. But today, they had been made louder and the call was strident, almost aggressive. She rushed through the streets, which were still quiet, but which now saw men and boys coming from their homes, purposefully hurrying to the mosques and the prayer mats spread into the alleyways to accommodate the overflow.

As soon as she came within hailing distance of the Mansions, she saw Mohamed in the street, looking as if he were waiting for her. She felt comfortable knowing the large doorman was there for her. She raised her hand in greeting and he returned it, standing and waiting for her.

Mohamed accompanied her as she climbed the stairs and did not turn away until she had put her key into the door. "Shukran, Mohamed," she said, pushing the door open. She had to bend and catch Badboy, who had decided to try for a 'runner'.

"No, you don't, little boy. YOU are not getting away from me."

Penelope met her in the living room. She took one look at Barbie's outfit and burst into hoots of laughter. "Where have you been dressed like a conservative Muslim girl?"

"More respectful and keeps the men quieter. I won't be going out again today, so I'll just take it off. Oh," she turned around. "Mohamed seemed to think I looked good, he gave me a great big grin and a nod!"

Penelope called Mitch and Rachel and the four of them met at the downstairs apartment for a big lunch, with fresh meat, and to watch TV. Llian looked in for a while and they exchanged news. Barbie said nothing, said she didn't have any gossip.

They watched the Friday prayers that took place in Tahrir, the imam broadcasting from the mosque at the corner of the Square. The sea of kneeling men were surrounded by lines of Christians, arms locked in a protective stance. The news commentator remarked that this was a show of solidarity of the Egyptian people, Muslim and Christian, to fight for their human rights. "No longer willing to identify only by religion, the people of Egypt have come together in this fight for freedom and democracy."

Mitch remained skeptical that this 'solidarity' would last, but applauded the thought. Barbie searched the sea of faces for a glimpse of David among the line of Christians. Then she chided herself for being silly, expecting that he would be there. She sat quietly, keeping her thoughts to herself as the others argued for and against the success of pushing Mubarak out, or continued violence against the demonstrators. They speculated on the meaning of the lack of police or any kind of civil control, except for the army, which all of a sudden seemed to be immensely popular. "The army in charge is a throwback," Mitch declared. "This isn't progress."

"It's security, it's not chaos," put in Llian.

"But you must admit, something has happened to the people. They have always been so timid when it comes to the rulers and their rules. Now, they seem to have found their voice. I think a genie has been let out of the bottle. And no one will ever put it back again. The Egyptian people deserve better than

Mubarak. I hope they get what they deserve," Rachel weighed in.

Barbie watched the sea of faces on the TV while contemplating the opinions swirling around her. Suddenly she thought she saw Parker Hampton. The camera had swept over the faces, so she couldn't be sure. Why was he in Tahrir? Well, a lot of people were there, and if this was live, then it meant that he wasn't here, in the Mansions. She trembled and tried to will the camera to revisit that part of the sea. She watched in vain.

Her phone rang and Barbie reached for it. When she saw his name, she suddenly felt shy and rushed into the kitchen, shutting the door with a solid 'clunk'. "David, I thought I would never hear from you again."

"Hello my sweet Barbie. Yes, this may be the last time. I need to tell you that all is well. He has been taken care of. You may hear some rumors, but please, never say anything. Deny any knowledge. This is best for you. You must go on."

"But David, what happened?"

"Please don't ask too much. Only let me say that I have connections. I have friends, and many enemies. He will no longer bother you, or anyone. Only let us say that he has gone. Now, I will say goodbye."

"Goodbye, David. When will I see you again? Can I call you?" Barbie felt bereft, as if he were breaking up with her, cutting her off without her consent.

"I'm afraid where I am going, you will not be able to find me. My phone will disappear. Now, goodbye for the last time."

"David!!??"

Silence greeted her cry. She knew he had not hung up, the line was still engaged, but there was no answer to her cry. Finally she whispered, "Goodbye." She waited for half a minute for any reply, any answer, any word or sound at all. She knew that he was waiting for her to hang up. She reluctantly closed the phone.

Chapter Twenty-eight: The End of One Mystery

The afternoon at Barbie and Penelope's apartment was filled with a stream of visitors. Llian ventured over again with rumor and gossip. The demonstrators were in secret talks with Mubarak, Mubarak was in secret talks with foreign governments, the demonstrators were in secret talks with possible new leaders like Mohammed el Baredei, military leaders, the Muslim Brotherhood, or someone else. The huge demonstrations had grown bigger and in the early evening, reporters from BBC, CNN and al Jazeera were reporting the biggest crowds yet. Penelope avidly listened to all. Barbie was quiet, jumping up every time the doorbell rang.

Between visitors, they read, played with the cat and talked about things other than the Revolution. They felt as though it was out of their hands as to what would happen to them. Barbie felt tense, insanely tense. She kept her phone by her side, waiting for it to ring. Wait, that is what they did, only wait.

Rachel came to get them and escorted them downstairs for another meal of spaghetti. Barbie only played with a small pool of noodles on her plate. The TV reported that one million had gathered in Alexandria, a city of four million. Mitch controlled the TV channels and flipped through them rapidly, trying to find the latest or the most interesting news. Another rumor flew, the Muslim Brotherhood was in secret talks with Suleiman, the current Vice President. No one knew what to believe.

The evening grew dark and the news was inconclusive. At 10pm, Barbie made noises about bed and pointedly looked at Penelope, who replied, "Go ahead, I'm not tired yet. Life is too exciting to sleep." Barbie thought to herself that she felt otherwise. Sleep was what she wanted.

A knock and the doorbell rang together. Mitch went to open it. Barbie steeled herself for who might be there, and she found herself involuntarily shrinking behind someone else, to make herself smaller, to hide. She heard shouts and laughter, and then Mercedes and W.B. were inside, followed closely by Llian and two of the other teachers.

W.B. held up two bottles of wine and Mercedes a bottle of scotch. "We heard there was a party going on here. We've come to join!" W.B. boomed to all. Mitch fetched some more glasses. Barbie felt as though they had consumed more alcohol in these few days than in all the months they had been in Cairo. What was it about being cooped up and helpless that made them all turn to the bottle? She accepted a glass of wine.

"Whoa, want to hear more news, more private like? Apparently Parker Hampton, the eminent AUE Egyptologist, has gone. Just up and left. Never thought he would do a runner," W.B. said.

Barbie stared wild-eyed at him, "How do you know?"

"Cornelius heard the news, maybe a phone call or an email, but he is certain that it is true. You know, that old man knows everyone and he keeps his ears open. But I haven't seen Parker since yesterday in any case. Whoosh, gone, no nerves maybe, this might have really gotten to him. Who knows?" W.B. accepted a glass of scotch and sat on the couch next to Barbie. "Oh, by the way, the scotch is from Cornelius."

"He must have a huge stash of it," laughed Mercedes. "He gave it to us to share with everyone."

"Good old Cornelius," said Rachel. "We need people like him and Mary around. Keep us supplied with booze and stories. A toast, to the Old Ones, the keepers of our history. Cheers!!"

Shouts of 'cheers' sounded all around. In the middle of all of the shouting, cheering and back-slapping, Barbie heard the doorbell. Everyone else seemed not to notice, or didn't care, so she got up and slowly opened the door. With her heart in her mouth, she looked out into the murky dull light of the hallway.

The enormous form of Mohamed emerged from the gloom. He reached around behind himself and gently pulled and pushed a small child forward. He was dressed as a miniature Mohamed in a long grey gallebeya, with a small white turban wrapped around his head. He looked up at Barbie with enormous dark eyes.

"Small boy come. Help me." Mohamed gave a push to the small figure's back and the boy lifted his hand to her. In the palm was a small white box, tied with a thin red ribbon. He thrust it towards her.

"For me?" she asked.

He nodded slightly.

Barbie pulled the ribbon and it fell away easily. She lifted the lid and peered inside, turning slightly to catch some light from the doorway behind her. A small piece of paper lay folded on top. She picked it up and opened it. "He is gone forever, do not worry. D." Underneath the paper, nestled in a thin layer of soft cotton batting, lay a silver bracelet. A stone scarab was set into a silver oval. She knew at once that this was an old piece. Fakes were easy to make; so much like their ancient cousins that it was extremely hard to tell. Had David had given her a real piece of ancient Egypt? Or was it an 'old fake'? Impossible to tell.

"Thank you, walid," Barbie said, calling him 'boy' for lack of anything else. "What is your name?"

A look of sheer panic spun over his features as the young boy struggled to determine his next course of action. He understood the question, but could not formulate the answer.

"Ahmed," answered Mohamed.

"Oh no, doesn't he have another name, Ali, Omar, something?" Barbie asked.

"His name, Mohamed Ahmed Mohamed."

"In that case, Ahmed it is. We can't have another Mohamed and we know the name Ahmed already." She turned to Ahmed, "Thank you, Ahmed. Shukran. Ahlan wa sahlan fi

Hatshepsut's Mansions. (Welcome to Hatshepsut's Mansions.)"

Ahmed stood taller and Barbie realized that he was older than she originally thought. Small, but not so young. He grinned at her, showing a row of large white teeth that gleamed in the dark.

"I'm your English teacher," she said to him. "Tomorrow we will start studying English."

Mohamed quickly translated and Ahmed became more animated. He whispered to her as he turned to leave, "Shukran."

Barbie waited in the doorway and watched them leave. She now let her fears fade. It was true; he was gone and she was safe. She had a new student and a new bracelet. Now, Egypt needed a new leader.

Chapter Twenty-nine: The Pharaoh Resigns

They had all huddled in front of the TV at Cornelius' on Thursday evening, almost two weeks later. They waited for Mubarak's' speech. Half expected him to resign, others were sure he would not. He had vowed to stay in Egypt, to die in Egypt, and many felt he meant it. Cornelius thought he would not resign, but feared that if he didn't, worse was to come.

"The army has the loyalty of the people now, but Mubarak does not. In reality, the military runs this country. As long as Mubarak was a good leader, he had the support of the generals. But when he lost the love, or fear, of the fellaheen, he was a cooked goose. Whether he resigns tonight or not, he must resign sometime." Professor Smythe sat back in his chair as they had listened as Mubarak defied the pundits and the people by refusing to hand over power to his Vice President.

They watched as the previously jubilant crowds in Tahrir turned their joy to anguish and then anger. Mohamed el Baradei, the darling of the Western press and the intellectuals in Egypt, warned, "Egypt will explode."

The expats who had gathered to celebrate Mubarak's departure left quickly, as disappointed and frustrated as the rest of Egypt. Wanting to catch Cornelius alone, Barbie waited for a few minutes. Then she had the old man to herself.

Barbie looked at Cornelius sitting in his favorite chair, a glass of amber liquid clutched in his right hand. He looked old and tired, and for once, Barbie thought, quite drunk.

She burned to ask him. She knew he would know all that was to be known. She had tried to do as David suggested, forget everything and go on. But she was Barbie, tenacious, contrary and curious. "Cornelius, tell me about Ahmed and Gamal. How did they die, and why?"

"Ah, my dear girl, I have waited for you to ask those questions. Do you really want to know? No one comes out of this story looking good. No one."

"For me, truth is easier than endless questions with no answers."

"Truth, you want truth? The elusive, ultimately unknowable 'facts'? Well, here is the outline. Gamal and Ahmed went to the Museum that night. Gamal, to protect treasures, or steal them, humph?! Ahmed, I don't know why. Only he knew why he felt compelled to go. But Gamal had crossed Parker Hampton, who was there to protect, or steal, who knows? Gamal McCall needed to be silenced, eliminated. Whether the knife that was plunged into his heart was by Professor Hampton's hand or another is immaterial. He took the opportunity. That is the way of civil disturbances, riots, revolutions – they present the perfect scenario for hiding nefarious deeds of revenge."

"And Ahmed? Why was he killed?"

"Because he was there and because he knew, he needed to die as well. We know that little Ahmed was very smart, very resourceful and not always so honest. Perhaps he tried to play his hand at blackmail. If so, he lost. He paid for his folly with his life. I do not know, but suspect, that another person was involved besides our missing Professor Hampton."

Barbie sat still, letting this information seep into her understandings of the people she knew. "I don't believe Gamal was there to steal treasures from the Museum. I don't want to believe that."

"I don't want to believe he was a thief either, but neither was he so 'clean' as we would want to believe him to be. Ahmed was 'collateral damage'. What more can I say?"

"And Parker Hampton?"

"Ah, my dear Barbie. This is something I know, but will not tell you. He was already a person of interest, but he tipped his hand the night he lured you to Tahrir. He must have known you were asking too many questions. And our friend Dawood was instrumental in making sure he fell into the 'wrong' hands. Messy business, not suitable for the ears of the innocent. Let us just leave it at the accepted story that he departed."

Barbie asked, "And he's not coming back?"

"Never."

Barbie sat silently. She dared not look at Cornelius' face. Her left hand reached involuntarily to touch the scarab bracelet on her right wrist, but she pulled it back to rest in her lap. There was one person she had not asked about and she did not want Cornelius to know how much she cared about knowing his fate.

She stood and thanked Cornelius for his time. "Oh, I do hope this all ends soon."

"Ah, young people, so anxious for action. Wait…" He stared into the distance.

The man servant silently appeared and pointedly walked towards the door. "Good night, madam," he smiled, holding the door open for Barbie.

Now it was Friday and the news outlets were reporting that two million people had flocked to Tahrir. Rows and rows of men had prayed in the open and then were joined by even more people, whole families, and gangs of youth, all emotional and ready to do something. The crowds began to gather at the Presidential Palace, the state TV building and they vowed to not let anyone in or out. Unbeknownst to the protesters, Mubarak and his family had already fled to their house in Sharm el Sheikh by helicopter. Everyone at Hatshepsut's Mansions stayed inside, waiting nervously for developments.

Barbie gave Ahmed another English lesson, but neither could settle to the task at hand. 'Ahmed II' was as apt a pupil as the first one, but he lacked the zip and drive of his predecessor. Perhaps that was all to the good, as times were unsettled and a young boy roaming the streets alone was not the safest course of action. Ahmed II had been introduced to everyone and had taken over many of the tasks that were needed by the inhabitants.

After the non-event of Thursday evening, the Mansion's inhabitants had settled in for a long wait for the Revolution to resolve itself. So, when the TV stations began to anticipate an address by Vice President Suleiman, many felt exhausted and ill inclined to watch. But Cornelius Smythe insisted that they again gather at his apartment to listen and watch. Tahrir Square fell silent as a large screen broadcast the reptilian face of Vice President Suleiman across the Square. Mitch read the line by line simultaneous translation to the assembled group.

"In the name of God the merciful, the compassionate. Citizens, during these very difficult circumstances Egypt is going through, President Hosni Mubarak has decided to step down from the office of president of the republic and has charged the high council of the armed forces to administer the affairs of the country. May God help everyone."

Two seconds of stunned silence greeted the announcement, and then an excited murmur spread amongst the teachers and professors of the University who had gathered. "It's over!" "He's gone." "Celebrate." The noise from the TV threatened to drown out the comments as they turned to look at the TV. It looked as if the entire Square was a cauldron of moving, shouting ants. Fireworks began to go off and flags were unfurled and waved overhead. Two million people shouting created a roar that none had ever heard.

They went outside. Some of the younger members of the group headed immediately to Tahrir, but others just sat on the steps of the Mansions and watched the crowds in the neighborhood celebrate. Young children with flags, sparklers and glow-in-the-dark wands came by with their parents. Everyone greeted the foreigners as if they, too, deserved to celebrate. Boom boxes appeared, turned up to a deafening volume, playing Egyptian dance music, or songs from the

Revolution, written for the people who had been demonstrating against Mubarak.

Barbie watched as old men and women, wearing pajamas, were helped down the street in their walkers and wheelchairs. Small children pranced around them, shouting and singing happily.

"Look at the old people. I wonder when the last time they were outside. They look like they have one foot in the grave," Penelope wondered.

"They were alive when the king left in 1952; this must be the same thing. Another revolution, sixty years on. And those little ones, think of what they will tell their grandchildren sixty years from now. 'I was there, I went out into the streets.' How could anyone want to miss this night?" Barbie answered.

Mary Bell came to join them and answered that question. "I am happy to be here tonight. I wouldn't have wanted to miss this. Truly historic. I have lived in Egypt for so many years and never have I experienced such an event. Of a lifetime!"

A gang of young men arrived, waving flags and carrying a portable recorder, turned to dance music. They set a small barbecue fire into the middle of the circle and began to dance around it. It was a wild dance, an abandoned celebratory movement of bodies. They danced as soldiers have danced from time immemorial as a victory celebration. It was hard not to feel happy with them.

"How many died?" Barbie asked. "How many martyrs?"

Mary answered, "About 800. It is hard to tell."

Penelope weighed in. "There were so many isolated deaths, like the one in Alexandria, a woman shot from a rooftop by a sniper. And those that went into jails and have not come out again. And others, caught in the web of chaos."

Barbie murmured, "Like Gamal and Ahmed. Revenge. We'll never know how many are dead because someone took advantage of the absence of police, the opportunity to do away with their enemies. And the disappeared..." Barbie mused.

"Like Parker Hampton. No one seems to have heard from him at all. He went home, but surely he didn't just disappear?" Penelope said.

Mary began to say something, then stopped herself. She started again, "This is the time to disappear if you don't belong on the right side."

Barbie was silent. The Revolution was over and no one knew what lay ahead. She murmured, "It will never be the same."

Epilogue: 2015

Four years after the events described in this novel, Egypt has resumed a more even course of events. There is no less oppression: innumerable journalists lay rotting in prison cells, members of the ousted Muslim Brotherhood undergo trials and harsh sentences, and opposition figures have gone underground or are in prison. Mubarak is still in Egypt and still has supporters, although he is currently hospitalized. The lucrative tourist trade has not fully recovered, although the infrastructure remains intact and plans go ahead for the opening of a new Egyptian Museum as well as newly discovered tombs and other sites of antiquity. The Egyptians as an entity have endured for 5,000 years, sometimes independent, sometimes ruling vast territories outside of Egypt and sometimes being ruled by others. They have long memories and the events of the 18 days of the Revolution of 2011 will not be easily lost to them. The threat of future demonstrations hangs over the heads of all who think to 'rule' Egypt and those in power must know that even though the people are quiet now, they know their own strength, their collective power. The Egyptian Revolution unleashed a voice that had not been heard in many years. Barak Obama, the US President, said at the end of the Revolution, "The people of Egypt have spoken, their voices have been heard, and Egypt will never be the same."

End note: Hosni Mubarak died in February 2020.